THE
ICE WOMAN
ASSIGNMENT

by

Austin S. Camacho

ISBN: 978-0-9794788-8-8
Cover design by Iconix.com

Published by:
Intrigue Publishing, LLC
11505 Cherry Tree Crossing Rd. #148
Cheltenham MD 20623-9998

Printed in the United States of America

THE
ICE WOMAN
ASSIGNMENT

Prologue

Two tall blood-colored candles lit the room. Highly polished gold plates stood on edge, filling the shelves that lined every wall. Light reflected from these plates played about the room, illuminating the naked woman behind the desk and the young man on the floor in front of it.

The man, or boy, was less than a week into his eighteenth year. His young, muscular body glistened with sweat. Wearing only shorts, he sat cross legged, in a mild state of convulsion. He was accustomed to it. It happened every time he received a vision.

"What do you see?" the woman demanded. She stood, but she could barely see over her desk.

"Two come. They will threaten you." The boy was a full six feet, tall for a Colombian with no European blood. Skin glowing golden in the candle light, he shook with gentle tremors.

"They are a danger? To me?"

The boy's head snapped back and forth for a moment. Then his brown eyes focused on the woman.

"One is the puma. One is the hawk. They come to pluck the serpent from its lair."

"Describe them."

"The man...is black," the boy said. His teeth clacked twice and he paused to avoid biting his tongue. "He is big, with the feel of a soldier. He is...most dangerous. He knows danger, feels its approach. The woman is pale, tall, red hair, green eyes. A trickster, and...so beautiful. She also can sense danger."

The woman sat back in her high, scaled-down chair. "It

is time for the serpent to leave her nest," she said. "We will go to meet this cat, and this bird of prey. You may stop now."

The boy's tremors subsided as he focused on the woman's shining eyes. They glinted like polished silver mirrors, flashing a signal, drawing him on. He moved quickly behind the desk, kneeling, and nuzzled his face into the black floss between her legs. Her feet, suspended above the floor, started swinging forward and back.

"I may have to kill them," she said. Her breathing was shallow, and her waist-length hair hung over the chair's back, swaying behind her like a huge charmed snake. "They will find the serpent to be dangerous prey. Ah, yes!" she gasped, her fingers tangled in the boy's hair.

-1-

"This raggedy kid?" Morgan asked. "This is the incredibly dangerous threat to society you brought us here to see?"

The three figures lay at the roof's edge, across the street from the boy they watched. At the other end of their binoculars, a teenager with Mexican features was about to enter a crumbling building half a block away. He had stopped at the door, reached inside his white baggy pants, and produced a thick wad of bills.

"Just keep watching," Chuck Barton said. Four men trotted toward the door. The pair coming from the left wore gray suits and carried big revolvers. The other two had on blue jumpsuits. SWAT team uniforms. One carried an automatic, while his partner held a shotgun. Morgan didn't envy them. Whoever chose those SWAT uniforms had not considered Southern California summer temperatures.

"Your boys, Chuck?" Morgan asked over Felicity's head. "CIA?"

"No way," Felicity said, turning her green eyes on her partner. "The two suits are FBI. I could spot them a mile away."

"She's right," Barton said, stroking her waist length red hair. "The other two are DEA. You just might get to see the first joint raid on an ice house that doesn't..."

The Spanish boy started into the door. One of the gray suits shoved him forward and dived in after him. An explosion of a shotgun blast, and the FBI agent flew out the door before he was completely in. Gun barrels smashed out windows on the second floor and a hail of automatic fire showered down.

One of the DEA agents dived and rolled behind a car to return fire. His partner was down, his body bouncing as bullets continued to punch into it. The second FBI agent sat leaning back against the front of the building, alternately holding his left arm and shooting into the door until he ran out of bullets. Rifle fire burst from the building facing the target house, but it sounded feeble compared with what the criminals sent out their three windows.

"What have they got?" Felicity asked.

"From left to right, I see an Ingram Mac 10, an AK-47, and that looks like a Skorpion machine pistol," Morgan Stark said.

"Still think it's kid stuff?" Barton asked. As they watched, five very young men darted out the front door, firing submachine guns as they moved. One stopped to coolly put a bullet in the seated FBI agent's head. Gun fire from the facing building slapped him onto the sidewalk a moment later.

"The building's too well covered," Barton said, running stubby fingers through his brown curly hair. "The back's sewn up. The boys on this side are expert snipers. If they'd put their guns down..."

"They won't," Morgan said. "They'll all die. For the ice."

"We need one alive," Barton said. "If only..." He stopped because the boy in baggy white pants was edging slowly up the street in their direction. He moved like a professional, from car to car, firing two machine pistols in a deadly spray. In front of the building directly opposite Morgan and Felicity he fired out his two guns, then dived backward, up the four outside steps and into the door.

"I can track him," Felicity said, leaping to her feet. She

was racing for the stairs, her long graceful legs pumping.

"Red!" Morgan shouted in his rough baritone, jumping up. "Get back here!" He sprinted after her. Barton followed, but Morgan and Felicity easily outdistanced him. He had on a suit coat on this hot July afternoon, while his friends wore only jeans and tee shirts. He was working. They were supposedly only observers.

Felicity was down the stairs and across the street before anyone could stop her, but she knew Morgan was right behind. In her tennis shoes she figured she could move silently enough to follow the youth to ground. Then she would let the men take over. She did not fear running into danger. Her finely honed senses always warned her in time.

She reached the door about two minutes behind the boy, but once inside the building she knew he was gone. She flowed up four flights of stairs without a sound, but sensing no life inside. She had not spent much time in the barrio, but she doubted these buildings had secret passages or trap doors. Only one option remained.

Felicity opened the door to the roof. At the other end of that tar paper expanse, the boy was just putting his foot down on a fire escape. Felicity raced after him.

A rending squeal of rusted metal set her teeth on edge. The boy leaped back onto the roof and looked over his shoulder, eyes wide with hate. She could hear what she knew was a large iron structure tearing away from bricks and, seconds later, crashing to the ground. The fire escape had given way, falling into the empty lot below. As the boy turned toward her, she realized he was no longer fleeing prey. He was now a dangerous, cornered animal.

She saw surprise and perhaps confusion on his face. She imagined she was just about the last thing he expected to see: a tall, beautiful Anglo standing in the center of the roof in designer jeans and a tight tee shirt.

"You cannot win," she said with a slightly Irish accent. "There are too many guns, and yours are empty."

"Who needs them?" The boy said with a laugh. Dropping both machine pistols, he pulled a butterfly knife from a pocket in his baggies. There was a swish-swish sound and suddenly, a knife's blade pointed at Felicity. With a sick grin he stepped forward, his movements slow but his breathing accelerating. Felicity considered her situation. She had thought of him as a boy, but he stood a good six feet tall, weighing maybe a hundred and sixty pounds. Very thin but wiry, and probably hopped up on drugs, making him all around a dangerous customer. She wished she had gotten further in her martial arts lessons.

When she saw the boy's face fall, she knew it did not matter. She turned and Morgan, her martial arts instructor, was there.

"Get behind me, Red."

The boy's smile returned when he realized this big black man's hands were empty. Nothing had really changed.

"I'll leave you both bleeding on this roof," the boy said. Morgan's massive shoulders dropped.

"Look again, son. I've got you by two inches and maybe fifty pounds. You don't want to mess with me. You don't know what you're facing here."

"Fuck you," the boy shouted, advancing slowly. "Fuck you and the bitch."

"Move out of the way, Morgan." Barton's voice came from the roof door. His revolver was drawn.

"He's mine, Chuck." Morgan's angular face settled into an expression of resignation. Then, to the boy, "I don't know what your story is, son, but to face down sniper fire like you just did, you must be serious. Trust me, kid, it ain't worth it."

"Don't matter. I'll kill you." The boy leaned in, taking a vicious swipe at Morgan's stomach. Morgan dodged to the side, his steps light for a man so big.

"Now that pissed me off!" Morgan snarled, dropping into a deep ready stance. The boy seemed crazed and frantic, but nerves and drugs gave him maniac speed.

"End it," Barton said.

"Morgan, don't hurt him," Felicity said.

"Shit," Morgan said. The boy thrust lightning fast for Morgan's midsection. Morgan dropped to the roof on his left side. Hot tar burned his hands as he thrust a side kick up into the boy's armpit. The knife arced skyward. The same leg curled and snapped a foot into the boy's chest. He hit the roof before the knife did.

"Pretty," Barton said.

Morgan was on top of the boy in an instant, pressing a forearm across the boy's throat. "Why?" he asked. "Why take such a stupid risk? Huh?"

"Fuck you."

"Let's try that again." Morgan pulled a double-bladed dagger from his boot top and pressed its edge against the boy's throat. "Now. Tell me why you'd walk into the middle of a fire fight with no cover when you could just give up and live."

After a moment's silence, the boy croaked out "I need the ice, man. You can't get it in prison. I'd have died anyway, without the ice."

Morgan kneeled up straighter, his nostrils flaring. He remembered that odor from younger mercenaries he had worked with: the sharp, stagnant smell of the speed freak.

"Drugs," he muttered. Before standing, he reached into the kid's pocket, pulling out a plastic bag. Its contents looked to Morgan like lumps of rock candy, like his grandmother used to give him.

"Ice," Barton said. "That's the drug I was telling you about. Maybe now you'll reconsider the job." He turned to Felicity. At six feet tall, he only had an inch or two on her.

He slipped a hand around her waist and looked her almost directly in the eye. "Well my buxom lass, will you and Morgan be able to help us get these drugs off the streets?"

Felicity looked at the boy. Then she glanced at her well-muscled partner, who gave an almost imperceptible nod.

"Make an appointment and we'll talk," she said.

-2-

"So, what do you think?" Felicity asked, pulling out of the underground parking garage of the Manhattan Beach building that housed Stark and O'Brien's offices.

"I think this'll be the most boring briefing in the history of talking," Morgan said, turning on the radio. "Still, we need the facts to decide if we want to get involved."

"You know, I just keep seeing that kid's eyes." She eased into traffic and took her position among the luxury vehicles that clogged the street. She drove her Jaguar XKE, in an attempt to at least enjoy the drive. Like all her customized sports cars, it was jet black with an emerald interior that matched her eyes. She pushed it onto Route 405 and opened it up. The car was not new, but time's passing had no effect on the V-12 engine's incredible smoothness.

"Funny, my mind keeps going back to those poor FBI boys trying to crash the house," Morgan said, raising his voice over the throaty roar of the engine. "Those guys aren't anywhere near ready to fight these people. I mean, they're in the dark ages."

"You saying the FBI isn't up to dealing with a pack of children hustling drugs?" Felicity asked. She frowned as the predictable glut of traffic forced her to cut her speed in half.

"I'm saying Al Capone didn't have this kind of armament, and his boys weren't all hopped up on drugs, you know?" He stared out the window, watching the city fly past. It kept on changing, like a living thing. Freeways no longer got you around seeing the parts of town where the living happened. South Central Los Angeles had become downtown.

Their meeting place was a nondescript hotel hidden in L.A.'s central business district. Neither of them had ever heard of it. From habit, Felicity drove past it and around the block. They trusted FBI security measures about as well as they trusted IRS auditors.

Felicity parked a block away from the hotel in a small parking garage. Once they reached the sidewalk, they saw Barton in the hotel doorway. He glanced at them and gave a slight nod. Barton free-lanced for years before joining the agency. If he checked the area, it was probably okay.

Felicity and Morgan walked at a moderate pace toward the hotel, all the time scanning the area. They saw no loiterers or anyone out of place. But just before they reached the door, Morgan spun around, his right hand moving halfway to his holster. It was not a danger warning, really, but something pulled his attention.

A long Mercedes limousine pulled past them, just a bit too slowly. It had frosted windows, but a back one powered down an inch or two as the car slid past. All Morgan saw was a pair of silver eyes. Then it was gone.

"What?" Felicity asked.

"Nothing. Trick of the light."

Barton led them out of the elevator and down the hall. They stopped at the door to a suite. Felicity was surprised this hotel even had suites. Barton took a deep breath, exasperated in advance.

"Now, do you suppose you two could go in here and just listen a while? I mean, you don't have to piss these guys off."

"Well, yeah, we probably do," Morgan said. Inside, two

grim faced men greeted them, rising from straight chairs around a small table. Felicity smiled at them, while placing her attaché case on the table. She and Morgan both wore tailored navy blue business suits, while everyone else in the room had on gray suits, clearly off the rack, and most likely the same rack.

"This is Mister Alvarez, representing the Drug Enforcement Agency," Barton said, indicating the stocky Hispanic man. "This gentleman is Mister Conrad, of the Federal Bureau of Investigation." The tall balding man with big ears nodded. "I'm here to represent the Agency. Gentlemen, this is..."

"Not yet," Felicity said. Morgan pulled a device no bigger than a television remote control from Felicity's case and started scanning the room.

"The room's been swept already," Conrad said.

"Not by us," Felicity said, still smiling and controlling her reaction to the federal agent's terse comment. "Our equipment is a little more sophisticated than what you use. Yours isn't the best on the passive devices." Barton looked embarrassed, but Morgan finished in two minutes.

"All clear," he said, putting his listener detection device away. "I'm Morgan Stark." Morgan shook hands with both strangers. "The lady is Felicity O'Brien. Chuck tells us you guys can use some help, so we're here to listen. What can we do for you?"

"You can help with some street surveillance," Alvarez said, stepping to the bar. "Want a drink?"

"No thanks," Felicity said. "What we want is to know what your problem is." She sat on the sofa, hoping no one would notice her nose wrinkling. This had been a room for smokers, and the odor seemed to puff up out of the cushions when she sat. Morgan continued to stand.

"The problem, as always, is drugs," Alvarez said. "We have a new thing taking over the streets."

"This stuff called ice?" Felicity asked, leaning forward to protect her clothes. "So what is it? I thought crack was the latest thing in suicide."

"You're behind the times," Barton said. "Crack is yesterday's news. This stuff's a lot worse. It's really a form of methamphetamine."

"What, like crystal meth?" Morgan asked. "Okay, so it's speed. I met that stuff in the Far East. Guys used the stuff to stay alert. What's so dangerous about that?"

"What is so dangerous, Mister Stark, is that this is in a purified crystal form," Alvarez said. "Technically it's not the same thing. It's a different but related chemical called 4-Methylaminorex. It has effects comparable to methamphetamine but with a much longer duration. Sometimes on the street they call it euphoria, spelled U4Euh. It looks like crack and it smokes like crack but it's not cocaine. Crack might keep you high for half an hour. This stuff can keep you flying for twelve, fourteen hours."

"Can't be," Morgan said.

"Don't kid yourself," Conrad said, speaking for the first time. "This stuff's synthetic and what we've found on the street is unbelievably pure."

"It must be serious stuff to convince the FBI, DEA and CIA to work together," Morgan said. "Where's the stuff coming from?"

"Originally from the Philippines, Korea, and Hong Kong," Conrad said. "It made a big hit in Hawaii. Now it's all over the West Coast. We believe the operation's been taken over almost completely by a Colombian organization."

"There's news," Morgan said, rolling his eyes. "Drugs from Colombia. So? You want us to drive down to Medellin and bring in a drug lord for you?"

"You don't seem to take this very seriously," Alvarez said, a little louder than necessary. "There's more than five hundred people every month getting turned on to this stuff, and they might not matter to you, but..."

"Easy," Felicity said, maintaining her smile. "I think you misunderstood my partner's meaning, although we do want to maintain a realistic view here, right? After all, I doubt all those people using this ice are being force fed it. Let's agree that all these victims won't be asking for a drug enforcement effort, or be too willing to help us out with getting the drugs off the street. However, I think what Morgan meant was, what is it that you need from us? We're not the police; we deal with security matters."

"The point is," Barton said, "I thought you guys might have the connections to find out who the distributors are at this end. Your record indicates you're very good at getting information. We don't want you to take any real risk, just help us find out how this stuff's getting distributed."

"Your people on the street can't find these boys?" Felicity asked.

"You don't know about the organization pushing these drugs up from Colombia," Alvarez said. "They are called the Escorpionistas, and they demand incredible loyalty. Like the Yakuza in Japan, or the Triads out of Hong Kong, these people defend their security with their lives. We've been at them for a couple of years but we just can't break in."

"You don't know enough about them," Morgan said.

"You're right," Conrad said, "but we know a little about you two." He picked up a brochure from the small table. Its glossy cover said "Stark & O'Brien, Security and Risk Management Services."

"Pretty complete services," Conrad continued, opening the pamphlet. "VIP close protection, surveillance, counter-terrorism, hotel and corporate security, conference guards, even security training according to this. And your rep supports it all. Barton convinced me you might have a chance at finding something out. But we wanted to meet you before we agreed to bring you in."

"Barton also told us a little about the events involving the ill-fated Piranha project," Alvarez added. "It looks like you can work with the government, and the bad guys don't spot you as good guys. Perhaps you can get us a name. Just a starting point to track back to the woman at the top of this organization."

Felicity looked up, her interest piqued. "Woman?"

"Anaconda," Barton said. "And that's all you get until you say yes or no."

-3-

"I'm just too damned dedicated to the cause," Barton thought, feeling sand slide down into his shoes. A warm desert breeze flapped back his blazer, flashing his waist holster.

He had not told Alvarez or Conrad that he had been Felicity's lover since the Piranha affair. When in Los Angeles, he spent nights at her penthouse apartment. Most times he could count on a leisurely morning in bed with her. However, this morning she had dragged him out early. They had picked up Morgan and his friend at Morgan's apartment. Felicity had let Barton take her Nissan 350ZX after dropping them off and sent him back to the hotel room the CIA was paying for. She wanted Anaconda's dossier before noon, and she planned too spend the morning in the air.

Sand whipped across his cheeks. He tried to ignore his stinging eyes and focus on his goal, a blanket on the edge of the flat basin he trekked across. A stone at each corner pinned the wide, Indian print affair down. A slender, beautiful, black woman held down its center.

"Bonjour, Chuck," Claudette Christophe said, flashing impossibly white teeth. Her black jeans and white tee shirt accented her long model's legs and small but perfect breasts. She waved him down beside her, picked up a large jug and poured him a glass of iced tea. As she leaned in to hand him the drink he picked up the scent of her perfume which, to him, just smelled expensive.

"My name sounds funny in that Haitian accent of yours, Claudette," Barton said, sitting. "I'll bet living in Paris you only meet guys named 'Sharles'."

"Yes, and one 'Chuck' is enough for me." She handed him a pair of binoculars and pointed over his shoulder at the sky. "Look. There they are." Chuck turned and focused on a slow moving dot arcing across the vast blue field. A bank of cotton ball clouds rolled like tumbleweeds away from the dot. Claudette frowned, and then picked up what looked like a large walkie-talkie.

"Chuck just arrived," she said.

"Good," Morgan's voice answered. "He can gather Felicity's pieces while you get mine. We're going to make one more circle, then we'll be right down."

"You know," Barton said, leaning back on his elbows, "She didn't tell me why they were out here. I take it he's teaching her how to skydive."

"Oh, she already does," Claudette replied, reaching out to brush some sand out of his brown, curly hair. "Says in her jewel thief days she sometimes got on roofs that way. What he's teaching her is how to make HALO jumps."

"As in High Altitude, Low Opening?"

"Yes." Claudette followed the dot as it arced lazily across the sky. "The poor girl gets bored so easily."

"I know," Barton said. "I might have brought a cure for that. How high are they?"

"He said a little over eight hundred meters. Is it not...windy for this?" Did Barton hear a slight waver in her voice?

"I wouldn't worry," he said, focusing his binoculars on the distant plane. "Morgan was a professional mercenary for years, like me before The Company hooked me. He's probably done this dozens of times."

"Still it is far. It is sand. And for people who go looking for danger, sometimes things happen."

Barton looked away from the plane. "You really love him, don't you?"

"There they go."

Barton looked back. He had missed their exit from the plane. Now he watched two forms dropping spread-eagled toward the Southern California desert. Soon he could distinguish which one was the female shape. He could see Felicity's long hair trailing her like a flag. The wind pressed her jumpsuit against her, as tight as the shrink wrap on a new toy. Her defiant breasts thrust toward the ground. Then she flipped to the side, unexpectedly. Her arms flailed. She seemed out of control.

Barton was on his feet now. The wind seemed cooler, but it was just the new sweat on his brow evaporating. "Pull the cord, lover," he whispered.

Morgan was tacking toward her but he was above her, unable to make contact. When Felicity got so low Barton could see the determination on her face, she suddenly snapped rigid. Her arms were back, her head thrust toward the ground.

"How fast?" Claudette's voice was a hoarse whisper.

"Easy a hundred miles an hour," Barton said aloud. To himself he screamed "Quit showing off and pull the damned cord."

Less than four seconds from the ground, two white sport parachutes blossomed simultaneously, and the ache in Barton's chest reminded him to breathe. A hundred yards away, Morgan came in at a trot, quickly gathering the billowing silk. Felicity seemed to land harder, rolling twice before coming up on one knee. Her silk canopy threatened to drag her off across the sand, but Morgan was there to help. Barton put down the glasses and moved to assist.

"Wait." Claudette put a hand on Barton's arm. "Give them time."

"They can use a hand," he said, but he moved slowly

toward the pair. As he got closer he could hear the tension in their voices.

"I ought to slap you." Morgan's baritone lapsed back into the Bronx. He whipped off his helmet. Light brown eyes shot fire at his target.

"You said five hundred feet, for the love of Mike," Felicity snapped as she dropped her helmet. "You know I had it timed to the second, even without the altimeter."

Watching Felicity, Barton thought only a native of Ireland could have hair so red, eyes so green or a brogue so thick. And only this woman could be so irritating and at the same time so exciting.

"I said five hundred feet if everything went smoothly," Morgan said. "You were up there doing fucking barrel rolls." They stood eye to eye now. After a tense moment, Felicity's voice changed from steel wool to amber honey.

"Morgan, I knew I was okay. I was in control. My hair just got caught in the harness, that's all."

"You could have been killed, Red."

As Barton could have predicted, Morgan melted before Felicity's charm. Morgan was twice as wide as she, but she could always turn him with a word and a smile. Then Morgan looked away from her and came face to face with Claudette. Without preamble, he took her into his muscular arms and dropped into a deep kiss.

"Well she's glad to see him," Felicity said. "Of course she came all the way from Paris for that kiss. Do I get one?"

"I thought all you wanted from me was this folder," Barton said. "Should I take it you've made a decision?"

"Well, there's good news and there's bad news," Felicity said.

"And the good news is?" Barton asked.

"I'll take that folder and we'll take the assignment," she said as they gathered her parachute into a bundle. I've got some ideas how we can find the connection here in L.A. Morgan wasn't really in favor of this, but I convinced him it would be fun to get a check from the CIA."

"And the bad news?"

"We'll be getting help from some people you might not approve of, and who may not like you much. Now, can I still have a kiss?"

"Well I sure don't want to disappoint you." He pulled Felicity close, covering her mouth with his own, enjoying the warm moment before pulling away and trying to get his mind back on business. They embraced and walked with his arm around her on their way back to her car. Chuck wished he had not missed Morgan and Felicity's takeoff that morning when he left them at the airstrip. He was happier than he wanted to admit that they could now return together.

Chuck had parked the car more than a hundred yards away. The two couples meandered back toward it, moving unevenly across the sand. Then, about five yards from Felicity's sports car, Morgan pulled up short. He separated from Claudette, slowly walking around the car. Claudette hesitated, and then took a step back.

"Morgan?"

"Something's wrong," Felicity said. She stepped lightly to her car, stopping a few feet from the driver side door. Morgan circled to the other side. She faced him across the Nissan's black roof.

"A bomb?"

"Maybe," Morgan said. "Did Chuck arm the anti-theft device?"

"I didn't show him how," Felicity said. "I knew he'd only be driving her for a couple of hours. He was only away from the car long enough to go into his hotel room and get the packet, so I wasn't worried about anybody stealing it. And I didn't think there'd be anybody way out here to steal it."

Morgan gave a slow nod. "Right. Okay. Chuck. Over here, please." When Barton got close, Morgan said, "I'm getting underneath. Hold the hood down, would you?"

It never occurred to Barton to doubt Morgan's instincts. He was one of the very few people aware of Morgan Stark's danger sense. Confidently, he rested both hands on the car's hood and waited. Morgan, he knew, would crawl under it to look for signs of an explosive.

Deep in shadow beneath the car, Morgan searched mostly by hand. After four minutes' exploration, he failed to find anything. Reaching up in front of the engine compartment, he tripped the hood release lever.

"Let it rise about an inch," Morgan said. Chuck did it, estimating a little low. Morgan stood and turned to look into the engine compartment.

"Red, do you have..." Morgan stopped as Felicity placed a penlight in his hand. She always kept a small light in her bag. Morgan smiled, stooped, and shined the light under the hood. After a moment's silence he straightened, waved Barton away and slowly raised the hood until it stood completely open.

Nothing.

Barton and Claudette sighed with relief, but Morgan remained tense. Felicity stepped closer to her ZX.

"Inside?" Morgan asked.

Felicity crouched at the side, looking closely. After a moment of silent examination she said, "Yes. Right here. Barely a scratch by the edge of the door. Whoever got into the car was good. Damned good. And look. There's a note on the dashboard."

Motioning Felicity away, Morgan gently gripped the door handle. He pulled slowly. The latch clicked. It was not locked. He opened the door gradually. Chuck knew he was feeling for any resistance from a wire. Again, nothing. With the door open all the way, he and Felicity stared inside. Chuck tried to look over their shoulders, adding his eyes to theirs checking for anything out of place, searching for danger possibilities.

"Contact poison?" Morgan asked.

"Maybe. How about a pressure bomb under the seat?"

"The seat?" Morgan said. "Unlikely."

"Then maybe...oh no. Morgan, look there. On the seat."

"What? I don't..."

"Look close," Felicity said. A shudder ran through her voice as she pointed. Barton slipped up behind them to look between their shoulders. Following Felicity's finger, he saw movement. Morgan pulled a knife from his boot and poised it over the seat. With a quick jab, he speared something. Lifting it up, he stepped away from the car. Tiny legs and a tail flipped around in the desert breeze.

"Scorpion," Barton said. Just under an inch long, it writhed on the boot knife's tip. Some dye made the insect a brilliant emerald green. Its color perfectly matched the car's interior. After a moment's struggle, it was still.

"How many, Red?" Morgan asked, flipping the tiny creature away.

"I count eight, if they all stayed on the driver's seat," she said. "I don't see any on the floor but I suppose they could have crawled under the seat, or even under the floor mat. They're so small they'd be easy to miss. Now what do we do?"

"Stay out here an extra hour or so," Morgan replied. "The dye covers their spiracles."

"Their what?" Barton asked.

"Spiracles. The openings to their respiratory organs. They probably sprayed the dye on them and covered the spiracles. So with that dye on they won't live long."

Barton shook his head. "Why do you know that stuff?"

"The sting is deadly, is it not?" Claudette asked,

hugging Morgan tight.

"Not really. A scorpion's sting sure hurts like hell though. Like a major bee sting. Two would make you sick as a dog."

"And eight?" Felicity asked, shivering slightly.

"Well, a person might die from eight before you could reach a hospital from here. Let's see the note, Red."

Felicity reached in, quickly snatching the slip of paper from the dashboard. Five long steps away from the car she read it.

"One word. It says `Don't.'"

"A warning for me," Barton said.

"Oh, it's not for you. Morgan and I are the targets of this thing."

"Is it addressed to us?"

"No, Morgan, it's not addressed at all, but there's something taped to it. A long red hair. Mine, for sure."

-4-

"I still don't know, Morgan," Barton said, setting his cup on the large oak cube that served as Felicity's coffee table. They sat in her apartment, one of two penthouse flats atop the building that held their offices. "Maybe you guys shouldn't get involved in this thing. These people are dangerous. And you certainly don't want to get your lady mixed up in this."

"We're already in it," Morgan said, pulling Claudette into his arms at their end of the couch. Music from David Sanborn's latest album almost relaxed him, but Felicity's huge living room, so sparsely furnished, reminded him of their vulnerability. "That little warning means the bad guys know us. I don't run from that kind of thing. As for Claudette, I flew her in for two reasons. First, her business is industrial espionage. She might have some information you don't. Also, these South American cartels often have a mystic angle to them, and being Haitian she could give us some insight into that stuff."

"I agree and that's settled," Felicity said, standing to walk past Barton. "Now, since the men both have copies of the folder, let's kind of flip through it. Starting with the Escorpionistas. Who or what are they? Another terrorist group? Or is this a drug cartel, like the one out of Medellin?"

"Well, neither really," Chuck said, tracking Felicity with his eyes. "They're kind of like the old Cosa Nostra in Sicily. They're into all kinds of crime, terror, extortion and like that. A scary bunch, but they were flying under the radar because they stayed local in Colombia until very recently."

"They are vicious fanatics," Claudette said, staring out the floor to ceiling window panels that served as the room's back wall. "They rule their areas by terror and magic. Even Baby Doc and Papa Doc before him would not bother the Escorpionistas. They keep seers and shamans..."

"Yeah, well, like I said, until recently they stayed local," Chuck said. "Then, according to my intelligence, a new leader rose up about three years ago. You rise in this organization only because those above you have unfortunate accidents and your team keeps you alive. And she seemed to have definite ideas on how to take the Escorpionistas out of Colombia into more profitable endeavors. It looks like she wants to play on the world stage, like al-Qaeda."

"She?" Felicity stopped in her pacing. "You said before a woman's running the show, this Anaconda. How does a woman get stature in an organization like that? I thought those South Americans were all about the macho stuff. And what's with the name? Isn't the Anaconda a snake?"

"Biggest in South America," Barton said. "Kind of an ironic title she chose. We don't have a picture but we have pieced together a pretty good description. The story is the woman's only four feet eight inches tall."

"Four foot eight?" Morgan asked, flipping pages. "A midget, or dwarf?"

"No, our information is that her proportions are all normal. She's just short. And that's not all. We're told she has straight black hair hanging almost to her knees."

"Doesn't it get in the way?" Claudette asked with a smile.

"Mine sure does," Felicity said, pacing in front of her couch. "I'm thinking about cutting it."

"Don't do it if you're headed to Central America, cheri," Claudette said. "The hair would be symbolic of fertility, or strength."

"Our information is she's pure Indian," Barton said.

"In Colombia?" Claudette sat straighter. "This is another powerful symbol. Not one in a hundred in Colombia is pure Indian. The Spanish were very thorough. You must understand that in that part of the world, just being unique gives you influence. This is ancient tradition."

"In that case, she's got it hands down," Barton continued. "Word is her eyes are silver. That probably means white, or real pale, but..."

"No, they're silver." Morgan picked up and emptied his coffee cup. "I saw her."

"What?"

"She's here, Chuck. I thought it was an illusion at the time. People just don't have silver eyes, after all."

"In front of the hotel the other day?" Felicity asked. Morgan nodded. "Sure and you looked like you had the enemy in your sights. Too bad we didn't know then. And if she was outside your hotel, Chuck, then she's watching you or one of the others on the joint task force."

"But this should simplify things, no?" Claudette asked. "If the woman is here, can't you just arrest her?" All eyes turned to Barton.

"Not without iron-clad evidence, which we don't have. She's a foreign national, and probably in the country legally. Got no way to know, because who knows what name she might be using. Besides, this organization's very influential in the Hispanic community here. It's all tied up in this mysticism thing. If we arrested her, they'd call it false arrest, racist harassment. There'd be riots in the streets. That's why we need her connection. With the distributors in hand we might be able to get enough to move legally."

"Your people on the street can't get anything?"

"All right. Customs has any number of people on the street, all Hispanics, all trained undercover agents. These guys are pros, but they get nothing but the run-around. Ditto CIA people in Colombia. Same for the FBI guys in Texas. We're stumped. It was my bright idea to bring you two in, but I'm really grasping at straws."

"What's Texas got to do with it?" Felicity asked, refilling everyone's coffee cup from a thermal pot.

"Customs reports connect the Escorpionistas with Gold Heart Shipping," Morgan said, holding up a sheet of paper.

"You're kidding. The international mercy organization?" Felicity asked.

"The same," Barton said, tasting the hot coffee and sighing with pleasure. "They've got a ship that regularly goes from Corpus Christi down to Colombia with powdered milk, clothing and books."

"Their own shipping line?" Claudette asked. "A smuggler's dream."

You'd think so, but we've gone over that boat with a fine tooth comb and haven't found a thing," Barton said. "I think it's a red herring."

"So, if Morgan and I can make contact with one of the drug dealers..."

"Just one step up, darling," Barton said, reaching to grab her wrist, pulling her down onto the couch next to him. "Not the street dealer, but the next guy up. That would do it."

"I've got an idea that might work," Felicity said, nuzzling Barton and brushing her hair back. "But first, Morgan and I have to go shopping."

-5-

A flashing neon sign over the club's door said "El Noches," the night. Morgan and Felicity stood across the street with a man who did not look like he belonged in that neighborhood. And yet most passersby averted their eyes, not looking at him. Paul was not as tall or as broad as Morgan, but something about him made even the toughest men want to pretend he just wasn't there. They certainly didn't want to attract his attention.

"I could come in with you," Paul said to his two bosses. "Backup isn't really backup at this distance."

"Sorry Paul," Felicity said. "In this place you practically define sore thumb. Have you seen another Anglo pass through those doors?"

He nodded, an island of chilling calm. "I take your point ma'am. My role is to cover your backs if you are pursued coming out of that door."

"Good man," Felicity said, heading across the street. Morgan paused for a moment to rest a hand on Paul's shoulder.

"The only person on earth I trust more than you is going into that bar with me. You know that, right?"

"And I would never betray that trust," Paul said with a straight face. Morgan smiled and followed his partner across the street.

Once inside El Noches Morgan went straight to the bar to check his look. The face in the bar room mirror did not look much like Morgan Stark. Oh, it was his face, but with reddish hair above it. Contact lenses made his normally light brown eyes almost black. And he had a silly little scar on his chin. He wore leather from head to toe. His shoes and pants were black. His deep red jacket had obscure symbols on its back. And there was the earring in his right ear.

It was a dark, crowded room, clogged with cigarette smoke. Everyone inside was Cuban, or Puerto Rican, or Mexican or from points further south. Music, loud and bass heavy, never stopped. The bar ran the length of one wall. The opposite half of the club held a dance floor, ringed with small tables. A row of booths stood against the front wall. Only three other doors were visible, two beside the bar marked as rest rooms, and one beyond the dance floor. Morgan looked around, folded his arms and leaned back against a wall, reflecting on the two tense conversations that had led him to this spot.

First was his talk with Felicity three nights ago in her apartment bathroom. While he tried on his new outfit, she rubbed a dye on her exposed arms, gradually tanning her normally pale skin. Her hair was already straightened and dyed black. While she squirmed into a tight red mini dress and four inch spiked heels Morgan averted his eyes. There was no physical modesty between them. He just felt it was the polite thing to do.

"You know, that warning we got was potentially lethal," Morgan said. "I mean, these people are serious."

"Are you scared?" Felicity asked, popping in brown contact lenses.

"Not the point, Red," he said, pulling on his custom-made shoulder holster. "There's no point in taking stupid chances. They know who we are and where we are. Maybe we should just leave this one alone. If the CIA, the DEA, and the FBI can't handle it, could be it just can't be handled."

"Relax, Morgan. Nobody going to spot us. It's a simple undercover deal. We'll make a buy, track the seller, and save the U.S. government a bundle. You know they'll never do it alone." She turned her back to him.

"Felicity..." Morgan began, zipping her mini dress.

"Felicity? Oh my. This must be serious."

Morgan took a deep breath, trying to swallow his frustration. "Look, it's a dumb idea. Pulling one local distributor off the street is just going to piss these people off. One lesson I learned as a merc was, never do your enemy a minor injury. Just tell me why you want to do this job so bad. To please Chuck?"

When Felicity turned to face him she was a different woman. She had a hint of dark hair on her forearms and her eyebrows were darkened. She was suddenly Mexican.

"Do I have to say it? All right! I need the rush, okay?"

Felicity stepped over to the bathroom door. She smiled at Barton who was waiting in the living room, then pushed the door closed. She turned back toward Morgan, pointing a finger at him.

"You know, pal, we do a lot together, but we're not Siamese twins," Felicity began, her Irish brogue becoming more pronounced as she went. "You take off maybe a couple of weeks every three months or so. On business, you say, sure and it's true, but I know where you're going when you go. You're out getting your fix."

"What?"

"Come on, Morgan," Felicity said, moving closer until only inches separated their faces. "You're leading big game hunts, or flying surveys, doing movie stunt work or 'advising' in some little country's local troubles. Why?"

"I...I like to keep my hand in."

"Call it what it is, boyo," she snapped. "You need the rush. And that's fine. Whatever you do, it always ends up helping somebody. And, near as I can figure, you can do all that stuff legally. When you go out of the States you even get the approval of the U.S. government. But what about me? I can't just go out and nick a painting or pull a jewel heist."

She turned and started pacing, talking as much to herself as Morgan. "You don't know how I sit in that office, and ideas come. Sweet little cons, or spectacular robberies I'll never pull. Don't you see, Morgan? I need to get loose once in a while, just like you."

Morgan had come away from that conversation with a chill. He thought it bad business, starting a caper for the wrong reasons. Still, she was his partner and in the end he had agreed. That was how he ended up in the Barrio, a part of town he knew little about. The bar, on the other hand, felt familiar. He had sat in a dozen just like it when he and Harlem were much younger. Still, the late seventies seemed a lifetime away.

He hung over the bar and ordered Bacardi dark. Across the room, Felicity flashed her long, shapely gymnast's legs while talking with a smiling Chicano, undoubtedly in perfect Spanish. Three stools down the bar, a tall Mexican in a yellow silk shirt and gold chains everywhere watched Morgan too closely. A scar ran down the side of his face, just missing his right eye. Morgan looked back, just long enough to make it clear he noticed, and then knocked back his drink. He hoped he passed the silent test.

Yellow Shirt could be the reason for things being the way they were that night, as they had tried to explain to Barton three days back.

When Felicity bounced down the three stairs into her sunken living room Morgan only nodded but Barton stood up. He looked at this tall, tanned girl with new respect. The hair, the eye color, the bright red nails, it all fit. She even held her mouth differently.

"If I didn't know it was you, I might not recognize you," Barton said, as Felicity twirled. "The dress and the shoes are perfect, too. And... your face is different. Are your cheekbones higher?"

"Very observant," Felicity said. "Wax pads over my top gums. They're small but the effect is pretty good, I think. Es muy bueno, si?" She spoke, not merely with a good accent, but an authentic Mexican accent.

"Do you really think you can make contact?"

"They're wanting to sell," Felicity said. "I'm wanting to buy. I know how to make the approach. Yeah, I'm thinking I can. And with Morgan for backup, I'm not in any real danger."

"When you go out tonight, I'll alert a couple of the local agents to watch out for you," Barton said, grabbing her waist.

"No thanks, Chuck. No backup. In fact, I'd like you to take a little vacation to Corpus Christi. I think we can trace the drugs back there."

"Darling, I've got to watch out for you," Barton said, leaning in for a kiss. "I care too much to let you just step onto the bull's-eye like that."

"I'm sorry, Chuck," Felicity said, pulling away from him after the slightest lip contact. "It's nothing personal. I just can't work with the CIA. Too noisy."

"What?" Barton raised an eyebrow, then turned to Morgan as if he needed an interpreter.

"In terms you'll understand, she means your signature," Morgan said, staring at the blackness beyond the all glass wall. "You boys are just as bad as the FBI and the DEA. You're all big machines and you move like tanks. You know how you spot a tank in the field?"

"Sure," Barton said with a nod. "By its signature."

"Right. It ain't just the noise. It's the heat. The radiation the optics give off. The dust raised. The radio bleed. The exhaust smell. The tracks it leaves. When a machine that big is on the move, there are just too many signs."

"Yeah? What about the Escorpionistas?" Barton asked, a little harsher than he intended. "Anaconda's machine is big, but it sure don't make much noise."

"Sure it does," Felicity said. "You just can't hear it."

For three consecutive nights, Morgan and Felicity had followed the tracks. It was a trail of young men with too much money and not enough time. It was overdressed boys who always stayed high. There was no way they could afford that, unless they were dealing. The most reliable sign was the fear in someone's eyes when anybody raised the subject of the Escorpionistas. Fear of a rumor got one reaction. The fear of a terror known got quite another.

The trail had started in the "V" between the Pomona and Santa Ana Freeways, not five miles from City Hall, the Civic Center and Little Tokyo. Here, at the edge of East Los Angeles, the city suddenly turned Spanish. With Morgan driving Felicity's black Corvette they moved through the night from bar to small store front to bar. As they went, the music, mostly driving salsa rhythms, became less and less flavored with hip-hop. They moved about, being seen and asking just enough questions. Felicity was sure that if they stayed visible and moved slowly, the right person would find them.

They had not noticed the small man with big front teeth who slid into a phone booth as soon as they left the first bar.

Now, in the most recent hot, dark, crowded night spot with continuous music, Felicity sensed she was getting close. Out there, the Barrio moved out from Los Angeles proper into an area of Los Angeles County that did not really belong to any city or town. The Barrio, "the neighborhood", with almost two million Chicanos, was its own city with its own rules.

Five minutes before Morgan and Felicity arrived at El Noches the small man with big teeth walked in. He stood on tiptoe to get the bartender's attention. When the barman leaned forward, the small man said "Prepare the back room."

Felicity's companion in the booth was gaunt and dry, with short cropped hair and a thin mustache. One heavy gold chain looped under his lapels, hanging down to the edge of his sternum. He had a wide smile, and chain smoked some short regular cigarettes.

"Carlina, you say? You come here from New York?" he asked, looking directly into her cleavage.

"That's right, Rico," Felicity said, leaning just a bit farther forward. "New York. You know a man named Felix Rojas? About five foot six, wears his hair long in the back, drives a white El Dorado?"

Rico snickered and shook his head. "Still driving that Caddy? Yeah, I know Rojas. He never mentioned you, though."

"That's lucky for him," Felicity said with a smile. "But you can check me out with him. He wasn't sure you were the man for me to talk to, but I try, eh?"

"So tell me, beautiful Carlina, why you want to muscle in on my business?"

"Muscle in?" Felicity sat back, looked hurt, and sipped her wine. "You misunderstand Rico. Think about the East Coast, eh? Boston is still the hub in the north and the Guineas own that, still pushing doogee. Horse breeds unhappy customers."

"Doogee? Only people in the Big Apple call it that," Rico said, laughing a hard laugh.

"Yeah, well that's the North," Felicity continued. "To the south it's Miami, still working the reefer and, of course, coke. You have to go to war to get into that business. Me, I figure I'll open up the ice market in The City. In a couple years, I could maybe double your volume. I got the money, and I got distribution set up and waiting." She leaned forward once more, stroking Rico's hairy hand and offering him a generous view of her tangible assets.

"You know, chiquita, we might be able to do business, if you're in touch with the streets."

"What you mean?" Felicity asked, moving her hand up his arm a bit.

"Let's dance." Rico suddenly stood, grabbing Felicity's arm. She stood with him, glancing at the bar. Morgan had snapped rigid. Felicity pushed on the long silver spike that held her pearl barrette in place, then smoothed her dress down around her hips and tugged at one triangular earring. Morgan read: "I'm in control, but watch closely. It feels like a setup."

"What was all that?" Rico asked.

"I was just telling my escort that it wasn't necessary to come over here and tear your arms out," she said. "He's very protective and very strong. Of course, that's why he's there. He'd die for me."

"He could get his chance," Rico said. "But I would rather see you dance."

The music was so loud she did not hear it so much as feel it. On the dance floor, flashing lights from all direction gave an unreal feeling of isolation, since other moving bodies were merely shadow forms impossible to focus on. Rico was a strong dancer, and his smile grew still broader when he realized Felicity was too.

She had studied the Lambada for her own pleasure, and concentrated on it more in the last week. Now she moved with Rico, almost unconscious of the close contact his body made with her most intimate areas, concentrating on staying with the rhythm and maintaining a properly passionate facial expression.

In minutes sweat covered them, Rico's musky scent mixing with Felicity's expensive perfume as they grinded together, dipped, and thrust into each other.

Morgan watched admiringly as Felicity wove among the crowded clinging couples. If she pulled it off, they probably would move one step closer to Rico's boss, the man they really wanted to see. He smiled, turning back to the bar.

The man in the yellow silk shirt was standing in front on him, just a little too close.

-6-

"Are you a real drinker?" The man in the yellow shirt asked in Spanish.

"Whatever you name," Morgan replied. His accent did not match Felicity's, but years doing mercenary work in South America gave him a workable Spanish vocabulary.

Yellow Shirt tapped a finger on the bar, and two shot glasses appeared. Then a bottle of Ron Rico 151 thumped onto the bar. Yellow Shirt poured both glasses full to the rim. Both men lifted their glasses and poured their contents down their throats, never losing eye contact. They both maintained stern, unmoving faces.

The bar was an island of relative tranquility. Inches away, beyond some invisible wall, the room was a chaos of swirling bodies, dancing, moving toward and away from the bar. In the midst of it all, Morgan seemed to stand within a bubble of concentrated stillness. Two big Chicanos stood behind him, as if to separate him from the club's disorder.

Yellow Shirt's challenge did not end with one shot. A second drink was poured, then a third. Morgan knew how conspicuous it would be for him to stop drinking, but he did not want to lose his focus. He watched Yellow Shirt's eyes but also kept Felicity in sight.

Halfway through the bottle of rum, three things happened. Rico, looking tired, started guiding Felicity toward a door on the other side of the dance floor. Morgan's danger sense went off like a burglar alarm in his head. And Yellow Shirt pulled out a gunmetal gray Zippo lighter and spun the striker.

"Let's make this a little more interesting," he said, waving the flame near Morgan's glass. The alcohol ignited easily. Then he lit his own. Morgan gave him a half smile while picking up his glass.

Morgan had done flaming shots in bars in Vietnam, Hawaii, and New Orleans. The trick is to shoot it decisively. Hesitation could prove painful. He tipped his head back and threw the flaming liquid down his throat. The rum burned all the way to his stomach, a delicious, enervating burn. It felt too good. He hoped he was not getting drunk. What if something happened?

Something did.

As Morgan's glass hit the bar, the lights went out. Shadowy forms and smoky images were replaced by a wall of blackness. The other drinker's glass provided a lone spot of light, glowing on the bar. Each man behind Morgan grabbed one of his arms, just above his elbow. Yellow Shirt produced a thin knife blade and held it in front of Morgan's face. It was a smooth setup, and Morgan could appreciate its professionalism. It meant that these men would not get jumpy or hurt him out of macho bravado. Morgan would calmly go along wherever they took him, hopefully to meet more interesting people. Then he heard a shrill whistle.

It was Felicity's distress call. Her whistle cut through the roar of the half laughing, half frightened crowd, even above the DJ's assurances that their light problem was only temporary. Concentrating on the sound, Morgan fixed her location in his mind. Then he focused on the knife.

"Let's go outside for some air, Red," Yellow Shirt said. Morgan almost chuckled at being called by that nickname, forgetting his disguise for a moment.

"I've got another appointment," Morgan said. His left hand swung forward. He could not reach his enemy, of course, but he did manage to sweep the shot glasses off the bar. Flaming rum splashed on the man facing him. The yellow silk shirt became a torch, sending blue flames licking at its owner's face. He turned, hands covering his eyes, and raced through the darkness. People around him screamed, trampling each other getting out of his way. Morgan sent one heel crashing into a knee, then slammed his other down onto an instep, and spun away from his two captors.

Charging like a linebacker through the crowd, Morgan crashed into three or four bodies before a heavy masculine form stopped him. He thrust forward with stiffened fingers for where he figured the man's solar plexus would be and got a loud grunt in response. Then he got moving again, stiff-arming people out of his path. He could only tell men from women by how yielding their forms were. He moved steadily toward the source of Felicity's whistle. Then he heard her voice say "No!"

Morgan's knee hit a table he knew was not there before. Pain arced up his leg. Then a fierce blinding light hit his eyes. Through the floating blue spots he could now barely make out the open door and the darkened room beyond. The voices of the bar's scrambling patrons combined into a cacophony of white noise. The total confusion in the crowded space overwhelmed his senses, blunting his danger awareness. Something hit him in the back, forcing him forward through the doorway. As he stumbled into the room beyond, a heavy fist caught him in the stomach, bending him forward. Something harder than a fist hit the back of his head. The darkness got darker and he slid peacefully into it.

Felicity saw Morgan collapse. Sprawled on a carpeted floor, she heard the heavy door slam shut with grim finality. Then came the sound of a heavy bolt being thrown.

Beyond the door, she could hear voices becoming calmer. She figured the bar's lights had miraculously returned as soon as they were locked into this back room. The situation wasn't ideal but she remained calm. She knew where they were, and this would be a poor setting for murder. The room wasn't soundproof and she was not restrained. Besides, Morgan would not be out for long. Besides, being captured could pay off. Their captors could be taking them to Rico's connection.

Then she heard a low rumbling somewhere ahead of her. The room started vibrating like low level earthquakes she had felt in California. She jumped at an air blast noise like a dragon snorting, and the room slowly lurched forward.

A husky female voice with a heavy Spanish accent said "Relax yourself, mi amigos. This could be a very long ride."

-7-

When his eyes opened, Morgan had a worm's eye view of the room. His cheek scraped a businesslike brown carpet. Three pairs of men's shoes stood nearby. Two more pairs flanked Felicity's distinctive legs, which hung down from an office chair. She sat beside a small table. Beyond her, at the other end of the long room stood a desk flanked by two empty chairs. It seemed hotter in the room, which carried a faint jasmine scent.

Morgan heard a subtle background sound he could not place, and the world was vibrating slightly. Sitting up hurt, but he did anyway. His hands were cuffed behind him. Felicity's were too. He wished he could get out of them as easily as she could.

Track lighting on each side of the ceiling burned into his eyes. He did not recognize his three muscular guards, but one of Felicity's escorts was her dancing partner. He examined them all with care, evaluating how dangerous they might be based on their stance, their alertness, their hands, and the hard look in their eyes. Those eyes stole repeated furtive glances at Felicity, and the reason was obvious. Her dress, torn in front, revealed her left breast. Had she resisted capture? Or did one of the men just decide to debase her?

Felicity gave Morgan an encouraging look, her face telling him that she was relaxed and confident. Morgan returned a small nod, while thinking that he would have to figure out which of the men exposed her. He wanted to make sure he killed the right man.

Then Morgan saw the woman behind the desk. She was small, but not petite. In fact she was nicely rounded with black, straight hair. She had a strong face with the Native American's high cheekbones and reddish cast. And then there were her eyes.

"They really are silver," Morgan said, standing.

"They are indeed," the woman said with only the slightest accent. She jumped down from her executive chair and walked around her desk. With nothing for comparison, he would not know she was so short. She wore very tight black pants and boots. Her tank top revealed a flat, muscular stomach. As she walked her hair bounced against the backs of her thighs.

"So you're the ice woman," Morgan said. "And the room is moving."

"It's a tractor-trailer," Felicity said. Despite her torn dress, her posture did not reflect modesty or shame and she made no effort to cover herself. Clearly she had more important things to worry about than being gawked by lowlifes. Besides, she had reason to be proud of her body.

"So where are we?" Morgan asked.

Felicity faced the woman in charge. "We're wandering the freeways, aren't we? It's rather a nice setup. That door we came through actually opens onto a loading dock. They just park this thing up against it. Looks like any other room from inside the bar but it's really a very nice mobile office."

"I don't like being watched in your country," their hostess said.

"Oh, like we're supposed to know you," Morgan said.

"Of course you do. I am Anaconda."

"Seriously? Like the snake?" Morgan asked. "Your friends call you Anna?" The man nearest him punched him in the stomach. He slouched, but continued to stand.

"I wanted to meet you," Anaconda said, hopping up to sit on the desk like a child. "You are really quite remarkable people. I suppose I should be flattered that you chose to get mixed up in my business. Despite my resources you were hard to track. Oh, and my man Eduardo wants to meet you again, Mr. Stark. You ruined his whole day."

"Eduardo?" Morgan asked. "Tall guy, yellow shirt, gold chains for days?" Anaconda nodded, and Morgan returned a smile. "Boy seems to have a lot of trouble with his face." Morgan's nearest neighbor punched him in the side. He grunted.

"I've learned a great deal about you in the last few days," Anaconda said. "You, Mister Stark, were a professional soldier for hire for some years. Martial arts expert. Apparently gifted in judgment of distance and direction. Now you own a security firm with this woman."

"That's all a matter of public record."

"True, Mister Stark," Anaconda said with a serpentine smile. "The fact that your Irish-born partner spent years as a jewel and art thief, and is an accomplished escape artist, that is not in the public record. Nor that she has a photographic memory, and can apparently tell the time without a watch. Nor is it public knowledge that you are currently in the employ of your Central Intelligence Agency."

As she spoke, Anaconda played with several items on her desk. There beside Morgan's pistol sat his two boot knives, one for throwing and one for stabbing. His larger fighting knife lay on top of its sheath. Anaconda picked it up. In her hands, its seven inch blade made it look like a short sword. "What do you call this?"

"That's a Randall Model 1 fighting knife," Morgan said. "It belongs under my right arm, opposite the gun's holster. It hangs handle down in a friction sheath. You can return it now, if you like." That remark earned Morgan another punch in the ribs.

"Is this a part of your act?" Anaconda asked, replacing the knife. She dropped to her feet and walked over to Felicity. "He talks while you sit and listen? Very good. You are all my reports said you were. You are smart, skillful, and dangerous. But not smart enough or dangerous enough to interfere with me. I wanted you to see that you can be captured, even if you can see danger coming. And you can, can't you?"

"How is it that you're knowing so much about us?" Felicity asked. Seated, she was almost at eye level with Anaconda.

"Oh I've been checking on you for the last two weeks, my girl," she said, stroking Felicity's dyed hair. "It's really red, isn't it?"

"Two weeks?" Felicity snapped her head back. "Bollocks! We didn't even know you existed two weeks ago."

"Ah, but I knew of you," Anaconda said, smiling again. Her canine teeth seemed just a little too long. She reached out unexpectedly and slapped Felicity's face, a jarring blow that whipped her head around. "Didn't they tell you I was a priestess of the ancient religions? My slaves can see the future. Maybe if I show you, you will know not to cross my path again."

Anaconda raised her right hand and snapped her fingers. "Frederico," she said. For the first time, Morgan noticed two boys crouched in the shadows in the trailer's forward corners. One stood, the other ran to his mistress' side. This boy was really a young man, about six feet tall with a sleek but muscular build. He had golden skin, with pure Indian features. He wore only shorts. Anaconda nodded and he knelt before her.

Morgan saw teenage admiration in his eyes. Anaconda

turned her back on her guests and guards, locking eyes with the boy. She swayed slightly, setting her hair into a smooth wave motion. The boy sat transfixed.

"Tell me, Frederico," Anaconda said slowly. "Tell me, will these two bring me pain, or loss?"

The boy stared for a moment, and then began shivering. Tremors wracked his body, as if a giant invisible fist had wrapped around his form and shook him.

Felicity felt a chill at the bottom of her stomach. Scanning faces, she saw that ancient fears gripped every person in the room, even Morgan. Their eyes reflected folklore and legends from three continents. Witches, shamans, witch doctors, the stories are all the same. The air thickened, making the watchers strain for breath. Then, before he spoke, the boy looked at Felicity.

She felt as if her soul were laid bare for his inspection. His captive look triggered something within her and she reached out to him, not with hatred or fear, but with pity. She saw he did not control his own destiny, and she knew how very tragic slavery could be. Then the boy's teeth clacked. He got control of it, speaking at last.

"Mistress, you are in no danger from them," he said in Spanish. "The serpent will fly high. The Hawk and the Puma will fall beneath her." Then Anaconda had his eyes again. His tremors gradually eased, then stopped. He breathed deeply and sweat burst out on his body.

"Impressive," Morgan said. "Can you tell me what's in my pockets too?"

"You bore me," Anaconda told Morgan. Then she returned to her chair behind the desk, picked up the telephone and pressed one button. "Garcia. Pull over for a drop." Then she turned to the man on Morgan's right, "Renaldo. Take him out and hurt him. Break something."

Air brakes hissed again and the world ground to a halt.

One man opened the rear doors. Another gripped Morgan's shoulder and shoved him out. Three of the big men followed him, leaping to the ground. One of the two remaining men pulled the door closed and flipped the latch, locking it shut. Anaconda pressed the button on the phone again and said "seguir," and the truck lurched forward again. Felicity felt a shudder run down her spine, but not from the night air that had come in.

When the vehicle reached cruising speed Anaconda moved to stare down into Felicity's eyes. Her face softened, revealing something like empathy.

"You know why I don't kill you right now?" Anaconda asked. "We are two of a kind, you and I. Two women succeeding in a man's world. And of course, because Frederico assures me you are harmless. And he is never wrong." Anaconda walked back to her desk, but while she spoke Felicity watched the boy. Ignored by his Colombian mistress, he never let his gaze wander from Felicity. She finally had to close her eyes to refocus her attention on Anaconda.

"Tell me; is all this hostility just because you're a wee bit of a lass? Are you angry just because you're a shrimp?"

Anaconda whirled, Morgan's boot dagger in her hand, rage flashing from her silver eyes. She stepped deliberately toward Felicity, the knife held in front of her. The two guards moved aside allowing her plenty of room. Frederico scampered back into his corner. When Anaconda stopped, she held the knife less than two inches from Felicity's nose.

"You think you are better because you are tall?" Anaconda all but shouted, shivering with contained rage. "You could not survive what I have. Have you ever been raped by a man half again your size? Or been given as a sexual gift to seal a business deal, just because some men like young girls?"

Felicity spoke carefully in soothing tones. "I'm sure your

life has been hard. But you've done much more than survive. You're in charge here. I can't even imagine how you reached the top of this organization, in a business that is so, well, male dominated."

"No secret there, chica," Anaconda said, sliding the blade softly against Felicity's cheek. "I left my native country early, with a man who liked what I had to offer. He took me to Cuba. There I learned from the experts, some of Fidel's closest men. I learned how to use my differences to influence the small minded. How easy it was, being female, to turn one man against another."

Felicity was fighting not to move when the cold steel touched her skin. "If the communists trained you, I'm surprised you didn't stay with them."

"Oh they wanted me," Anaconda said, sliding the side of the blade down Felicity's neck. Felicity shivered, and sweat broke out on her face. "I returned to my own country because I knew I had talents the Escorpionistas could use."

"Talents?"

"Let's say gifts," Anaconda said, moving the knife so the point rested half an inch from Felicity's right eye. "I have a gift for organization. And I knew I had qualities that could be used to control these primitives. My racial purity. My eyes. These two brothers I found who can see what others can't. You see, I am a priestess in a religion you know nothing about. And I've created a very profitable international trade for the Escorpionistas."

Felicity thought that that little speech implied Colombians were superstitious and easily manipulated by ancient symbolism. She considered how much contempt Anaconda must have for her own people. Felicity hoped Anaconda felt the same way toward Morgan and her. Perhaps appealing to her ego might get Felicity out of this with a whole skin.

"All right," she said. "I get it. You're too much for us.

How about I admit it and you tell your friends to bring Morgan back in and just send us home?" She smiled in what she hoped was a humble way.

"Maybe you got something there," Anaconda said. "As you can't harm me, you are of no importance. And that would send a message to your CIA. Yes, maybe I should just let you go. However, you have been an inconvenience. Maybe you should carry something away from our meeting, eh? Something to make you remember your meeting with Anaconda, the most influential woman in this hemisphere."

There was no warning, except that Felicity's senses went crazy. Anaconda slid the knife downward until it hung three inches below Felicity's collarbone. Felicity involuntarily bared her teeth. Then Anaconda quickly slashed down. The razor edge of the blade slid effortlessly through Felicity's flesh, but cutting no deeper than her skin. Because Morgan kept his knife so sharp, a second or two passed before the pain hit like the touch of a red hot brand. Felicity sucked in a breath, biting back a scream. A diagonal red line appeared on Felicity's left breast, ending just before her nipple.

"Now your perfect body is not so perfect," Anaconda said. "Now you can learn to live with a physical flaw, as I have. Rico, take this bitch home."

-8-

It was a big Chevy, gold with red interior, model unknown. Cigarette smoke had filtered so deeply into the upholstery that Felicity could smell it now, even though no one was smoking. She leaned against the passenger side door, as they bounced down the street on nearly useless shock absorbers. Rico drove, with one friend in the back seat.

Felicity had perfected her cowering female act over the years but never before had she been able to base it on such a solid platform of truth. She was scarred, cut by a vicious person for no good reason. Hatred and self-doubt battled for dominance within her, but she maintained the haunted eyes and slumping body language she hoped would keep her captors at ease. She just wanted to be home, safe.

Why did she get involved in this anyway? She was no policeman or spy. Not so long ago, those people had been looking for her. She should have let them flounder in the same ignorance and incompetence that had worked to her advantage all those years. Instead, she had offended a major criminal for no personal gain. Anaconda had proven as deadly as her namesake, and she was backed by a huge and shadowy organization whose members showed absolute devotion. Felicity wondered what had made her think she could defy them.

Then Rico, looking straight ahead, reached over and stroked her knee. She shivered and said "No." He did not seem to notice. They turned a corner, and he reached again, rubbing her thigh.

"She said to take me home," Felicity said. "Please, just take me home."

"She didn't say we couldn't have some fun first," Rico said. "It don't have to be bad, you know. I know a nice place we can stop for a little while." The man in the back seat chuckled. Felicity looked out at the slow but steady traffic. She could see that Rico was avoiding the freeway. She hated to think he made that choice just so he wouldn't have to pay much attention to his driving.   Anaconda intimidated her but close up, these clowns did not.

"You're not going to do this," Felicity said.

"And why not, girl?" Rico asked. His hand slid painfully across her exposed breast, down her thigh, to land beside her knee on the seat.

Felicity startled the back seat rider when she reached up to her hair, useless handcuffs dangling from her left wrist. She yanked the long silver pin from her hair, letting the comb fall out.

"This is my stop, you bastard," Felicity said, stabbing down into the back of Rico's hand and pinning it to the seat. He screamed and swerved, driving the Chevy's left front fender into the driver's door of an oncoming car. Before the car was completely stopped, Felicity jumped out, running at top speed across the street. She dodged oncoming vehicles like a matador, silhouetted by rushing headlights. Horns blared, brakes squealed and above it all, Rico shouted obscenities in Spanish.

Felicity ran down the block, trying each parked car as she went. The seventh car, an aging red Chevy Impala, was unlocked. She ducked inside and reached under the dashboard. Twenty seconds later, the engine roared to life. Felicity glanced at the corner street sign, noting where she got the car from, and then pulled into traffic.

The sedan, an automatic with the stick shift on the floor,

was nothing like her usual choice of rides but right then it felt like luxury and the snarl of the V8 engine gave her comfort. She knew no one was following her, but Felicity drove an evasive course anyway, making last-second turns and timing her approaches to corners to slide under orange lights just before they turned red. Watching for street signs she soon figured out she was in the Pomona area. In short order she was able to find Interstate 10. From there getting home would be easy, just point west until she hit the coast. Just the thought of being in her own apartment made her feel better.

She rolled her window down to clear her head. Cool night air raised gooseflesh on her left arm, but she stubbornly left the window open, fighting to bring her breathing rate down to normal.

Thirty minutes later, Felicity coasted to a stop in front of her building. Her perfect time sense told her it was ten minutes past one. Tim, tonight's security man, would be sitting at a console inside, watching closed circuit video screens. She knew she would be visible on one of them, but of course Tim wouldn't recognize the car. She blew the horn six times before he went to the door and looked outside. While he stared at the strange vehicle, she pushed her head out the window.

"Tim!" Felicity called. "It's me. Felicity. Bring me your jacket, would you?"

"Miss O'Brien?" Tim, a tall ex-Marine, had a brush cut and a face too small for his head. He stared blankly at her. He had to recognize her voice, but she suddenly remembered he probably could not recognize her face.

"Yes, it's really me, Tim, I'm just kind of in disguise. Now be a dear and please lend me your jacket. My...my dress is torn.

Now he looked sure. Tim stepped out, locking the door behind him, and walked to the car, unbuttoning his uniform jacket. When he handed it to her through the window she pulled it on quickly but there was no way to avoid offering him a flashing glimpse of her exposed breast. He sucked air in between his teeth as if he had just cut himself. Their eyes met.

"Sorry," Tim said, embarrassed. "I didn't mean to... you got hurt."

Felicity leaped from the car and hustled into the building without another word. Tim followed her as far as the elevator. As the doors closed in front of her, she said, "I'll call you in a couple of minutes."

Upstairs, Felicity made sure her only neighbor was not in the hall, then sprinted past the bird of paradise plants in the center garden and punched the buttons to open her door's cipher lock. Inside, she ran down the hall to her bedroom. Once there she dropped the jacket to the carpet. In her full length mirror she stared at her new injury. The thin line of blood had become a long, narrow scab. She stared at herself in shock and horror, letting tears flow freely down her cheeks, onto her damaged breast.

She leaned over her dresser to drop the contact lenses out of her eyes. Only one fell. Amidst the tension and chaos she had not noticed that the left lens was missing. It must have flown when Anaconda slapped her. She shed her tattered clothing and wrapped herself in a big white terrycloth bathrobe. She felt an overwhelming drive to wash the color out of her hair and off her skin. Was this how a rape victim felt, this need to be clean? The desire to shower and shampoo, to get back to her own look, was strong but she knew she had more important matters to attend to first.

Morgan.

Perched on the sofa's edge, Felicity pushed buttons on her cordless telephone. After three rings a familiar voice said hello.

"This is Conrad, right?"

"Who's this?" the voice asked, too carefully.

"It's O'Brien. Listen, have you heard from Morgan?"

"I don't think I know any..." Conrad began.

"Look, don't give me any of your silly spy malarkey. Morgan's been taken by those Chicanos and he might be hurt, or worse."

"I'm sorry," Conrad said. "You must have the wrong number." Felicity heard a click, then silence, then a dial tone.

"Arsehole!" She screamed into space, and then dialed again. Her photographic memory kept her from having to look up any number she had ever dialed. This time she called Chuck Barton's hotel room but got no answer. He must have already left for Corpus Christi. Damn. Next she dialed a number in Panama. She waited impatiently through long distance clicks, until she heard the remote ringing sound.

"Yes?" It was Mark Roberts' voice. Roberts was Barton's control agent, an old acquaintance of Morgan's, and CIA bureau chief in Central America which for some reason included Colombia. She knew he would not talk to her until he could verify her identity and switch on a scrambler.

"It's O'Brien," she said. "Call in thirty minutes. Priority one." That meant life and death. Then she hung up, thought for a moment, and dialed again. "Tim, it's Felicity. I need some help."

"Anything, Miss O'Brien," the guard said. "After all, you're the boss." He meant it literally. Felicity and Morgan insisted on providing security for the building their offices were in, and her apartment above them.

"Tim, I need you to bring me a phone book." She paced as she spoke, her nerves on edge.

"Ma'am you sound nervous," Tim said. "And, seriously,

do they still print those things? I have no idea where I'd find one. Why don't you tell me whose number you need? I'll just look it up online, or call information."

"No good. I've got to find Morgan. I might need the phone number for every police station in the state. And all the hospitals." Her voice faltered, cracking. "And maybe the morgue."

-9-

In the dark, they could be anywhere. Six yards off the freeway they stepped into a patch of transplanted evergreen forest which could just as easily exist off the New York State Thruway or Highway 95 in Georgia. Morgan could not be sure they were still in California.

A soft breeze flipped his collar and cooled his face. The whoosh sound of passing cars was linked to lights rushing by, catching the three Chicanos in a chilling strobe effect. Morgan stood on soft, springy ground. He faced the trio, hands locked behind him. Again he wished he could open handcuffs as easily as his partner. As it was, he was prepared for a beating. Then one of the men popped a switchblade open and the rules suddenly changed.

"You faggot," Morgan said, addressing no one of them in particular. "Three against one, my hands are chained behind my back, and you need a knife?"

"Quiet," Renaldo said. Body language marked him as the provisional leader. He was broader than the other two but in the flashing lights, Morgan could not tell much else.

"You cowards," Morgan said, stepping back farther into the wooded area. "Maricone. No cojones, eh?"

Taunting them brought the desired reaction. The three men moved toward him quickly, but tightly placed trees kept them from reaching him together. Jogging left, Morgan got all three attackers on one side of him.

A big rig tooled past, leaving the scene lit for half a second. The light was at Morgan's back, in his assailants' faces. In that half second, Morgan kicked out, a side stamp that put Renaldo into his two partners. Then Morgan was behind them, kicking into the knife man's left knee. He went down howling.

The second man spun on him. Morgan put his head down and charged. His shoulder knocked the breath out of his attacker. A front stamp kick put the man on the ground.

Morgan was caught in the next car's lights, and Renaldo's fist hooked into his stomach. Another crossed his jaw. Morgan staggered back, fighting to stay upright. His face smacked into pine bark. The pungent scent of sap slid into his nostrils, clashing with the coppery taste of blood.

"Now you will hurt," Renaldo said. "I don't need a knife." Morgan heard the whistling sound just before he ducked. A length of chain clanged against the tree.

Where did he get that? Morgan wondered. Was it wrapped around his waist, or did he drop it out of the truck when he jumped down to the street? Morgan turned quickly as the chain arced again, hitting his back like a steel bar. Morgan ran forward, trying to escape. He dodged a tree, but stumbled and dropped to one knee.

This time when the chain hit, it forced Morgan to the ground. In a flash of headlights he saw the steel links spinning over Renaldo's head. He began rolling just as the chain arced down. It thumped the ground just inches from him, raising dead needles. Renaldo tried to stomp him, but Morgan kept rolling.

When his shoulder hit a tree Morgan grunted. Renaldo laughed. The chain spun above his head again. Morgan stared up, his back wet from the rotting forest floor. Headlights revealed Renaldo's grin and need for a shave.

Then Morgan reversed his roll. His body slammed into Renaldo's knees. After an instant of weightlessness, Renaldo fell over him. Morgan squirmed around quickly, but a root caught the handcuffs, limiting his progress.

Renaldo got to his knees, then to his feet. Lying on his side, Morgan hooked a foot behind Renaldo's ankle and kicked out at his shin. Renaldo dropped again. From that awkward position Morgan raised his left foot, snapping his heel down into Renaldo's groin.

While the other man howled, Morgan forced himself upright. Renaldo grunted and managed to get to his hands and knees. As a passing car silhouetted him, Morgan kicked once, to the side of his head. This time, Renaldo went down for good.

Morgan dropped to the ground, wondering how much time he had. On his back, he managed to get the handcuffs down around his feet. Now he stood with his hands chained in front of him. Exhausted and sore, he knelt to check Renaldo. He lived, but surely had a bad concussion. He would be out for a while.

He followed a low moaning to the man with a dislocated knee. From there he could just see number three. He was shaking his head, about to stand. Morgan moved like a wraith through the darkness, making sure his target never saw him approaching and had no idea he was there until the chain of Morgan's handcuffs settled across his throat.

"When are they coming for you?" Morgan asked in a chilling tone.

"Half an hour," the man croaked out.

"Who's got the keys to these handcuffs?"

"Left them on the truck," the Mexican replied. Morgan nodded, reflected on his recently acquired injuries, and tightened his grip. His captive's hands went to the thin chain, but dropped a moment later. When he passed out, Morgan dropped him to the turf. Then, out of habit from years as a mercenary, Morgan dragged him and Renaldo into the center of the wooded island where they would be harder to find.

A quick frisk confirmed the absence of any small keys.

Morgan stood on the graveled shoulder, fatigue settling on his shoulders like a wet woolen overcoat. His watch told him it was well past midnight. He had not eaten in six hours, bruises were rising on his back, and his lip was swelling. Pointed shoes worn to fit in at the clubs were a poor choice for hiking, but hike he would. His wallet was with his personal weapons aboard Anaconda's traveling office. No sane person would pick up a leather clad hitchhiker with a bloody face, wearing handcuffs on his wrists, carrying no money or identification.

Luckily, Morgan could rely on an infallible sense of direction. His mental grid map told him he was facing west, which meant toward Los Angeles.

The first green reflective sign he came to told him he was out on Route 60, almost five miles past the Montebello exit. Well, at the first exit he would find a gas station and call Felicity. He figured Anaconda would not hurt her if she kept her mouth shut a little better than he did. After all, Anaconda only sent him out for a beating as an example. She wanted to make a point about her power in this country, and Morgan showing up with a broken arm would have been sufficient.

With the crunch of gravel following him along the freeway's shoulder, facing the blinding headlights, he mustered one small smile. How would Anaconda react, he wondered, when she returned for her three flunkies and found them unserviceable?

-10-

Morgan's head snapped in a double take when he spotted Felicity, in a simple sweat suit, driving a red Chevy with bucket seats. He stepped away from the telephone booth, silhouetted by the light from the cover over the gas pumps. Felicity swung the car around so the passenger door faced him. Morgan's face curled into a smile as he settled into the vinyl seat.

"I've got about thirty better questions," he said as Felicity pulled the car back onto the highway, "but first I have to know where you got this car."

"I needed transportation when I escaped from those Spanish...oh my God." Felicity had started speaking before she looked at him. Even in the dim light of passing neon signs, she could see how swollen Morgan's face was on the left side.

"This is nothing," Morgan said, sitting back. "You should see the other three guys. But could we stop long enough to get these bracelets off?"

"Good Lord. Did you have to fight in these?" Felicity pulled onto the road's shoulder and slid a pick out of the wide elastic band around her hair. Morgan noticed she was a redhead once again. In seconds his hands were free and they were back on the road.

"Now, what's this about escaping?" Morgan asked, rubbing his wrists. "I figured Anna would just let you go."

"Anna? Oh, I get it." Felicity shook her head. "Anaconda sent me packing, but my escorts got a wee bit

56

frisky so I had to shake them and get my own ride."

"You stole it."

"We're taking it back right now," Felicity said. "Picked it up just off Firestone, on the edge of Watts. I figure if I park it where it was and leave a hundred bucks on the seat, nobody will be sore."

"Okay. We can catch a cab from there. Or, at least we can walk to someplace where I should be able to hail a cab. The question is, what do we do now?"

"Morgan." Felicity hesitated, a rare event indeed. Morgan waited in silence for her to continue, just watching the street lights fly past. "Morgan, I'm sorry I ever got us into this. You were right. We've got no business..."

"It's a job, Red," Morgan said out of the darkness. His partner's confidence was shaken more than he expected. "We signed a contract. Besides, nobody sends me out to the woodshed for a whipping. Let's not have any talk of dropping the case. I just want to know how we get to Anaconda from here. These people ain't no joke. They're dangerous."

"Well, I've got an idea." Felicity's foot seemed to gain weight, her speed increasing on the freeway. Morgan opened his window a crack and took a deep breath. She was showing more than just a loss of confidence. Something was really wrong, but what? He might expect this feeling if she was hurt, but was it physical or emotional damage? He would simply have to wait for her to tell him, and deal with the moment at hand. Right now presented enough danger.

"Well, let's look at it," he said. "The Escorpionistas got a lot of influence over the Hispanic population. There must be about three hundred thousand Latinos in L.A. East L.A. is a city all to itself. No way to crack in there. However, this is a widespread organization from what we were told. So, maybe the place to get at these guys..."

"Is in Texas," Felicity said. "That's what I figured. We

check out the shipping line and find out how the drugs are brought in. I'm betting when the payroll dries up, the power of South American voodoo hoodoo dries up too."

"I take it you don't believe the boy's prediction," Morgan said.

"That we can't harm Anaconda? I don't buy into crystal balls. But the situation there is kind of spooky, huh?"

"I read it a master-slave relationship," Morgan said. "Kid's so dominated he probably just says whatever he figures will please the woman." The words "I hope" got left off his sentence.

When they climbed out of the taxi in front of their Manhattan Beach office building, Morgan and Felicity scanned the area carefully. They could see no one watching them. Still, they knew he was out there.

Once in her apartment, Felicity checked her bedroom telephone for messages while Morgan picked up the living room's cellular phone. He heard three rings before a Haitian voice answered.

"Allo."

"Claudette. Hi." Morgan sighed in silent in relief. They had not targeted her. At least, not yet. He wanted to tell her all about the dangerous evening he had just had, but he saw no point in scaring her. "Listen, doll, this case is getting a little complicated."

"Where are you, mon cher?"

"At Felicity's. Look, her place is being watched. I don't think mine is, but these people we're mixed up with play the game kind of funny."

"Will you return here?"

"I don't want to lead them to you."

"Then I should go."

Pause. "Yes, lover, I think so. It might not be safe right now. Catch the first plane to Europe. I'll call as soon as the dust settles."

"I'll fly evasive, just in case," Claudette said. "The long route. If you get no answer at my place, don't worry. Just leave a message with my service. Je t'aime, mon cher."

"I kind of dig you too," Morgan said. He waited until she hung up to do the same.

"Oh, tell the girl you love her," Felicity said, returning to the living room.

"Any messages?" Morgan asked, dropping his jacket.

"Mark says he'll call again around two our time on a secure line. He's in contact with Chuck."

"Excellent," Morgan said, pulling his shirt off. "I'm taking a shower to clean out all these cuts and bruises. They didn't hurt you, did they? I mean, need any first aid?"

"Nope," Felicity answered, turning her back to him. "Never touched me."

"Good. Then you get some rest. I'll watch the phone. After the call, I'll hit the guest room."

"Twist my arm," Felicity said, smiling. "I'm beat. Let's plan on a late breakfast and an afternoon flight to Texas. I'm tired of doing things the hard way."

-11-

Felicity's eyes popped open, her face tense with anger. Why wasn't Morgan answering that phone? He said he would watch the phone. Was he just watching it ring?

Then she realized how light it was. Her all blue bedroom was positioned so her wide windows received the sunset, but she could still see the darkness was lifting outside. Her internal clock told her it was twelve minutes before seven in the morning. Surely Mark Roberts called long before this.

Maybe it was Chuck. Pushing only her right arm out from under her thick blue comforter, she reached for the phone on her side table.

"Hello." Felicity's voice was still slurred from her recent deep sleep.

"I know what you want," the voice at the other end said. "You can save me. I will do anything you ask."

Felicity's slender form snapped upright, and she filled her lungs with the cool air pumped into her apartment. In an instant she was completely alert. She knew that voice. She had heard it pronounce her doom in Anaconda's mobile office.

"Frederico? What is this?"

"I ran," the boy said. "Take me away from her. I lied and saved your life. Now you must help me."

How could he have escaped? Was this a trap? "Are you in danger?" Felicity asked. "Where are you?"

"The sign says Alameda Street," Frederico said. "I

passed City Hall a block ago, or maybe two. I can see signs I can't read. It's not English or Spanish. Senora, she will kill me if she finds me. I ran away."

Felicity's mind moved like a race car. If it was a trap, they would just have to chance it. Having an insider in hand would certainly make breaking the Escorpionistas easier, and less risky. "Listen closely. There's a restaurant not far from you. I'm going to give you an address. Go there and stay until I get there. Okay?"

Four minutes later, Felicity, in jeans, Reeboks, and a blouse over a tee shirt, was shaking Morgan awake. His sleepy smile faded when he saw her expression.

"No time for questions," she said. "Somehow Frederico found my number and he's hiding from Anaconda. We need to go get him. Get dressed!"

Morgan didn't question his partner's urgency. On their way out the door he had one question.

"If this deal is legit, you think the kid can hide from the Escorpionistas in this town?"

"Don't know," Felicity said, "but he made a good start. He at least found a place he's got a chance. One place where Hispanics won't be able to disappear in the crowd. He's holed up in Little Tokyo."

-12-

Felicity rolled slowly down the streets of Little Tokyo in her black Corvette ZR-1. She felt confident, but could sense her partner's coolness in the passenger seat. Right then, she knew he wished he was holding a desk phone instead of her car's cellular one. A desk phone he could slam down. The best he could do with the receiver he held now was stab the disconnect button as hard as he could.

"I am not happy," he said through clenched teeth. "We're heading into a potential combat situation in broad daylight with no backup."

"I take it Alvarez was no more use than Conrad."

"Refused to even admit he knew me," Morgan said.

"Guess they want Chuck to be their only contact with us. Mark told me he's already in Texas."

"Yeah, and neither of them can offer much help that far away."

Felicity did not share Morgan's feeling that they needed help. She had watched him in their office that morning, picking up new weapons. He preferred a basic Browning Hi-power as a fighting pistol, but he only kept a stainless steel model there. Its magazine held fourteen rounds, one more than the gun Anaconda took.

He slipped the gun into his shoulder holster, and another Randall model One knife went into the right side sheath. He slid a throwing knife into his right boot and a short double edged dagger into his left. His black denims covered both, just as his lightweight tan blazer concealed his shoulder holsters.

The environment comforted Felicity as much as Morgan's armament. The streets were almost entirely populated by Japanese Americans. There, Frederico could easily spot and evade Anaconda's Latin soldiers. She had not seen a Hispanic face in ten minutes, and they were closing in on Tanaka's, one of her favorite Japanese restaurants.

Aromas crowded the street, reminding Felicity they had missed breakfast. Her ears strained for any snippets of conversation in anything other than an Asian accent.

They approached the entrance of Tanaka's, easily spotted by the ornate lions and dragons capering up and down the door and its casing. A face poked out. Frederico. He recognized Morgan, glanced both ways, and darted for the car, carrying a small case. He wore only shorts, a tee shirt and tennis shoes without socks. When Morgan opened the door the boy dived into the back. No one had to tell him to stay down. Felicity powered through the intersection, barely making the light.

"No followers," Morgan said after they drove for two more minutes. "Let's head for Alvarez's hotel room."

"You're kidding, right?" Felicity asked. "You know that place is being watched. That's got to be how they got onto us. If they'd really hurt the kid, we can't take him there."

"Don't worry," Frederico said to the back of Morgan's head. "She is a woman of great power. I saw it in her eyes. She can take me away from Anaconda's evil. That's why I lied and saved your lives."

"Saved our lives?" Morgan pivoted, so he could look at their young charge.

"The vision came," Frederico said. "The puma, you, and the hawk, your mistress, pull the flying serpent from the sky. If I had told my mistress that, she would have killed you instantly."

"My mistress," Morgan repeated, breaking into laughter. Felicity resisted as long as she could, but soon she started chuckling despite herself.

-13-

Morgan sipped his coffee, trying to stay calm. Felicity had not stopped driving until they were down near Long Beach. They had found a small diner, and now sat in a corner booth behind three plates covered with eggs, hash browns and calamari.

Morgan had chosen this place, at the corner of a long strip mall. He sat so he faced both Felicity and the door. The place's front wall was glass from knee height to the ceiling. Frederico sat between Felicity and the wall. Frying grease clogged their noses. The juice was fresh, the coffee strong, the conversation strained.

"It's nuts to take him with us," Morgan said, as if Frederico were not there.

"If we abandon him, he's dead," Felicity said. "No way he can defend himself. Those clowns Chuck was working with certainly can't protect him. He's an illegal alien, for God's sake. And he's our best tool to crack this dope gang."

"If he's that important to her..." Morgan began.

"I am her talisman," Frederico said, all the time staring at Felicity. "I see more than my brother. And I am a symbol of her power. No enemy could reach her as long as I predicted trouble. She could always strike before they were ready. Men died if I told her they would oppose her."

"No wonder she rose up the ranks so quickly," Morgan said.

"And I am her possession," Frederico continued. "She will not tolerate my leaving."

"If he's that important, she'll be watching the airports," Felicity said, starting to squirm under Frederico's stare.

"And the trains," Morgan said. "And the border. Ports. Bus stations. Her network's pretty extensive. Not just Hispanics. Everybody who needs the ice can be a pair of eyes for her."

"You are not Mexican," Frederico said.

"No, dear, I'm Irish," Felicity said with a smile. "This is the real me, red hair and pale skin. The other was a disguise. Was that why you thought I was so powerful?"

"No." Frederico spoke as if he was about to tread on sacred ground. "It was your eyes. When I saw you, after my trance, your eyes were different. Only one was green. The other was black."

Felicity's smile broadened. "I get it. It was after Anaconda slapped me. You see, one of my..."

"They change color," Morgan said, interrupting. "A sign of her power." He glanced at Felicity, and she held her words. He knew about her contact lenses, but he feared Felicity might lose her hold on the boy if he recognized her as a mere mortal woman. For a woman to hold sway in his culture, she had to be something special.

"So where to now?" Felicity asked.

"The body of Christ," Frederico said, without hesitation. "Where the ships take the drugs."

"Christ's body?" Morgan asked, staring out the diner's window.

"Sure," Felicity said. "Corpus Christi. In Texas. We'll link up with Chuck and let this lad lead us to the ice." Her eyes locked on Morgan's and her smile disappeared. "Something's wrong, and it's nearby."

"Right," Morgan said. "Spanish guy outside looking at your car a little too closely. Wearing a windbreaker. Only one reason in this weather."

"Your play," Felicity said.

"Wait two minutes, pay the check and walk out to the car slowly."

Morgan wiped his mouth, stood and went to the men's room at the back of the diner. The smell would stop him from using the facilities but he didn't plan to anyway. Standing on the tank behind the commode he had no trouble climbing out the single narrow window.

Back at the table, Felicity stood up and dropped money on the table. Frederico rose with her, following like a faithful puppy. She moved toward the exit, looking through the glass door and the man on the other side of it. Outside, the Latin man had almost reached for the door. As Felicity approached it he stepped back, turning to avoid her view.

Behind him, at the edge of the building, another man flicked a switchblade open. Felicity read his eyes, his body language and, through them, the situation. He was back-up. Taking the boy was their sole intent. They thought they would find him alone, but they did not anticipate any real trouble from his new friends.

The knife carrier grinned at Felicity until an arm reached around the corner of the building and a strong hand gripped his jaw. His eyes bulged as his head was rammed into the brick wall. His partner turned at the sound of the impact. He stared up into Morgan's grim face. He watched his partner sliding to the sidewalk, leaving a red smear on the bricks. Behind him, Felicity and Frederico stepped through the diner's door. Her face showed an easy calm. Frederico's reflected something close to panic.

"Get in the car," Morgan said. Felicity grabbed her charge's hand, running into the parking lot. The Latin man reached under his jacket. Morgan rushed at him, trapping his hand against his chest. The stiffened fingers of Morgan's right hand thrust deep into the man's stomach. With a sharp twist, Morgan spun the man around and shoved him through the restaurant door.

Glass exploded into the diner, some of it speckled red. As the body hit the floor, an alarm began to batter Morgan's ears. The man laid still, blood trickling from his left arm and neck. Some diner patrons stood up for a better look but most of them screamed and scrambled to the back of the building. Morgan sprinted for Felicity's car. The door stood open, waiting for him. He leaped inside and the door had not quite closed when Felicity stomped the accelerator, leaving black patches of rubber on the parking lot asphalt.

"Where?" Felicity asked.

"Texas," Morgan replied after only a short pause. "Only safe play. But we've got a couple of stops to make first, if we're going to travel in peace."

-14-

It was Felicity's first smile in three hours, but she could not help it. The two men walked out of the department store looking much like father and son. Morgan's exasperation showed in the lines in his face. Frederico grinned like a seven year old after his first day in Disneyland. He was brand new top to bottom, from the simple blue cotton shirt to the jeans, socks and tennis shoes. Knowing Morgan, he probably had new underwear too.

They climbed into their newly bought car, Frederico as usual in the back. While Morgan put a new suitcase in the back seat, Felicity wrestled the column shifter into the "D" position and pulled away from the curb.

"He give you any trouble?" she asked. Behind dark glasses, her eyes laughed.

Morgan grimaced in apparent disgust. "You'd think the boy's never had clothes on before. He couldn't have attracted more attention. The faster we're on the road the better I'll like it."

"I have worn clothes before," Frederico said. "Just not new clothes. These are all new."

It felt good to relax for a bit. Their morning had been hectic. From the diner Felicity had driven in a random pattern for a few minutes until she was certain they could not have been followed and their destination could not be guessed. Then, at Morgan's direction, she pulled into a low key strip mall.

"This parking lot is a good choice," Morgan said.

"You've got good visibility in all directions and easy access to the street. We passed a used car dealership three blocks back. That's where I'm headed. Sit tight, but if you see anybody even a little suspicious, or if you get a nervous feeling, you get the hell out of here, understand?"

Morgan had started walking while Felicity and Frederico stayed in her Corvette, alert but trying to look relaxed. While they waited, she called her office to check in.

"Stark and O'Brien, how may I help you?"

"Sandy, good morning. It's Felicity."

"Ms. O'Brien, so good to hear from you." Sandy Fox's voice went from professional cool to personally concerned. "Mister Stark hasn't been in yet, and he's always here by seven-thirty. You can set your watch by him, except of course when he's on one of his special assignments."

"He's with me," Felicity said. "Sandy, I need you to listen closely. Mister Stark and I are on a job, undercover. Neither of us will be in today. Actually, I don't know when we'll be in."

"Yes, ma'am. But what about your appointments? Your calls?"

"You'll handle it," Felicity said, slouching down in her car seat. "You always do. Now listen, we're going to have to abandon my car. Take down this address and send Paul to pick it up later, okay?"

While Felicity waited in her black Corvette, Morgan went to get them something a little less conspicuous. Anaconda's intelligence had been good so far. From what Felicity heard, Anaconda had studied them carefully. She must have known Felicity collected high performance sports cars. To travel under Anaconda's radar they needed exactly the opposite.

When Morgan returned to pick them up, Felicity knew he had found it. The sedan he pulled up in was nothing she would have driven except in the most dire circumstances.

"I give up," she had said. "What is it?"

"This, my spoiled young passenger, is a nine year old Buick LeSabre. The finest automotive transportation you can buy for forty-seven hundred dollars. After three phone calls, he was willing to take a check. Don't you like it?"

"What? Primer gray with a taupe interior?" Felicity said, climbing in. "What's not to like?"

They abandoned Felicity's Corvette where it stood, moving to step two, preparing for their trip and making their charge harder to spot. This resulted in Morgan outfitting him in a department store, while Frederico looked in awe at the simplest things.

Despite being annoyed, Morgan had to admit he also felt sorry for the kid. Frederico obviously grew up in a very limited corner of the world. He was stunned when Morgan simply purchased a change of clothes and travel items for himself and Felicity, and a suitcase to put them in. Morgan figured Anaconda must have kept him as segregated as possible from other people to maintain his mystique.

From there Felicity drove them to a small gas station. Morgan filled the tank, bought and filled an emergency five gallon gas can, and bought five quarts of oil, just in case. He filled a second emergency can with water. Finally, he bought a map. When he returned to the car, he opened the driver's side door.

"I'll drive," he said. "You slide over and get some rest."

"How long?" Felicity asked, rolling her window down.

"Looks like about thirteen hundred miles, with a couple of jogs around the Mexican border," Morgan said, opening the map. "Maybe eighteen road hours if this thing will hold the speed limit all the way. And if we don't have to stop too often for gas, and food, and bathroom breaks." Then he folded the map carefully, put the Buick in gear, and pulled into traffic.

They drove with all four windows down because the air conditioning did not work. The radio did, but with such tinny sound that it soon became nerve wracking. The springs in the seats were shot, the shocks nonexistent.

"Got to admit, you were spot on about one thing," Felicity said. "No one who knew anything about me would ever suspect I'd be travelling anywhere in anything like this."

Thirty minutes down I-5 they stopped at another filling station on the outskirts of Santa Ana to deal with the final detail before they could really get underway. While Morgan and Frederico parked in the shade of a giant Texaco sign, Felicity dropped coins into a telephone for a long distance call to Texas. A clerk answered at the other end, then transferred the call into a certain bungalow.

"Yes?" It seemed the standard CIA telephone response.

"Chuck? Felicity. Pay phone. Unsecured line, but outside of Los Angeles. Okay?"

"Felicity. Thank God," Chuck said, sending a loud sigh of relief bursting through the phone. "Mark called. Tried to tell me you had some trouble but it got kind of garbled. What's going on? Are you okay?"

"I'm fine. Morgan took a couple of bruises. Is it okay to talk on this..."

"Fuck security," Chuck snapped. "My phone's clear. Damn it, I should have been there. No, I should have never gotten you into this."

"Chuck, I'm fine. No need to worry about me at all. Morgan's the best protection a girl could have."

"Yeah," Chuck said. "Thanks. You getting out, or digging in or what?"

Felicity hesitated only a second, and then decided Chuck, being CIA, was someone whose judgment she could trust on a security matter. "We're heading your way.

See you tomorrow, midafternoon. And we've got one of Anaconda's boys."

"What? A prisoner? If Anaconda spotted you, why are you still mixed up in this? You sure as hell can't go undercover to get any information now."

"It's the kid. Did Mark tell you about Frederico?"

"He said something about a boy who talked some psychic mumbo jumbo to keep Anaconda's men in line. Is it true she would have killed you if this boy said you were too dangerous?"

"Aye, that's the long and short of it," Felicity said. "He could have spiked us but he didn't."

"And you're saying that now he's with you and Morgan?"

Yes. He wants out of the Escorpionistas, Chuck. He's important to their boss and even if he wasn't they don't like traitors much."

Chuck took a deep breath. "If they want him you're putting yourself at risk, girl. Why should you…"

"He's got intel we need. He can help us find the drugs. Says they come in on the ships for sure. But we've got to protect him."

"Jesus, do you know what you're doing?" Over the phone, she could almost hear him sweat.

"We're not safe here. Just hold the fort until we can join you. I promise to be careful. Got to go, lover. See you soon." Felicity blew a kiss into the phone. After a brief pause, the line disconnected from the other end. Felicity cursed under her breath. What a caper. Here they were on the run, with excess baggage, ill equipped. The enemy had the advantage in manpower, intelligence, and resources. And now, her man was pissed off at her.

"Life was sure easier when I was a thief," she told herself.

-15-

"Yes sir, I'll make sure Ms. O'Brien is in touch with you as soon as she returns," Sandy Fox told the telephone. Whenever that is, she added silently. As she hung up the phone, Paul came into the office.

"Have you seen Mister Stark?" he asked in his cool, accent free voice. "I expected to meet him in his office five minutes ago, but he hasn't arrived."

"Neither of them is here," Sandy answered. Looking up at him, she brushed her hair back with her hand and pushed her glasses up from her pert button nose. Then she realized she was showing all her nervous habits and ordered herself to stop. "Ms. O'Brien called to say they were on a job, some kind of hush hush thing," she continued. "You're supposed to go pick up her car."

"I see. What was Ms. O'Brien driving today?"

"The Corvette," Sandy said. "The keys are in a magnet box stuck to the muffler." She liked Paul well enough, but he always made her nervous. She thought it must be his eyes, ice blue like the Alaskan malamute puppy her father gave her when she was ten.

"Right," Paul said. "Give me the location and I'll take a taxi over."

"Don't you think this is a little funny?" Sandy asked. "I mean, it just feels...I don't know. Anyway, I hope this doesn't mean she's in any kind of trouble." She looked up at the tall man, hoping for reassurance.

"Yes, I like her too," Paul said. "However, if she has

Mister Stark with her I'm sure there's nothing to worry about."

-16-

After tossing his jacket into the back seat and rolling up his sleeves, Morgan settled into the serious business of driving. Despite wearing dark glasses, he battled a merciless sun. Heat mirages laid silver sheets on the asphalt ribbon ahead, like shallow pools that were forever out of reach. On either side of the road, scrub grass and sand stretched out to the horizon. The car soon filled with dust, which Morgan washed from his throat with black coffee from Styrofoam cups.

A little after noon they rolled into a roadside truck stop. All three riders climbed out and stood to stretch and work out the kinks that accumulate on a long ride.

"I'll get us some food," Morgan said. "The boy stays here."

"Don't you think that's being a little paranoid?"

"Are you so sure he won't get spotted, even out here?" Morgan asked over the car's roof. Felicity glanced around, showing a flash of uncertainty.

"I guess you're right. But he's going to have to at least get to the loo."

Nodding, Morgan walked Frederico to the men's room on the side of the building. Then, while Felicity took her rest stop, he pulled his jacket back on and went inside to buy lunch to go. Outside he filled the gas tank, and within ten minutes they were travelling again. Felicity unwrapped her food, muttering under her breath.

"I should have gone in to order," she said, balancing

greasy French fries and a Jumbo burger on her lap. At Morgan's sharp stare she took a long drink from her large Coke. Behind her, Frederico was enjoying this American luncheon like any teenager in a mall food court. Looking at his calm, relaxed face made her smile.

"Lad, I don't see how you can be so confident," she said.

"I am safe now," he said. "Don't worry. The vision was clear. You will destroy Anaconda and I will be free of her. As long as my new mistress is happy, I am happy."

Conversation dwindled to a minimum. Morgan focused on the road while his two passengers dozed on and off. He had bought four coffees, which he drank at about one hour intervals. His mind soon began to turn his present situation over. With one bold move they had escaped Anaconda's surveillance, but what else?

Corpus Christi remained a mystery, complete with a smuggling scheme no one had been able to figure. Beyond that, what happened to Frederico when it was all over? Even if they succeeded in breaking Anaconda's drug operation, what would prevent a vengeance strike from the Escorpionistas? All in all, he did not like his present position.

Five hours after the first stop, Morgan pulled into another truck stop. A tiny building, it grew up out of the desert floor like a lone cactus, not far from the corner where New Mexico and Arizona met at Mexico's border. Before getting out of the car, he reached back and began struggling into his jacket.

"Wouldn't it be easier to just take off your shoulder holster?" Felicity asked.

"Easier. Not safer."

"Okay," she said. "Still, if you'll wait until I go to the bathroom I'll get the food." Morgan nodded, and his passengers bolted for the rest rooms as if they might soon explode. He pumped the gas, letting Felicity pay for it inside. They were using cash because like cell phone transmissions, credit card purchases can be traced and they still had no idea of the limits of Anaconda's resources.

Fifteen minutes later their LeSabre was speeding down the freeway. Silence ruled until just after eight-thirty. Felicity broke the stillness with a tentative request.

"Morgan? Do you suppose we could stop soon?"

"Well, I kind of wanted to make El Paso before we stopped for the night, Red."

"Where are we? I haven't seen a sign in a while."

"Well, over there, that's the Florida mountain range," Morgan said.

"Obviously misplaced."

"Yes, well the Texas border's a good seventy-five miles away," Morgan said. "It's not that much longer. Are you okay?"

"Honestly my bum just can't take it," she said with a pleading smile. "I simply cannot sit on a car seat another five minutes."

Morgan nodded, said, "Okay," and pulled off I-5. They were near Deming, New Mexico. He drove south, away from the city. A few minutes into the mountain range Morgan found a small town called San Simon. Hanging onto the town's perimeter, standing all alone, he found a small hotel called The Wagon Wheel Inn. He drove past a large standing half wagon wheel in front, around to a parking area in back. A puzzled look on Felicity's face caught Morgan's attention.

"What's the matter, Red?" he asked. "Are we being followed?"

"No chance. I've been watching. Besides, I'd sense it."

"Not if they were just watching," Morgan reminded her. "If they meant us no harm, presented no danger, I wouldn't get a warning, and I think you're the same. But something's bothering you."

"No, it's just...didn't we pass this town before?"

Morgan grinned, pulling his jacket back on. "We passed a San Simon in Arizona, not far past Bowie. It's not so uncommon for a town name. I think there's one in California too." When they all got out, Morgan grabbed the suitcase. They breathed dry, and thanks to the elevation, somewhat cooler air now than when their trip began.

The Inn, all white with black shutters, looked like it belonged in Georgia or Alabama, rather than a good fast ball's flight from the Mexican border. Instead of the expected Spanish influence, it showed almost Victorian styling. A staircase wound up to a second floor entrance. A row of seven columns supported big porches on the second and third stories which were surrounded by banisters.

Inside, the wide reception room had flowered wallpaper and that beige carpet only hotels and motels ever use. Morgan stepped to the counter just as a young woman in a gingham shirt, jeans and cowboy boots came from a back room to meet them.

"Welcome to the Wagon Wheel Inn," she said. "How may I help you?"

Morgan made a quick appraisal. Mexican with a little Caucasian blood, medium build, a little heavy in the chest. Straight black hair, parted down the middle, dark eyes, very prominent cheekbones. Small, pointed nose. About thirty years old. Her Spanish accent was slight but clear, her smile warm and genuine.

"We need a couple of rooms, just for the night," he said, matching her smile. "On our way East for a little vacation."

"We're happy to have you," the clerk responded. "I can give you two adjoining rooms right down the hallway." She reached for keys on a board behind her. Morgan couldn't remember the last time he had used an actual key in a hotel instead of a plastic card.

"Nothing upstairs?" Morgan asked, leaning an elbow

on the counter. "I'd be more comfortable. Especially if the room all the way in the back happens to be empty."

"I think I can take care of you," she said, switching keys.

"I'm sure you can, Mrs..."

"Miss," she said, quickly correcting him. "Miss Mary Carter." That answered Morgan's questions.

"Thanks, Mary. And is it too late for us to get something from the kitchen?" Morgan asked, accepting keys. "A sandwich and maybe some iced tea or something?"

"Why don't you folks sign in and get settled in your rooms?" Her eyes never left Morgan's. "I'll rustle something up."

Morgan led his team down the hall and pushed open the door to the stairs. He didn't like closed stairwells, because it was too easy for danger to hide there. Upstairs, Morgan opened one room door. All three walked into a room furnished in the style of the old south, with a small writing table, and a low bureau. It had a small private bath and two big windows flanking the door to the porch.

Pleased to have a room with two exits, Morgan went to one of the windows. To his relief, it opened easily and quietly. The fresh, sharp scent of desert flowers drifted in. It was quiet except for the most widespread sound on earth, the chirping of crickets. He sat on one of the three-quarter beds and opened their suitcase.

"I don't think we're in any danger here," Morgan told Felicity. "Normally we'd all stay in one room, but I think you can have a room to yourself tonight."

"But I must stay with my mistress," Frederico said. Morgan looked first at him, then at Felicity. Her brow furrowed, she took one deep breath and looked into Frederico's puppy like eyes. When she spoke to him her words were hesitant.

"Why don't you go to the other room? I'll be over in a minute. I promise." Morgan handed Frederico the key. The boy quickly gathered Felicity's things and his own and left the room. Felicity closed the door behind him.

"This is getting crazy," Morgan said in a sing song voice.

"I don't know," Felicity said, sitting beside him. "Scared, he is. He's thinking that I can save him. I got to admit, the attention is very flattering."

"Red, he can't be more than eighteen."

"I know," she said. "I'm not talking about a seduction scene here. In fact, I'm not sure why he hooked onto me like he did."

"You're not that naive," Morgan said, pulling off his jacket. "Like I said, Anaconda probably held him in a kind of master-slave relationship. He's kind of immature anyway. Maybe a touch masochistic. Maybe she got too tough on him. He wanted to break from her but he don't know how to stand on his own. So..."

"So he picks me for his new master, er, mistress." Felicity stared at her feet for a moment. "I think I can handle that better than what he might do if I rejected him."

"Your funeral," Morgan said, pulling off his shoulder holster set and hanging it in the closet. "I just don't think..." A knock on the door interrupted him. "Who?" he called, reaching his right hand back into the closet.

"Room service." The voice carried a slight Spanish accent. Morgan opened the door to find Mary with a tray in her hands. "Three steak sandwiches, potato chips and a pitcher of iced tea. Best I could do."

"Who made it?" Morgan asked.

"Me."

"Looks yummy," he said, reaching out. "I'll take this. We'll eat in their room."

"Their...?" Mary stifled her question as it was leaving her mouth. Morgan gambled and winked at her. His gamble paid off with a blush from her.

Felicity opened the other door and Morgan carried the tray in. Only one of the full size beds was turned down. Morgan set the tray on the other. A quick scan told him Felicity's clothes were already put away. He heard the running water sound stop just before Frederico emerged from the bathroom.

Sitting on the bed, Morgan poured three glasses half full of tea. Felicity sat on the other bed, her feet between the two. Frederico knelt next to her bed on the other side.

The sandwiches were hot, thick and delicious, stuffed with peppers, onions, mushrooms and a sauce that had to be homemade. Morgan had taken three bites before Felicity tasted hers. Frederico stared at her.

"Tell him to eat," Morgan said between mouthfuls. Felicity handed Frederico the third plate. He hesitated, then took it and went to the writing table.

"Man that was good," Morgan said, wiping the last bit of sauce from his plate with the final scrap of bread. "Guess I'll head on over to my room. Open that window just in case. Closed it won't keep anybody out, but open it might speed an escape. And plan to be up early. I think we ought to break camp around six. That will put us in Corpus Christi around three or four in the afternoon." Answering Felicity's bewildered look with a smile, he added "Have fun," and left.

Next door, Morgan pulled off boots and shirt and plopped heavily on the bed. He closed his eyes, trying to imagine their next move. Morgan believed in imaging, a technique his sensei taught him in Vietnam, where he first studied the Korean martial art called wharangdo. The concept was deceptively simple. He mentally created a plausible path down which future events could easily flow. In this way he controlled his destiny.

A ring from the old fashioned dial telephone next to the bed interrupted his meditations. He grabbed it, turned the bell down to minimum volume, and then answered it.

"Mister Stark?" Mary asked.

"Morgan, please, and what can I do for you?"

"I just wondered if you needed a wake up call," she said, a little hesitant. "I'm the night girl. You know, eight at night to eight in the morning?"

"I see. Thanks, but I brought an alarm." By which he meant Felicity. She was as reliable as any clock. Her mental time keeper would rouse her promptly at five-thirty. "It must get lonely though, up all night way out here in the middle of nowhere."

"Sometimes," she said, welcoming the opening. "I saw you're from California. Always wanted to move there."

"Really? Well, I don't need much sleep. If it gets too quiet tonight, stop up and we'll talk a bit about it." Morgan let the conversation lapse there, not wanting to push too hard. She would come up or she wouldn't. Either way, having your hotel's clerk on your side never hurt.

He had just hung up the phone and leaned back again when he heard Felicity scream.

-17-

Paul paid the taxi driver a little over a block away from his destination. He had no reason to expect trouble. He was simply a cautious man and chose to walk to his boss' Corvette.

He had had a busy work day, but that was not the reason he waited for moonlight to retrieve Felicity's car. It just made sense to make an enemy wait, grow bored and careless, on the off chance there was a reason Miss O'Brien and Mister Stark abandoned their vehicle across the street from a used car lot.

The city kept a quiet distance while Paul crouched behind the car and reached under the rear bumper. He felt along the cold metal until his fingers pressed against a small lozenge shape. Rather than pull the box loose he slid it open, dropping a key into his hand. When he stood, he neither saw nor heard anything in his environment react. Still, he chose to circle the car once, before opening the door.

Unfortunately, it was too dark to see inside the car, but he did not need to. He could see the shocks were slightly depressed in the front, on the passenger side. Moving only two steps away from the vehicle, he pulled his pistol out of its side draw holster and slid it under his waist band in the small of his back.

Then, maintaining his bored expression, he slid the key into the driver's side door lock and turned it. As he pulled the door open, the interior light came on and a man on the floor stabbed a revolver at him. There was an uncomfortable moment when the two men just stared at each other, neither quite sure what to expect next. Paul was not surprised, but the other man appeared to be.

"You are not the black man."

"That's pretty obvious," Paul answered, watching the man's eyes. "Nor are you. Not Mexican either. I'd say Colombian or perhaps Panamanian. Paul," he said, pointing to himself.

"Very good." The gunman shifted himself up onto the seat. "Alejandro. Now, where are the black man and the red haired woman? And where is Frederico?" Paul decided he knew those eyes. They were the cold eyes of a killer.

"You won't believe this," Paul said, taking a small step backward, "but I don't have any idea what you're talking about."

"We will see. You have a gun?" Paul frowned bitterly and slowly raised the right side of his jacket, revealing his empty holster. Alejandro flashed a broad, hateful grin and waved his gun, indicating that Paul should back away. Paul took one more step back. The gunman moved up on the seat, pivoted to face outward and slid forward.

An instant before Alejandro's foot touched the pavement, Paul moved. His body dropped to his left, his right hand darted to his back, and his left foot rose to kick out against the door.

Alejandro cried out as the door slammed on his ankle but his voice was drowned out by the blast of his pistol. The car's driver side window exploded outward, showering Paul with shattered glass. He stayed on the ground, his left arm supporting him, waiting for the door to snap open again.

Alejandro jumped out of the car as quickly as he could, waving his gun in Paul's general direction, but his night vision was gone, destroyed in the flash of his first shot. He hesitated, only a moment, unsure of the location of his target.

On the pavement, Paul squeezed his trigger once. His automatic jumped, and Alejandro's head snapped backward. By the time his body hit the ground Paul was up and climbing into the car.

The violent action had taken place in the space of half a dozen heartbeats. Paul took a deep calming breath and dropped into the Corvette's driver's seat. He slammed the sports car into gear and pulled away, quickly reaching the speed limit but not exceeding it.

Away from the city, out on the highway, the high half moon washed the color out of the world. Paul was sure no one had witnessed the shooting or his departure. Once he reached the office he would park the Corvette in the parking garage, throw a plastic sheet over it, and wait for further instructions. He would have to get a new barrel for his Sig Sauer P229. The bullet he left in his assailant could be traced to the present one. His biggest disappointment was that he had not learned anything.

He wondered just what kind of trouble his bosses had gotten themselves into this time.

-18-

Morgan burst into Felicity's room, his left arm forward, his right fist at his waist holding his boot dagger. Felicity stood before him, mouth and eyes wide. Frederico sat on the floor to Morgan's right, hugging himself and rocking. His teeth chattered and his entire body shivered spastically.

"My God, he's having a fit," Felicity shouted.

"Hold him," Morgan said, springing for the bathroom. Felicity knelt in front of Frederico, gripping his shoulders. Seconds later Morgan crouched beside his partner. His left hand gripped Frederico's hair and tipped his head back, allowing him to shove a rolled up hand towel between the boy's teeth. Frederico's head snapped back and forth. Morgan moved behind the boy, replaced Felicity's hands with his own. She moved her hands to grip Frederico's balled fists.

"Relax," she said, her voice soft and smooth. "Don't fight it. Relax your muscles. Calm your mind." She made eye contact and held it, speaking in the soothing tones of a first class con artist. She had removed all doubt from a dozen marks in just that way years ago. She repeated those same three short sentences, until they combined to become an almost hypnotic chant. Frederico seemed to merge with her mantra. Slowly his spasms gentled, finally stopping. The boy sat, soaked with sweat, breathing like he had just finished a marathon.

"Grand mal seizure," Morgan said, standing. "What a life he must have had." When Felicity looked at him in

87

confusion he added, "Your boy's an epileptic, Red, and a bad one."

"I am fine," Frederico said, pulling the towel from his mouth. "It never comes more than once in two days. I knew you could bring me out of it. Your eyes have the power."

"Red, do you want me to..."

"No, you go on," Felicity said, looking up. "You need to get some rest, and I think he's more relaxed with you next door."

Morgan looked at Frederico, shook his head, muttered "Your call. You're a big girl," and returned to his own room. Frederico stood up as if nothing unusual had happened and waved a hand at the bathroom.

"Mistress, your bath is getting cold."

"My bath?" Felicity asked, startled. Frederico's reaction, or non-reaction to having a seizure tilted her off balance.

"I made your bath before we ate. I couldn't find any oil."

"Oh. Thank you," Felicity said. She did need a good soak in a tub, and he looked like he would be all right. With a final glance backward, she went into the bathroom, securely closing the door.

Dropping her clothes in a pile on the floor, Felicity stared into the small mirror over the sink. She made herself look at the angry red line down her left breast, crusting where her flesh was starting to knit together. Her teeth tingled, like when she looked at bird tracks in snow, although she did not know why. She knew she should have had a doctor look at it right away, but she could not yet bear for another person to see it. Or was it that she just did not want to think about it?

Their whiteness further accented her breasts. The rest of her body was tanning smoothly for a change, without the usual peeling. Her normally pale skin had taken on a slightly golden cast, smoothly covering her face and neck. Then she noticed her arms. A line separated her dark brown right arm from the utterly white shoulder above it. During their long drive eastward her arm had hung out the window almost the whole way. This resulted in a line showing where her tee shirt sleeve ended.

Silently laughing at herself, Felicity turned and stepped into the deep, claw footed tub. The water was still pleasingly hot as she climbed in. Raising her knees let her sink almost chin deep. Leaning back, she could feel muscles unknotting all over her body. Total relaxation. Her body unwound completely.

Then, adrenaline flooded her system when Frederico walked in. Felicity snapped forward, her arms crossing to cover her breasts.

"Get out of here," she snapped.

"You need your bath," Frederico said, as if that explained everything.

"Sure and I do, but you can't come walking into the room when I'm sitting here starkers." Her eyes blazed and her brogue came through.

"Starkers?" Frederico asked.

"I'm naked, you twit."

"Yes," Frederico said, kneeling beside the tub. "To be bathed." As if it were the most natural thing, he wet a cloth, soaped it, and began washing her back in a smooth circular motion. Against her will, Felicity began to calm down.

"Look. Frederico. I'm sure this is what you were taught, but I'm a big girl and I can wash myself."

Frederico's hand froze in place. "Have I displeased you?" he asked. Looking over, Felicity saw fear cross his eyes.

"It's okay, Frederico, really it is, but you'll have to be going now," she said firmly. "I need to be having some time to myself." The boy dropped the cloth, bowed his head, and hurried out.

Felicity sat back and blew air upward. She could not

remember ever feeling so very naked, perhaps because she thought of him as a boy, despite the obvious fact that he was a man.

She remembered Morgan saying something about a master-slave relationship. She had heard the word "dominatrix" often in California, but thought of the whole idea as a joke. Women in leather with whips and so on. But this was not funny at all. Anaconda had apparently used Frederico, not just for his supposed psychic talent, but as a body slave. *How much more was there to it?* she wondered.

Felicity stayed in the tub just long enough to get clean. Standing, she found all her personal items in the bathroom, arranged very neatly. After powder and cologne, she pulled on a white terry cloth robe Morgan picked up for her. She had not thought of it, but he did. Expecting all three of them to share one room, he had anticipated her needs. As usual.

When Felicity went into the bedroom, Frederico stood up where he had been sitting, on the floor next to her bed. Felicity rushed to speak, to preempt any further nonsense.

"We have an early day tomorrow. We're needing to get some sleep. Your bed is there." So saying, she tightened her robe belt and got under her own bed's covers, face down. She pushed her face into the pillow as if she wanted to escape her discomforting situation.

"But mistress," Frederico said, undaunted. "Your massage." Before Felicity could react, strong, sure fingers were kneading her shoulders and neck. She started to snap at him but it felt so good it disarmed her completely. She lapsed into stillness, not even protesting when he pulled her robe down to her waist. As he worked slowly down her back, she forced herself to speak, trying to maintain some control.

"Frederico, how did you get involved with Anaconda and the Escorpionistas?"

"My former mistress came to visit my father in the village three years ago," Frederico said, probing for tight muscles in her back. "She had heard that Anthony my brother, and I, we had visions."

"Visions?" Felicity choked back a moan of pleasure as Frederico's sure fingers probed her lower back.

"The spirits come, take us over, show us things. Anthony's ability is not so great as mine, though. Sometimes, if I think about a thing, or a person, my vision will be about that person or thing. Anaconda gave Father a great deal of money, I think, and she took us away. She has great power. She was able to control the spirits, so I was not hurt so much as I used to be during the visions. Mostly I protected her from enemies. By knowing who might cause her trouble, she has risen quickly to take over the Escorpionistas. But they are all very bad people."

"I know," Felicity said. "And while you protected her, she taught you to do these things?"

"She taught me how to treat a mistress," he answered, pressing a thumb down to free a knotted muscle in her right thigh. "I had to please her. I...she was my mistress. But the people around her were bad and they used my visions to hurt others. I did not like that. Then, when I saw you, and the spirits told me you would stop my former mistress, I saw a chance to escape. Anthony said this was my chance and encouraged me to go."

"Frederico." Felicity took a deep breath, prepared to tread delicate ground. After a moment, she decided to be direct. "Were you her lover? Did you have sex?"

"No," he answered simply, squeezing her calves. "Only the...my English fails." He gave the Spanish term for oral sex. "I pleased her with my hands, and my mouth. Shall I...?"

"No! Thank you. We will not be as you and Anaconda were. Understand?"

"Yes, mistress," he replied, massaging her left foot.

"How long have you been epileptic?" When he looked at her quizzically she said "The fits, how long? The shaking."

"The visions?" he asked. "The spirits have visited me since I was ten years old. There is hair."

Felicity looked around after that seeming non sequitur. Across the room, Frederico rummaged in his small bag.

"I have what I need, here," Frederico said. "Razor and slave creme." Now she saw. He meant her legs. As he massaged her he noticed her legs needed shaving. A lazy smile touched her lips.

"No, son, you mean shave..." she stopped, realizing he probably said exactly what he meant. Anaconda had conditioned him to be a slave, even used him for her personal hygiene and her selfish sexual satisfaction. Well, she had to admit he gave an excellent massage. Carefully pulling her robe up around herself, she turned over and leaned up. She was about to protest and put a halt to his attentions when he again startled her.

"The man, Chuck, he really loves you."

"What?" she was too startled to stop him from spreading white foam on one leg below her knee.

"That was my vision tonight," he said, his voice calm as he drew a straight razor smoothly down her leg. "He is very worried about you. And he is jealous."

"What, of you?"

"Oh no, mistress," he said, turning her foot to reach her inner calf. "Of Mister Stark. He fears he can never be as close to you as Mister Stark is. Shall I shave here?" To Felicity's surprise Frederico pointed up her robe at her crotch.

"No! No, thank you. That can...leave that part alone." She wanted to be shocked and offended. But secretly, she did not know if she could stand it. Having a man shave her legs was, to her surprise, a very sensuous experience. It may have been fine in a different context, but she did not want that kind of relationship with this boy. Once it was clear that it would go no further she decided she would just lay back and enjoy it.

While her body floated in some physical pleasure zone, she played back Frederico's words. She was beginning to believe he really was psychic, somehow in connection with his epileptic seizures. She thought he might really be able to predict future events, so it unnerved her when he spoke again.

"Your Chuck, he searches for a way to prove he is as worthy of your trust as Mister Stark. His search will have a bad end."

-19-

Manuel Alvarez did not know exactly why he woke up. Was it a sound? A vibration in the room? Or maybe just a feeling. The feeling of being watched.

"Hello, Manny." The voice chilled him, coming out of the darkness in his hotel room. The voice was neither high nor low, and it carried no accent at all. His first impulse was to reach for his gun, but he doubted he would make it to the closet alive. Something about that voice.

"Who are you?" Alvarez tried to harden his own voice. "What do you want? How did you get in here?"

"First, understand that you are in no danger," The voice said from across the room. "My name is Paul. I'm visiting this way because you clearly want to maintain a certain distance from a friend of mine. I need to know where Morgan Stark is."

"Stark?" The stocky DEA agent sat up. "How the hell should I know?"

A bored or frustrated sigh came from across the room. "Mister Stark keeps excellent records. His appointment with you is documented, but the assignment is not. I know you represent the Drug Enforcement Agency. I know you refused to communicate when he needed more information. I know he's gone."

That sounded like an accusation to Alvarez. He rolled toward the closet. Paul racked the slide of his automatic. The metal-on-metal sound was loud in the little room. Alvarez sat back, grateful for the darkness. The other man could not see him sweat.

"Okay, Stark and O'Brien did accept an assignment for us. He's undercover. Probably they both are. But I couldn't talk to him because I can't be linked to it. Same reason I can't tell you."

"I visited this way so you wouldn't be linked to me," Paul said. "No one saw me come. No one will see me go. Two men were watching you tonight. Was one of them yours?"

Was? "Yes, I had a man on lookout." The room was very stuffy, and Alvarez worried that his visitor might smell his fear now.

"They are both sleeping comfortably. What are Mister Stark and Ms. O'Brien looking for?"

"No," Alvarez said.

Paul sighed. "Don't move please." His pistol's slide slammed back louder than the silencer-covered blast. Alvarez heard the bullet punch a small hole into the wall three inches from his own mouth.

"It's late. I'm tired. If I have to ask someone else, news of your death would make him more cooperative," Paul said. "What are Mister Stark and Ms. O'Brien looking for?"

Alvarez took two deep breaths, staring hard into the darkness. How could the other man see him? Or did he shoot based on the sound of Alvarez's voice? His hands were clammy, his mouth dry. How important was his secret? Not worth his life. Besides, maybe this mystery man could help him do his job.

"They're helping with an investigation," Alvarez said. "Looking for a connection to trace the import of a drug called ice. It's being imported by a Colombian criminal syndicate called the Escorpionistas. If they're in trouble, that's who's making it."

"Thank you. I assure you your security will not be compromised. Now lie down. Close your eyes. Count to fifty. Then, go back to sleep. Tell no one of our meeting and I promise not to come back."

The implication of that last remark was clear. Alvarez started counting. He never heard anything but his own voice but by the time he got to thirty-five he was pretty sure he was alone. At forty-five he turned on the bedside lamp. He was alone.

Still, he kept counting to fifty. He would do everything this Paul told him to. Except one thing.

He would not be going back to sleep.

-20-

A light tap on the door just before midnight snapped Morgan's eyes open and drove his right hand under his pillow to grip his automatic. Then he relaxed, realizing no enemy would knock before entering. Besides, his danger sense would have awakened him. He slid out of bed and into his pants. At the door he quietly asked who it was.

"Is it too late to talk?" Mary asked. Morgan smiled and opened the door. "It does get lonely down there," she said.

Morgan waved her in and turned on the writing table lamp. Mary took the chair, looking nervous. Morgan recognized these mixed signals: a woman fighting to project an air of experienced worldliness, and simultaneously a feeling of "I've never done this kind of thing before." Morgan guessed the truth was somewhere in between.

"Did you have any complaints about noise?" Morgan asked, sitting on the bed. "Something scared my friend a while back and she screamed."

"Not likely," Mary said. She tried crossing her legs, uncrossed them, and settled on sitting with her hands between her knees. "You three are the only ones on the second floor." She smiled, and silence hung thick between them.

"So you think you'd like California, eh?" Morgan asked after a moment.

"Well, I've been kind of thinking about it for a long time," Mary said. She was dressed as before, but her shirt's top three buttons were open. Soft light from the lamp beside her had a dual effect. It washed years away from her face and accented her breasts with heavy black shadows. Morgan's pulse quickened just enough for him to notice.

"It's not as laid back as this place," Morgan said, suddenly realizing how unnatural this setting was. "You know, I'd like to offer you a cup of coffee or something, but I guess you'd have to go get it." That made her laugh a bit and they both relaxed a little.

"We both know I didn't come up here for coffee," Mary said, standing. Morgan stood also and they met beside the dresser. She had to look up to see his eyes. Morgan slid one arm gently around her, feeling her warmth pressed against him. It was moving quickly, which only increased the intensity.

"I can't be gone too long," Mary said, pulling his mouth down onto hers.

"How long?" Morgan whispered after their first kiss.

"An hour maybe," she said. He kissed her neck, her shoulders, the top of her breast. "Maybe an hour and a half," she said.

-21-

Morgan sat bolt upright, his right hand suddenly filled with his Hi-power. With widened eyes he probed the darkness for any immediate threat. Seeing none, he released his held breath, but did not relax. Over the next ten seconds, he reviewed his most recent memories.

Mary had lain in his arms, wrapping him in the afterglow of intense, vibrant sex. She was a fully giving partner, sensitive and responsive. At the end, when he could endure the pressure no longer, she had drawn her nails across his back, mewing, almost sobbing, deep in her throat. Afterward she had covered his face and chest with small, soft kisses.

After a long warm moment she had said "I guess it doesn't matter now, but...well, are you married or anything?"

Morgan had chuckled and said, "No, as it happens I'm not attached to anyone. You?"

"Free, Red and twenty-one," she answered, giggling at the joke they could share. "Guess that's why this place is getting me down."

"Well, now you know somebody in California," Morgan had said. He regretted the implication as soon as the words left his mouth, and he knew Mary felt him tense.

"Hey, I'm not looking for a husband if that's what you're thinking," she said in her soft voice. "But maybe somebody could help me find a job and a place to stay."

"That I would be happy to do," Morgan had said.

Five minutes later she was looking at her watch and offering energetic apologies. She slipped out of bed, leaving it cooler than before, gathered her clothes and crept to the bathroom. Morgan opened the door for her when she left, giving her a final deep kiss. Then he got back in bed, missing Mary's warmth, and dropped into a deep sleep…

Until he was jarred awake, his scalp tingling as it did only when danger approached. Ten seconds after he sat up, the soft purr of the room telephone jolted him. Without turning from the door, he lifted the receiver to his ear.

"Morgan? Mary. Two guys were here a minute ago asking for you."

"For me specifically?" he asked, getting to his feet.

"Well, no, not by name. They were looking for a young Mexican, a white woman and a black man. I told them you were here and they left. After they were gone I thought, well, they didn't look right."

"Mexican guys?" Morgan asked, starting to sweat in the room's warmth.

"What? Yeah, how did...are you in some kind of trouble?"

"Listen to me very carefully," Morgan said with an edge in his voice he realized might frighten her. "Those are very bad men, and I don't want you hurt. When they return..."

"They're coming back?"

"For sure," Morgan said. "When they do you tell them anything they want to know. Don't try to lie or fool them. They're going to want to come upstairs and when they do, you stay behind that counter. You understand?"

"Yeah. What's going to happen?"

"Nothing bad if you do as I say. Just playing a trick on some friends. I'll be down when I can." When he hung up, Morgan's stomach was clenched like a fist. How in hell had they found them? Anaconda must have a better machine than the FBI.

He rethought it as he dressed. Would it be any different trying to hide from the Mafia in Sicily? Or the Yakuza in Tokyo? He had to remember that in this part of the country he was a foreigner in a foreign land in some ways.

When Morgan opened his hallway door he was in black jeans and pullover. Holsters hung under his arms, but he held his gun in his fist. When he poked his head into the darkened hallway he made eye contact with Felicity who had looked out at the same time.

"You felt it too?" she whispered.

"They're here," Morgan said, tossing his gun to her. "Stay in that room. Point that at the door. If it ain't me, shoot it." Felicity nodded and closed her door. Morgan locked his room and crossed the unlit hall. He opened the door opposite his own without a sound, pushing it almost closed behind him. Then he lay prone on the floor, and drew his fighting knife from its scabbard under his right arm. He knew that violence was coming, and he knew it would be a quick, quiet fight, either way it went.

In hotspots all over the world, Morgan's long experience as a Special Operations solider and then as a soldier for hire had trained him to lie still for days. That life was far behind him, but the discipline he absorbed in the U.S. Army and as a mercenary remained. To his mind the present situation was close enough to war to count. He breathed slowly through his mouth, silent as a two day old corpse.

Somehow they found us, he thought. They came into the hotel, but left again. That must mean they needed to report in. Maybe their orders did not include what to do if they got lucky and found their targets. But now they would be ordered to return and finish their assignment. To kill him, maybe rape Felicity and take Frederico back to their mistress for punishment. They would strike hard and fast, not wanting to involve any other hotel patrons.

The hair on the back of Morgan's neck tried to leave his

skin, and he knew they were back. Cautiously he glanced at his stainless steel Rolex Seamaster. Its luminous dial said five thirty-two. Scant minutes before dawn. The best possible time to strike. The time when most people were their least alert or most soundly asleep. The timing implied that a pair of true professionals was pursuing them.

They made no sound, but Morgan felt their menace coming up the hall. He drew his legs up under himself, and then withdrew his aura, becoming one with the carpet, just another piece of furniture. In the dark he saw the deeper blackness of a body standing in front of his room door. Then another form joined it. They wore no cologne, so no leading scent would give them away. They would carry automatic pistols, he knew, equipped with silencers. Everyone in the building would hear any shots, but it was such an unfamiliar noise they would assume it was something else.

Morgan closed his eyes to avoid any possibility of a reflection from his pupils, or of his attackers feeling they were being watched. One stepped toward him, then quickly away. He heard the sound of a heavy shoulder hitting a door, popping its flimsy lock loose from the frame.

As the door to his room burst open, Morgan sprang to his feet behind the two men. He dived into the darkness, even as he heard the first coughing sound of a silenced shot fired into his empty bed. Then his right shoulder hit a broad back and he slid his fighting knife's razor honed blade into the man's kidney. They continued forward, falling onto the bed.

In movies, when somebody gets stabbed they stiffen, groan and collapse. Real life is not so simple. A deep stab wound does not paralyze or shock a healthy man. He fights violently, thrashing and kicking, until he loses a lot of blood, which might take thirty seconds or more.

Morgan got his right arm around the shoulder of the man

under him and heaved. Still thrashing, the stabbed man actually helped Morgan turn him. Morgan rolled back, facing the door, in time to hear two more coughs and feel heavy lead punches thrown into the man who now shielded him. His wet, slippery hand pulled his knife free. Then with a grunt, he heaved the body forward.

The standing gunman, struck by his partner's body, staggered backward until his back hit the edge of the open door. Morgan crashed into him an instant later, reaching around the dead man to grab his live enemy's neck. The gun rose to point toward Morgan's ribs. Morgan slashed downward across the man's wrist. The gun dropped to the carpet with a dull thud. The man stifled a scream. A pro, Morgan thought again.

Then Morgan stepped to one side, spinning to get behind his still living foe. The man managed to catch Morgan's head with an elbow just before Morgan got a grip on his enemy's chin.

The sun peeked over the edge of the horizon, staring through the open window. Just as the first rays of light filled the room, Morgan drew his knife's edge across the unknown man's throat.

Six seconds later, Felicity tensed, then lowered the pistol as Morgan stepped through her door. In the near total darkness Frederico gasped. Felicity turned the gun around to hand it over to her partner.

"How did you know it was him?" Frederico asked.

"I always know it's him. Just like I sense danger, we sense each other. Comes in handy." Then the sun crept up another inch and it was Felicity's turn to gasp. "Jesus," she said through clenched teeth and turned away.

Morgan's face showed confusion for a moment, but then he looked down at himself. His left arm was solid red from the elbow down, dripping someone's warm life on the carpet.

Felicity's face contorted in a rictus of fear, and a shiver shot through her. She knew her reaction was irrational, but she could not turn her mind away from the fact that one of Morgan's knives, honed by that very same fist, had so recently tasted her own blood. Now, seeing Morgan himself holding one of his blades, covered with evidence of its ultimate use, chilled her like death's breath on her neck.

Morgan didn't know why Felicity would react so strongly, but her expression was enough to prompt him to race into the bathroom and pull off his shirt. He scrubbed himself quickly in the sink. While he was lathering his arm it struck him that he had never seen either man's face. He had no idea who he just killed. He wondered if that fact should bother him, but he had more pressing concerns. Time was escaping like the night, but he had to make sure he would not draw attention when they left.

"We're ready," Felicity said when he returned to the room, her voice just a bit shaky. "Pull on one of my tee shirts for now. Have you got a backup plan?"

"I think so," Morgan said, dropping his shoulder rig and forcing himself into the tee shirt. It was too tight, but made of some sort of stretch cotton fabric that clung to him like a second skin. He had only seen men in shirts this tight in Cirque do Soleil performances, and he knew that under other circumstances Felicity would crack wise about his appearance. As it was he though the did catch the shadow of a smirk on her face.

"Not a word, miss. This was your idea, and maybe it's get-back for the times you've borrowed one of my tee shirts. I can never wear them again after the way you stretch them out in front."

He left Felicity and Frederico in the hall long enough to pull on his jacket and pick up their suitcase. Then all three moved, as quickly as possible without running, down the hall and down the stairs to the big reception room.

Pale and shaken, Mary stood behind the counter, her knuckles white from gripping it. She appeared to have held her breath for the last five minutes. When she saw Morgan she released it, deflating slowly. Morgan went to her, grasping her arm.

"I need some help," Morgan said. "Do you really want to see California?"

"I...yes. Yes."

"Do you have a car?"

"Didn't you drive here?"

"Do you have a car?" he asked again.

"Yes. Well, a Bronco out back."

"A four by four? Okay." Morgan glanced at Felicity who somehow understood and began writing on a piece of hotel paper. "I'm going to give you the key to the car we came in. It's now yours. It ain't no prize but it's yours. Felicity will give you money."

"Five hundred dollars?" Felicity asked, opening her small purse.

"Should do," Morgan said. "I need you to take that car and drive to Los Angeles. There's the address and phone number. Go there and tell Miss Fox, the office manager who you are. We'll call her today so she'll be expecting you. She'll put you up until we get back, probably in a couple of days. Right now we need to get moving. If we can use your Bronco we'll return it when we get back. Okay?"

"I guess so, but what about those two men?" Mary asked.

"Just don't go upstairs," Morgan said. "Eventually someone may question you, but you're in no danger with what you know now."

Mary gulped and handed Morgan her keys. He pulled

her over the counter and kissed her hard on the mouth.

"Just enjoy the drive," he told her, "and be there when I get back."

-22-

Morgan put on his sunglasses as they climbed into Mary's black Bronco. Although he was most comfortable driving a four wheeler, he wished for any other vehicle because even a casual glance at this one revealed all the occupants, and they were a combination that would stand out anywhere.

"Think they'll follow her?" Felicity asked after a time.

"Hope so." Morgan's jaw muscles were working, clenching his teeth.

"How long?"

"At least until the first stop," Morgan said. "Until they can get a good look at her. No one was watching the hotel. When they come looking for their boys, they'll find quite a mess. Or if they're slow, they might find the police. Either way, they'll look for the car."

"If they buy it."

"Even if they don't it ought to at least split them up," Morgan said, easing the Bronco around a curve on the mountainous road. "They have to watch the car in case it's one of us, or she's going to meet us. That in itself is a help."

"Lord, how many men can she have to send after us?"

"Who knows?" Morgan said. "But I can tell you one thing. They just lost two of their best."

"I'm not sure what you did, but I know you saved my life," Frederico said slouching in the back seat. He looked at Morgan in the rear view mirror. "Thank you. I see that you are part of my mistress, and part of my mistress's power."

Morgan cranked the wheel, pushing the Bronco off the highway. He drove across sparse brown grass, raising a tall plume of sandy dust behind them. Once out of sight of the road, he hit the brakes.

Without a word, Morgan left the Bronco and walked aimlessly for a few steps. Felicity got out and followed. He stood holding his belt, staring down at a small round cactus. Felicity stopped four steps from him and spoke to his broad back.

"All right. What is it?"

"We leave him," Morgan said without turning. "Put him off in El Paso."

"No."

"Red, he's what they're after," Morgan said, turning. Painted mountains loomed behind her in the distance, making Felicity seem very small. "They're not chasing us. If they found him, we'd have some room to move and I wouldn't have to be watching your neck every minute."

"Yeah? And what about him?"

"She won't kill him," Morgan said, brushing her objection aside with his left hand. "She needs him. He's her power. How many psychic fortune tellers you think she's got?"

"Maybe two," Felicity replied. When Morgan stopped to stare at her, she continued. "Last night he told me Anaconda took on him and his brother. And when he told his brother about me, he encouraged Frederico to run away."

"I don't get it," Morgan said, but he was beginning to see. The distant sound of tires on asphalt was like the whine of battered children.

"Frederico says his brother gets visions too, but not as good. Maybe he found us."

"Hold it." Morgan glanced at the Bronco, but Frederico

was oblivious to their conversation. "Even if you're right, why would his brother send her after him?"

"Remember what you said about a master-slave thing?" Felicity asked, brushing hair out of her eyes. "Maybe the brother wants to be number one boy. He couldn't while Frederico did the job better. But if Frederico was out of the picture..."

Morgan considered. Her theory fit with all known facts. And Felicity was right: only Frederico's uniqueness would have saved him from Anaconda's anger. She probably would gladly trade an unwilling instrument for one not as good, but more loyal. He silently weighed their options, but he kept coming back to the same answer. After two long minutes exploring the problem, he finally muttered "damn" under his breath.

"So? What now?"

"Damn it, I'm no hero or some crime fighter." Morgan kicked the cactus in frustration. "We don't belong in this. This ain't personal protection and it sure as hell ain't security work."

"Morgan, you're right." Felicity gripped his shoulders and turned him to her. "Okay? I said it. For no good reason except I wanted to and it would have helped a friend, we got involved in something that's none of our business. I'm sorry. God, I'm sorry. But we're in it now. We owe Chuck a finished job. It looks like we owe this kid our lives. And I owe that bitch something for... hurting us. So. What now?"

"Now we continue on to Corpus Christi," Morgan said looking into her deep green eyes. "We hope we can figure out this smuggling thing soon." Shaking his head, Morgan climbed back into the Bronco and started it.

-23-

Mary Carter hated everything about the gray Buick LeSabre. She hated the power steering that yanked the big car in any direction at the slightest move of the steering wheel. She hated the grabby breaks. She hated the automatic transmission that always seemed to shift way too late. She hated the rough, ragged ride reflecting shock absorbers that had long passed their usefulness. But more than anything else she hated the fact that it was taking her in the exact opposite direction from the tall, muscular stranger who gave it to her.

On the other hand, she knew she would see him again, and that brought a smile. It was a beautiful day and she had gotten on the road early enough that she would have the golden sun at her back for a while. There was almost no traffic on the I-5 at that time of morning, and California waited in the distance. It was not the Promised Land, of course, but she knew it had to be a big step up from the rural outpost she had been stuck in all her life up to now.

She pushed a button and was pleased to learn that the radio worked. While she familiarized herself with the controls she noticed movement in her rear view mirror. A black vehicle was slowly gaining on her. Someone driving in a much more practical Ford F-250 had somewhere to be. Well, she did too, but she did not want to push the LeSabre past seventy miles an hour. Not with its spongy suspension and overactive steering. She missed her Bronco. But all she had to do was get to the address Morgan gave her. She had no reason to hurry and there was plenty of room for the other driver to pass her if he wanted to.

She hit the scan button, hoping to find one of those sunny summer songs that she associated with California.

"Why would they go back?" Marta asked. He drove the black Ford truck with his seat pushed back as far as possible so that, with his left hand on the wheel, his arm was stretched out to its full length.

"How the hell should I know?" Quesada asked. "And why should I care? Our orders are to follow, not second guess. When they settle someplace we'll take them out. Doesn't matter to me where that happens." Quesada rode with his right elbow hanging out the window, scratching at the scar running down from his right eye.

Marta leaned back, huffing with exasperation. "We could end up driving all the way back to California to take care of this. Just to get Anaconda's boy toy back. What a bullshit job."

They drove in silence for a few minutes. Marta maintained a comfortable distance behind his quarry, occasionally dropping back far enough to be out of sight. He didn't know who these two were, but he heard how the Black man had fought his way out of a three-man attack. If he was that good, he might spot a tail.

Beside him, Quesada lit up one of his little cigars. After he took a drag he leaned forward, as if he was looking for something. When he spoke he blew acrid smoke toward his partner.

"Hey, pull up a little closer."

"No way," Marta said. "I don't want them to see us following them, dumbass."

"As long as they can't see us, we can't see them," Quesada said. "And I want to. Look up there. You see Frederico?"

Marta eased the truck a bit closer and looked hard. "No I don't see him, but so what? He's probably laying down in the back. The boy's a pussy. He's probably taking a nap."

"Yeah? And what you heard about this Black guy, you think he's laying down with the boy?"

"Hehehe, no, I don't think he's that way," Marta said.

"Yeah? So where is he?"

Marta leaned forward and eased the accelerator a little closer to the floor. He didn't want to be obvious, but he did want a better look into the gray car ahead. Now it was clear that the only visible person sat behind the wheel. Too short to be a man, and with long black hair. Quesada was leaning forward too.

"Damn it!" Quesada thumped the outside of the passenger door with a fist. "There's only the girl. They must have split up. Now what the hell are we supposed to do?"

Marta was quiet for a moment, and eased off the pedal to allow a little more distance between the truck and the LeSabre. "Something ain't right here. I thought the girl target was a redhead. And ain't she a mick?"

"Idiot," Quesada said, thumping his partner in the shoulder. "She dyes her hair. Don't you remember? She was disguised as a Mexican in California."

"Si, I remember," Marta said. "But the description also said she was tall, maybe five seven or eight. You see where that bitch's head is, just over the back of the seat?"

"Maybe she's just slouching down," Quesada said. "What difference does it make? We know they're not all in the car, right? We need to call in and report." He took one last long drag off his little cigar, flicked the butt out the window and pulled out his cell phone. Marta all but snarled at him.

"Report our failure? Our stupidity? Not without knowing all the facts. I want to see for sure."

While Quesada stared at him with wide eyes, Marta pressed the pedal to the floor. The Ford truck surged forward, closing fast on the old gray Buick. Quesada, wary of the reputation earned by their quarry, slid his Glock out from under the seat.

Two car lengths behind the target, Marta pulled the truck into the left lane, as if he planned to pass. The LeSabre neither sped up nor slowed down. He hoped to catch a good look at the driver's profile as he eased past. She would keep her eyes forward, not wanting to be seen. This he knew because she was from all accounts a professional.

Marta and Quesada wore plastic smiles as they eased past the LeSabre. The sound of a Beach Boys song Marta couldn't name came through the open window. To his surprise the Buick's driver turned toward them, smiled back and waved. Marta stared into that golden round face for a moment, and then eased the truck back behind the car. Anger was rising behind his eyes.

"That bitch is about as Irish as I am. We got played."

"A decoy," Quesada said, pulling out his cell phone. "Now we don't know where the hell they are with the boy. This is bad, chico. Very bad. For us." Quesada tried to push the button to report in but missed it because his body was slammed back into his seat. Marta had mashed the accelerator to the floor, spurring the big F250 forward.

"What the hell?" Quesada snapped.

Marta replied through clenched teeth, not looking over at his partner. "We got played. I don't like getting played. This bitch got to pay."

As they approached a gentle curve, Marta pulled the big truck forward until the LeSabre was in its shadow. There was still not another car in sight on the I-5. Quesada could see a narrow curve up ahead. He looked down through the two vehicle windows at the woman gripping her steering wheel with both hands. She looked up through thick black hair as terror slowly overwhelmed her face.

Marta's face reflected only rage.

Quesada managed to say, "I don't think..." just before Marta pulled the wheel to his left and then yanked it hard to the right. The truck's front quarter panel smashed into the Buick with a grinding squeal. Quesada leaned left, away from the impact, but was thrown against the door when the two vehicles met. Then the truck slowed and dropped behind the car. The LeSabre, pushed onto the shoulder, jerked left as the driver apparently tried to correct for the unexpected impact. The car's rear wheels broke loose and the Buick swung in a radical swerve. Marta chuckled as the left side tires left the pavement. The right side tires caught the edge of the shoulder and the LeSabre rose into the air as if in slow motion. The truck rolled past as the car's right side hit the ground, then the roof. In his rear view mirror Marta saw the car do another complete roll, finally coming to rest on its right side.

Marta pulled to the side of the road and hopped down from the truck. He leaned against the lift gate, shaking his head. Quesada walked back to stand beside him.

"Well, that's one bitch that won't be fucking with us no more," Marta said.

\"You think?" Quesada asked. "Know what I think? I think that was a damned amateurish move, amigo. What if somebody saw us?"

"But nobody did, moron. And she sure as hell ain't gone tell nobody nothing."

"Really, Marta?" Quesada asked. "Really? Are you so sure she's dead?"

Marta laughed one hard laugh. "Are you shitting me? Look at that car? It went over twice? And she was a little broad anyway. You don't think she's dead?"

Quesada was not smiling. Without answering his partner

he took four long steps toward the car. Then he lifted his nine millimeter and raised his left hand to shield his eyes from the sun. He fired once into the underside of the car. Marta heard the bullet pierce the steel with a plink sound. Quesada fired again. Clear liquid flowed out of the second hole, as if the car was bleeding.

Quesada's third shot must have caused a spark because the gas tank erupted outward. The explosion was fierce enough to rock the car over onto its roof where it settled into the sandy earth and the flames spread to completely engulf the LeSabre's body. Quesada stood quiet for a moment, then slid his gun into his waistband and turned.

"Now I'M sure she's dead," he said as he walked back past Marta to climb into the truck.

-24-

Morgan, Felicity and Frederico all entered Corpus Christi with some surprise. Aside from being their journey's end, the city was a welcome departure from the tumbleweeds and ten gallon hats that typify the rest of the second biggest state.

This coastal city felt urban to her, in a way even Dallas and Houston were not. Felicity was surprised to find restaurants and hotels trying to appeal to a continental class of tourists. And she knew that if she were visiting under different circumstances she would love shopping there.

Barton stayed in a cottage in a cluster of cottages near the coast. Despite the mid-eighties temperature, a gentle breeze toyed with Felicity's hair when she stepped down from the Bronco. She noted the difference between the smell of a Pacific wind and the somehow tangier gulf breeze that she thought carried a slightly oily aroma. The cottages, scattered about at land's end, were a sandy color that made them seem natural growths, rising up from the beach. When she stared out toward the ocean she was startled by riders in motion.

"Are those horseback riders racing out there?"

"Yep," Morgan said. "That's Mustang Island. Not really an island, it's just one part of Padre Island. It runs this way," he said, pointing, "for sixty-six miles."

"You spend way too much time watching the Discovery Channel," Felicity said. Morgan chuckled but stopped when Felicity jumped like a startled mustang herself. A jet ski engine coughing somehow reminded her of a silenced pistol shot. Smiling at herself, she turned toward Chuck's door. When she knocked she had a brief flash of seeing Morgan at a similar hotel room door, one arm coated with blood. She closed her eyes to erase the image. When she opened them, Chuck Barton was reaching for her, pulling her inside, spinning her off the floor.

"Lord I missed you," Chuck said into her ear. "I was so worried. Mark called, but he didn't know where you were or anything."

"You're breaking my ribs, lover," Felicity said, giggling. "If you'll just be putting me down now I'll tell you everything."

"We're fine too, thanks," Morgan said, brushing past the couple to drop the suitcase beside a sofa. It faced a love seat and was separated from it by a low coffee table. Across the big room four straight chairs surrounded a square table.

"Wait a minute." Chuck put Felicity back on her feet to stare at Frederico. "Who's this guy?"

"That's part of the everything I have to tell you," Felicity said. "But I hope I can get settled first. Would you be so kind as to drop my suitcase in the bedroom?"

Burton smiled at the implication and dragged the suitcase off. As soon as he was out of sight Felicity touched Morgan's arm.

"What?"

"You're awful jumpy," Morgan said in a low tone.

"Is that what you were frowning about?"

"Well, that and this place," he said.

"What about it?"

"You kidding?" Morgan asked. There's windows on every wall and a hatch over the sink in the little kitchenette area that opens to the attic and probably the roof. That adds up to way too many access points. Plus, the front door directly faces the bedroom door. A guy with Chuck's merc experience should know better than to pick a place like this. I'm telling you, Red, CIA life is ruining him."

Before Felicity could respond, Barton bounced back into the room. "Your stuff's all put away, baby. Now, want to go see the town?"

"Well, if it's all the same to you I'd sure like to be getting a shower first. All right?"

"I guess so," Barton said, stepping back to look into her deep green eyes. "But then you get an official decent welcome to the Texas Riviera. I'm taking all of you down to Aransas Pass, the shrimp capital of Texas."

***

A cloud of laughter followed them back to Barton's rented cottage. During a delicious dinner Felicity introduced Frederico, explaining his part in their story. Morgan picked up the narrative at breakfast the day before. When he got to the sneak attack in the hotel, he said simply, "Two guys came after us at dawn. I left them there." Then, conversation turned to the excellence of the shrimp, the beauty of the weather, and what Barton had been able to find out during his short stay in Corpus Christi.

Somebody said something about tequila's potency compared to Irish whiskey. Morgan declared himself designated driver, while Felicity and Barton initiated scientific research on their theories, bravely using themselves as test subjects. When Frederico told them he was seldom allowed near alcohol, they insisted he become involved in their experiment.

By the time Barton pushed his door open, using Felicity for support, the sky was a field of sparkling lights, slightly blurred from either of their viewpoints. Morgan entered last, visually checking the perimeter and frowning.

"Morgan, would you relax?" Barton said, flipping on the light.

"Yeah, Morgan," Felicity joined in. "We're safe here. In

fact, we've got the initiative for the first time since this whole stupid job started. What have you got to be so uptight about?"

"Guess I'm just paranoid," Morgan said with a half smile. "But I did notice that half the faces I've seen in this town were Mexican." He settled on the sofa and pulled off his boots.

"So, we need a plan for tomorrow," Felicity said, sitting at the table. "Chuck, you checked the area, right?"

"I told you, I looked it over." He pulled a chair up next to Felicity's. "Look, that mercy ship follows a predictable path every month. It always leaves here loaded with food, clothing, books, sometimes with seeds. It always docks in Cartagena. Its cargo is unloaded, then it turns around and comes right back here."

"What comes off the ship here?" Felicity asked, leaning toward Barton and swaying just a little.

"Not much," Barton answered, starting to rub her foot with his own. "Golden Heart Shipping has a major warehouse downtown. I was there yesterday when the ship, El Corazon de Hielo, docked. I guess some books were sent back. No surprise there. These people want food, not literature. They emptied the hold, then loaded up with the usual powdered milk, clothing and more bibles."

"El Corazon de Hielo," Felicity repeated. "The Heart of Ice. They're bringing it in, all right, and laughing at us all the way."

"But how?" Barton asked, stroking Felicity's arm. "We've been all over that warehouse, opened any number of crates. Nothing."

"We need to look it over in the morning," Morgan said, hanging his shoulder holster over a chair.

"Yes, I'm thinking that's tomorrow's job," Felicity said, yawning. "I am so tired. I think tequila wears me out. I'll think better after some sleep."

Felicity stood, Barton stood, and Frederico rose as well, watching his mistress' face. Glances were exchanged all around. Morgan studied his feet.

"Let's go get some rest," Chuck said, taking Felicity's hand. Her eyes widened, just for an instant, then narrowed to slits.

"Chuck, I don't think..."

"I must stay with my mistress," Frederico put in.

"Not tonight, kid," Barton said, smiling and shaking his head.

"Chuck, I do need some privacy tonight," Felicity said. Barton looked at her as if he had not heard correctly. "And I'd feel pretty uncomfortable sleeping with you with Frederico looking on."

"Then we put him out. Right?" Chuck said, his smile a little smaller.

"This is kind of delicate," Felicity said, taking a step backward. "I'll explain it tomorrow, honest. For right now, just let me go in the bedroom..."

"With him?" Barton's smile had become a stern straight line.

"You can't be thinking that I'm sleeping with him," Felicity said, putting an indignant cutting edge into her voice. "Look, I don't have to explain myself to you and you don't own me. I said we'd talk about it in the morning. I'll be going to bed now."

Felicity tossed Morgan a terse good night and went through the bedroom door with Frederico at her heels. Barton stood with his mouth open for a moment, then cast a bewildered glance around the room. Morgan stood up, stretched, and moved to the love seat. He lay down with his legs up on one arm, as if he were settling in for the night. Barton staggered over and plopped onto the sofa.

"What happened between L.A. and here?" Barton asked himself aloud.

"Wish I knew," Morgan said, his eyes closed. "I don't think she's doing anything with the kid. He's just a boy and she feels responsible for him is all."

"Yeah, she told me, remember?" Barton answered, squirming around, trying to get comfortable. "He saved your lives with his psychic mumbo jumbo. I get that bit, but what's it got to do with her and me?" Morgan sat back up, turning to face Barton. His lips curled in.

"Chuck, something happened to her in Anaconda's moving office," Morgan said. "I don't know. Maybe this woman really scared her. Anyway, something's different. A little less confidence, maybe? Something dulling her edge."

"What are you talking about?" Chuck said. "She's just doing one of those woman things nobody understands." The words came out rough. Maybe, Chuck realized, a little rougher than he intended.

"Yeah, well maybe so. Just don't push her, and keep your eyes open for clues."

"Right now, I'm just going to keep my eyes shut," Chuck said. "I got a feeling I'm going to need my rest for tomorrow's fun and games."

Morgan's head moved as if he was about to rise. Frederico came through the bedroom door as if on cue and turned off the light.

-25-

Gulls screamed in the early morning light. Through an open window, Morgan watched one trace a wide invisible circle against a cloud. After five circuits, it seemed to see what it wanted and steered into a power dive. Inches from crashing into the surf it pulled up, touched the water with its talons and stroked hard, driving back into the air. Its talons now grasped a small, wriggling fish.

That's how it happens, Morgan thought. Just like that. He filled his lungs with salt air and turned to the bed. Felicity's long red hair coated her pillow, a white sheet covering her to her chin. Like a faithful guard dog, Frederico slept on the floor on the other side of the bed. Morgan reached down, gently touching her shoulder. Her eyes snapped open. She smiled up at him for an instant, until she focused on him. Then her smile faded. His face was tense, carved from stone.

"We have to talk," he whispered. As she sat up, he stiffened for a moment. She had on a tee shirt with a print of a dragon on the front. Morgan had never known Felicity to sleep any way but nude. He knew this because she had never been modest about her body, at least not around him. He turned and went to the table in the great room, sitting in one of the straight chairs. Seconds later, Felicity followed, having pulled on a pair of shorts.

Gulls' calls seemed shrill in the early silence. Waves slapped the beach violently, almost callously. Barton's light snoring filled the otherwise silent room. He lay on the sofa, sleeping more heavily than a professional should. Felicity stood beside Morgan, a hand on his shoulder.

"Been out already?" she asked in hushed tones.

"I woke up, so I walked down to the 7-11. Picked up some donuts and the paper."

"And?" She must have known something was up, but it was not her way to guess. Morgan appreciated her trust.

"Sit down. Take a look."

Felicity sat behind a cup of coffee Morgan had poured for her. She felt the morning was already off to a shaky start, but she wanted to force it in a better direction. She knew that was not going to happen when Morgan pushed the paper toward her. She sipped her coffee, scanning the page Morgan indicated. A small fire. Local politician says he will not seek reelection. New statistics on wind surfing accidents. She took a bite of her doughnut. Then she saw it.

Felicity's stomach clenched tight and her breath caught in her chest. It was an auto accident. One passenger, female, average build. Rolled the car on I-5, near Gila Bend, Arizona. Trapped inside, she died in the fire caused when the gas tank ruptured. Must have been driving at a high rate of speed to leave the road on that shallow bend and flip the car. Old model Buick Lesabre. Paint down to the gray primer. Passenger as yet unidentified. If you have any information, please contact...

"Oh Lord." Felicity squeezed her eyes shut, then forced herself to look up at Morgan.

"I killed her," he said.

"Nonsense," she snapped, still in a whisper. "They killed her. They were mad when they figured out they followed the wrong car. Instead of just leaving it, those sadistic bastards ran her off the road. Nothing to gain, just being bastards."

"I knew better," Morgan said, fingering his cup's handle,

but never quite picking it up. "You never get amateurs involved in this kind of thing. She had no way to know. Poor kid never did anything to anybody. She just wanted to get to California."

"Well, aren't we the early birds?" Barton sat up, stretched, and stood.

"Change your clothes and get some breakfast," Morgan said, closing the paper. "We need to see this warehouse. I want to finish this business, now."

After looking at his friends' faces, Barton chose to say nothing. He simply went to the bedroom to shower and dress. Morgan, restless, explored the small refrigerator. Inside he found frozen orange juice and a dozen eggs.

When Barton returned from the bedroom, Frederico followed him. Morgan was busying himself at the two burner electric stove, scrambling eggs. On the table were juice, coffee and the two dozen donuts Morgan had bought earlier. Felicity had not moved. She gazed out the window the way people do when they see a bad storm approaching from far away.

"Morgan do all this?" Barton asked, dropping into a chair and sipping some juice.

"Yeah," Felicity answered. "Good thing, too. I can't cook worth a darn."

Breakfast was a sullen affair. Felicity filled Barton in about the news story while they ate. As she spoke, Frederico's eyes grew wider and flashed from her to Morgan and back.

"Hey, I think wonder boy here is getting the idea."

"I trust that you and my mistress can keep us all safe," Frederico said. "It is just that…"

"Yeah," Morgan said. "You've figured out that the danger didn't end when we left the hotel. Good. Hang onto that lesson. It might keep you alive."

"I am sorry about your friend," Barton said. "I know it

won't undo what's done, but the Company might be able to work some kind of compensation for her next of kin."

"Appreciate the thought," Felicity said.

Barton let a moment of silence pass before pushing into business again. "I know this is a tragedy, but it sure looks like your strategy worked. This death might not be in vain if it gives us the chance to stop Anaconda's ice from destroying more lives."

When the meal was finished Felicity cleared the table and cleaned up, despite Frederico's protests and assistance. Morgan checked his pistol again and looked over his knives. Barton also performed a final check on his gun.

"What do you carry these days?" Morgan asked.

"The Agency's been hot on these for a while," Barton said, offering Morgan his pistol. "Glock 20. 10 millimeter's got to be half again as effective as the nine or the thirty-eight specials we used to get issued. Packs 15 in the clip, but still pretty light."

"You using an issue gun?" Morgan asked, turning it in his hand. "Very nice. Quite a handful, though. I mean, it's a good fit for me but I hope you don't have any women in the field trying to hold this thing. Anyway, my old Hi-power's always put them down to stay."

"Still loading those hollow points with the explosive tips?" Barton asked, accepting his gun back.

"Yeah," Morgan said, sliding a full magazine into his weapon. "I found some commercial exploder ammo, but it turned out to be kind of erratic. My stuff just performs better. Besides, it's more personal that way."

When they stood ready to go, they made an odd picture. Felicity, in her shorts and tee shirt looked appropriate, but her two escorts wore sport coats over their tee shirts, and long pants. Morgan still wore boots. Frederico headed for Felicity's side, but Morgan stepped in front of him and planted his hands on the boy's shoulders.

"Listen very closely," Morgan said in a voice no one could ignore. "No one knows you're here. A woman who didn't even know you paid for that with her life. We're not about to parade you all over the city. There's food in the fridge and a radio in the bedroom. Now you stay in this little cottage and you don't poke your nose out that door until we get back. Don't even unlock the door." His powerful hands tightened on the youth's shoulders and pain sprang up in Frederico's eyes. "Do you understand what I'm saying?" Frederico nodded. "Okay. Now lock it behind us."

Outside, the sun was a fierce spotlight. Barton burst into sweat immediately. Heat never seemed to bother Morgan. It did not matter. They decided to take Barton's car, a modest gray Chevrolet sedan. Before he put his seat belt on or turned on the radio, Barton started the air conditioning and pushed the fan to high.

Corpus Christi is a wide, city with bright streets and natives who are aggressively Texan. Barton took them to the heart of the business district for a look at the corporate headquarters of the nonprofit organization known as Gold Heart Limited. Barton put the car in park but Felicity dropped a hand on his thigh.

"I'd love to do a site survey, but we're not about to underestimate these people again. Someone inside might recognize me or Morgan from a description. I'm thinking we stay in the car. Besides, I'm not thinking these people would keep anything like drugs in their offices."

"They might have records worth looking at," Morgan said.

"Yes, but I'm still liking the better part of valor here."

Gold Heart's offices filled the fifth floor in a modern, glass fronted office building. The trio circled the block, examining access. Behind the building was a large parking lot and at the back, a loading dock.

"This is where charitable donations get converted to

goods. Everything is crated up right here to be trucked out to the warehouse, then loaded onto El Corazon de Hielo," Barton said.

From the back seat, Morgan said, "I bet powdered milk is great for smuggling drugs in."

"Maybe," Felicity commented. "But this stuff's going out. I'm betting that not much that's edible gets sent back."

"You got that right," Barton said. "Not much ever comes back, except the propaganda that goes with the handout."

"Right. Let's follow the trail, lover."

Traffic got heavy and they wasted most of an hour getting across town. Streets got narrower and darker and suddenly they were in what appeared to be a separate city.

"This must be the part of town the locals call The Docks," Barton said.

"Reminds me of when I was a kid and I'd go down to the Brooklyn shipyards," Morgan said. Dark, narrow streets alternated with vast wide driving areas for prehistoric looking tractor trailers to maneuver their wide doors up to loading bays.

"It's a lot bigger than I thought," Morgan said. "I always thought this was mainly a resort town."

"You kidding?" Barton said, swerving around a long trailer. "Corpus Christie's a major seaport. Handles about fifty million tons of cargo a year. That's why it would be so easy to hide stuff here. Now let's take a look down warehouse row."

They parked in front of a vast building, reminiscent of an old airplane hangar. Giant doors on the front had man size doors cut into them. A ring of windows ran around the top of the warehouse, fifteen feet up the walls. The walls were painted a dull gray, like every other structure in the area. The men walking these streets were mostly dull, mostly black, and all big.

Facing the warehouse, Felicity's back was to the ocean.

The air seemed saltier here than in the cottage on the same ocean's edge. Loud voices bounced off her ears, with violent and abrasive profanity. She heard heavy machinery grinding along and the clatter of wooden crates being manhandled into position. Her attention was drawn to a four by eight foot sheet of plywood leaning against a hydrant in front of the warehouse. Some crude artist had outlined a human form on it in grease pencil.

"This is Gold Star's warehouse, I take it," Felicity said. "Contributions must be good to warrant a place this size. Sure would like a look around inside, without their knowing about it."

"You can get inside, can't you?" Morgan asked, examining the doors. "I mean, there's nowhere you can't get in."

"I need my gear," Felicity said, leaning back against the car. "There could be motion detectors, infrared or microwave beam sensor nets, hidden micro cameras. Without electronic detection equipment or extensive research, I wouldn't even be trying it."

"And I thought it was all about picking locks and using glass cutters," Barton said, hugging Felicity. "Guess I'd never made a decent thief." Felicity's response was friendly, but not warm. If Barton heard the difference, he gave her no clue.

"If they really do smuggle through this place, I'm surprised we don't see guards posted," Morgan said.

As if on cue, one of the small doors opened. A man in canvas pants, a sleeveless shirt and heavy work boots walked out. A chain belt hugged his waist. He was heavy for a Mexican, average height with small hands.

"You want something?" the guard asked in a heavy accent.

"Just looking around," Barton said, smiling.

"Tomas don't like it Anglos looking around here," the

guard replied. When he saw Morgan he added, "Tomas don't like nobody looking around here. Is bad luck."

"Really?" Morgan said. "For who?"

"Bad luck for lookers," Tomas said. He turned to face the drawing on the plywood sheet, twenty feet away. Then Morgan saw that the chain around his waist was in fact a bandoleer of some kind. Double edged knives surrounded him. Each was not much more than three inches long including a short handle.

Tomas glanced at his audience, slipped one of the knives out of his belt, and tossed it. The blade thudded into the plywood man's right biceps. Morgan maintained a bored expression.

Tomas pulled a knife with his left hand. This one he sent into the drawing's left arm, and now Morgan thought he might be hitting where he was aiming. Felicity looked at Morgan when Tomas pulled a third blade from his belt. This one flew into the plywood man's left thigh. Now Barton looked uncertain. Tomas turned his left side to the target, drew a fourth blade and flipped it behind his back. The action was all wrist, but the knife flew true into the target's right thigh. Finally he pulled a knife with his left hand and turned to face his watchers.

"Looking around can be dangerous," Tomas said. Without losing eye contact with Felicity, he brought his arm down. The final knife landed in the target's throat. When Tomas grinned, he revealed a gold tooth on the right side of his mouth.

-26-

Rodney was feeling that itching under his skin again. It was the first sign that he was coming down from the ice high. Time to score again.

His mind had started to wander, and he almost walked into the man on the corner. He was tall and thin, like Rodney, but he certainly did not belong here. First of all, he was not Mexican. He was white, with short brown hair and spooky blue eyes. And he had on a light blue suit and a tie. Rodney started to move on, but the man lightly touched his arm.

"You look like the man I'm looking for."

Like most teenagers, Rodney liked being called a man, even by a stranger. "Yeah? For what?"

"I'd like to give you this." The stranger held up a hundred dollar bill, and then headed down the street slowly. The sun was hurting Rodney's eyes, one of the things that happened when the ice faded. He turned to follow the tall stranger.

"Okay, you the man," Rodney said. "What you want? Not much I can't handle for a hundred dead presidents."

The man never looked at Rodney, but kept his eyes straight ahead. Still, it felt as if he was looking everywhere. "I just want to know who you get the drugs from and where they are."

"What, you think I'd rat out my connection?" Rodney grabbed the man's arm and felt unexpected strength there.

"I look like a cop to you?"

He did not. Rodney was not thinking too clearly, but he took the time to think now. None of his usual posse was on the street. He was broke and he needed the cash now. But turning in his connection might make it hard to get his next fix. He jammed his hands down into the pockets of his baggy pants.

"Give me the money," he said. "I'll take you."

Paul had followed the Mexican teen for ten blocks on a winding route which took them down a seemingly endless string of narrow streets. He was sure the boy was a drug user. He had the wiry build and the distinctive body odor of a speed freak. He could only hope the boy would lead him to his connection, which might put him on the trail of his two bosses.

Finally, the boy came to a boarded up tenement. Kids played in the street, shouting at each other in Spanish, but none came near this place.

Rodney shoved the door open a few inches and darted inside. After the slightest hesitation, Paul followed.

Light filtered in through loosely boarded windows, creating an imitation dusk in the musty room. Rodney turned and Paul subtly shifted his balance.

"All right. Where are we?"

"Right where they'll find you if you don't give me more money." Rodney pulled his butterfly knife and flipped the handles apart, exposing the long blade.

Paul remained calm. "You're a hundred dollars richer. Why not keep this simple?" He began to slowly circle through the long, dark shadows criss-crossing the plaster dust covered floor.

"You got that much, I know you got more," Rodney said, carving small figure eights in the air with his knife. His movements were fast, but somehow disjointed and all the more dangerous for that. Paul heaved a heavy sigh.

"You're out of your depth, son. You don't want to play this game with me. I used to do this strong arm stuff for a living."

"Fuck that!" Rodney shouted. "Fuck you! You don't give it up, I'll take it off your bleeding body."

Paul heard the commitment in the boy's voice and resigned himself to the unavoidable outcome. He moved his hands to his sides, farther than some might consider wise. His feet shuffled on the floor, covering his shoes with a fine white powder. Crumbling plaster. His eyes were on Rodney's belt buckle, the leading indicator of a thrust.

Rodney feinted once, twice at Paul's midsection. Paul did not react at all. He was waiting for the real thrust. When it came, it came fast. Rodney stabbed forward with all he had, right on target. Except somehow, when the point of the blade arrived, Paul's body was no longer there.

Paul's right hand crossed his body to land on Rodney's wrist. He swung his arm up, around and out in a big circle. Rodney screamed as his shoulder joint rolled around and out of its socket. The knife clattered to the floor just before Rodney landed on his back, raising a small dirty cloud. In the semidarkness, Paul could see his face twisted in a rictus of pain. He pressed his left foot into the boy's armpit and rotated his arm out just a little more.

"I understand your confusion now," Paul said, his voice still tightly controlled. "I'm nothing you've ever seen before. I'm not a policeman constrained by rules of law. I'm not a drug addled junkie or one of these, er..." he reached for the right word, "one of these gang bangers you meet. I'm the genuine article, sonny, and I'll twist your arm right off unless I get a name and a location real soon."

But pain and the need for drugs had already broken Rodney. He began to babble wildly, words spilling out of his mouth like the pitiful meanderings of a wino with delirium tremens.

-27-

"This Tomas is special help," Morgan said around a mouthful of scampi. "Too special to be guarding a warehouse where nothing shaky's going on."

"Got to get in there," Felicity said, sipping her wine. "Somehow Chuck's people missed it, but I'm sure the stuff's held in that warehouse."

They had found a small, peaceful restaurant and chosen from four pages jammed with shrimp dishes for a late lunch. They had an ocean view from their seats through a wide picture window.

Barton sat back from his shrimp Creole and took a long swallow from a Coors bottle. He swung a hairy hand up and slapped Morgan's shoulder.

"You guys have changed a lot since that fiasco in Panama," Chuck said. "I seem to remember you smiling a lot more, Morgan."

"At the time I hadn't killed any young women recently."

"You're not responsible for that," Felicity said, pushing her Newburg away.

"And you, my fine beauty, you're different too," Barton continued, sliding a hand into her hair. His fingers slid down her neck, probing toward her chest.

"Jesus, don't you ever think of anything else?" Felicity snapped, brushing his hand away. Morgan looked up from beneath hooded eyes. For the first time since he had known her, he could not read her face.

"I think you're right about the ice being in that

warehouse," Morgan said between sips from his beer. "You got a way to get in?"

"Nope," Felicity said. "Don't even have any contacts around here to get detection equipment to defeat their security, but I'll think of something."

"I'm telling you we went over that damn building with a fine tooth comb," Barton said. "Where could drugs be that we couldn't find them?"

"Good question," Felicity said, looking up. "If it's not too late on the continent I might be able to get the answer." Then she left her chair, heading for a pay phone just outside the restaurant. Both men watched through the window while she pushed one button and started talking.

Morgan knew Felicity was talking to an operator, which meant an overseas call. She would not want to use her own credit card, so she was most likely arranging a collect call. After a pause, she started talking, eyes wide and rocking her head the way she did when her voice was filled with excitement. After a time, she turned to the picture window and signaled for them to join her. Morgan moved outside while Barton settled their check. When Morgan was close enough to hear, she mouthed "It's Raoul" and held the phone a little away from her ear.

"Cheri, you know I never handle narcotics," the man at the other end said. Morgan knew him, a professional smuggler who lived in Paris, and Felicity's friend and lover from years back.

"How do you stay in business without it, lover?" Felicity asked, only half joking.

"The law of supply and demand does not only apply to illegal addictions, ma petite," Raoul said. "Right now there is a lot of money for anyone who can get American cigarettes into Russia. Also, moving legal medicinal drugs into the Middle East is highly profitable these days."

"Well, darling, we're chasing this new drug called ice,"

Felicity said, caressing the telephone as if Raoul could feel it. "A synthetic crystal it is. How would you move such a thing so it can't be seen?"

"Is this business, ma chere?" Raoul asked from across the Atlantic.

"I'm on a job, love," Felicity said. "I don't do vendettas. Just give me an idea."

"When I was handling jewelry and art you brought me, it was the same," Raoul said. "The secret is in misdirection, just as it is for a thief. With drugs, like jewels, you must change the form. And thanks to good misdirection, what is being smuggled is right where you thought."

Barton finally joined them just as Felicity threw Raoul a good-bye kiss.

"He's right," Felicity said, stepping away from the phone. "Let's head for the cottage. Sure and I've got to think this thing through."

The bloated summer sun was half way to the horizon as they approached Barton's cottage. Daytime beach dwellers packed three lanes on their left, crawling past them, returning from a day's sun worshipping. With traffic so light in their direction, Barton drove at a relaxed, unhurried pace.

"I still don't get it," Barton declared, stopping for a red light. "Our DEA partners are experts at this sort of thing. Why would you spot a smuggler when they wouldn't?"

"I knew a guy once who did a mind reading act," Morgan said. "A panel of experts in psychic phenomena were convinced he was genuine. They were experts, see, but in the wrong thing. Know who busted him out? A couple of professional magicians. Felicity's an expert at getting stuff past the cops. Since she just thinks like a crook, not a cop, she's got a chance."

Felicity interrupted Morgan with a sound very close to a scream. He spun, scanning for whatever could shock

Felicity so much. He followed her gaze across the wide avenue. It was a suburban scene filled with casual wanderers dressed in bathing suits, cowboy hats and shorts. In front of a small drug store, Frederico was trying to get gum balls out of a machine.

"Damn," muttered Barton, and Felicity saw why. They were one car back from the light. Two cars had pulled up behind them, preventing Chuck from moving. She stared at the tableau playing itself out on the sidewalk. A low slung white sedan slid around the corner and pulled to the curb just past Frederico. He turned, as if to cross the street, tossing the gum ball into his mouth. Tiny beads popped out on Felicity's forehead, despite the car's air conditioning.

Two Latino men in cheap suits with their sleeves pushed up jumped out of the white sedan. The one with a scar on his face ran past Frederico but then turned around. The other, a darker man, walked purposefully up to Frederico and swung a fist up into his midsection. Frederico doubled over, his knees buckling. Felicity's stomach flipped and clenched as if she had taken the punch herself.

She heard a car door slam and saw Morgan, running across the street. The light must have just changed, because cars suddenly rushed at him from his right. On the sidewalk, the dark, weasel faced man shoved Frederico forward, while Scar Face grabbed his arm. They had him in their sedan in seconds.

Morgan had a hand on the car as it sped off. He reached under his jacket, then hesitated. Felicity could imagine him considering the density of the traffic, the number of people on the street, the likelihood of nearby police. She saw anger twist his face as he reached the same conclusion she had. Pulling a gun here, now, was not only pointless, but dangerous.

She bounced against the car door when Barton could finally whip his car into a U-turn. He locked the brakes in front of Morgan, who got in and slammed the door, much harder than necessary.

"No chance to chase, not in this traffic," Morgan said.

"Get a license number?" Barton asked, driving forward anyway.

"Sure, but they'll have a new one by now," Morgan said. "Just like back at the hotel, these guys are pros. Sorry, Red."

Felicity's teeth hurt, making her realize the extent of her tension. She took three deep breaths before answering. "Nothing to be sorry for. He was safe as long as he stayed indoors. I should have known he wouldn't do as he was told. He never really believed he was in any danger as long as...he thought I was some kind of magic protection." She dug her nails into Barton's shoulder, betraying her desperation. "Can't we get after them? Chase them down somehow?"

"Felicity, sweetheart, they're gone." Barton put one of his hands over hers.

"He's gone," Morgan said, hitting closer to the mark. "The Escorpionista's machine is bigger than we thought, and it don't make anywhere near the noise we figured it would. Nothing to do now, Red, but get down to the business of hitting Anaconda the only way we can. Cripple her drug empire."

Barton drove on to his rented cottage and parked in his designated space. Morgan got out and looked around, cautious even though he felt no danger warning. Barton walked around the car and opened Felicity's door. She stared up at them both, her eyes moist.

"It won't do," she said. "He saved us. We couldn't save him. It won't do."

-28-

It sounded loud when Barton hung up the phone, but Morgan realized it was only in contrast to the silence in the room before and after his calls. He did not speak right away, just sat looking at Felicity. Her face was blank, her body lifeless. She stared into the darkness just outside the window. Morgan wondered what she saw there.

"Well, that's it," Barton finally said. "I've talked to the agency, the FBI and just for fun, the local police. The dragnet's about to drag over every Hispanic in the state."

"They won't find him," Felicity said. "They've gone to ground with him, or maybe taken him to California or even back to South America by now." She paced around the cottage's main room in a rough figure eight pattern.

Morgan, sitting at the table, watched her closely for a clue to what was happening. He understood Felicity being depressed about losing Frederico, but this was something else. Usually, Felicity was filled with fire, like good Irish whiskey. Now her green eyes were dull and her face had lost its usual light of creative intelligence. Morgan had never seen her really at a loss before.

They had driven to a small place Barton knew for dinner and brought back take out Mexican food. The table was littered with wrappers and half eaten bits of chimichangas, burritos and tacos. Felicity had tasted everything, but eaten very little. Since dinner she had paced, as if measuring the distance the sun dropped with her tread. Now the moon was out and it looked as though she might walk the floor until dawn.

Morgan, knowing what kind of night it would probably be, had bought five more pounds of coffee when they were out. Barton had picked up a bottle of scotch. Half a bottle later, three glasses had been poured into, but only Barton's had been emptied, and that several times. He lurched to his feet, weaving in front of Felicity.

"Look, you been doing your imitation of the mummy for half a day. You need to finish that drink."

"Hey Red." Morgan spoke as if Barton was not in the room. "This can go two ways. You want a hot shower and a rub down? Or, you want to make a plan to go save the kid?"

"Sure and I don't know if we ought to..." Felicity's voice trailed off, and Morgan saw an unfamiliar look of indecision cross her face. Morgan was ready to fight or drop it, but he understood Felicity's emotional investment and was prepared to let it be her choice. In the past, deciding who should lead in a given situation had been easy for them, but this time Felicity was not responding as usual.

"I know what you need, baby," Barton said, putting his glass down. He walked up to her, stared into her eyes, and put his right hand on her waist. Morgan could see Felicity was trying to smile, to be receptive. He knew this man had given her comfort in the past. They shared a gentle, tentative kiss and she pressed herself to him. Her tensed shoulders dropped.

Then Barton's hand slid up her side, toward her breast. Felicity jerked away. Anger flashed on Barton's face, just before he could hide it.

"You want to help me, or help yourself?" Felicity asked, her voice slowly heating up. "I don't need company and I don't need comfort. I need to be left alone and I need for all of this to just go away." At the end she was on the verge of screaming. She spun around, taking Morgan in with her glance, and then walked into the bedroom as if she were leaving the site of a messy accident. The door slammed, and a deep silence rushed in to fill the room again. To build the strength to break that silence, Barton emptied his glass yet again.

"Why don't you go in there and comfort her?" Barton sneered in Morgan's direction.

"You know it's not like that between me and Felicity," Morgan answered, keeping his voice low.

"Too bad," Barton said. "Her problem is, you're what she always wants. Nobody can compete with your image, pal. If it's broke she figures you're the only one can fix it."

Morgan did not feel any response was necessary. He stood up, stretched, and moved toward the door. "Think I'll leave you two lovebirds alone for a while," he said. He heard no response, no call for more conversation as he stepped outside. When he pulled the door closed behind him, Morgan heard liquid pouring from a bottle. The night air was cooler and the ocean breeze brought a pleasantly briny smell. A walk would clear his head, perhaps bring him some idea what to do next.

-29-

It does not always take a lot of input to create sensory overload. Sometimes, it is just too much at one time.

A key turning in a lock woke Morgan up. Someone was trying to open the door quietly. A siren in the background almost drowned out the sound. Morgan, topless and barefoot, reached under the sofa. He had thumbed his gun's hammer back before he noticed the still empty love seat.

He had returned from walking the night before to an empty living room. Either Barton and Felicity had found common ground, or the CIA man was out getting drunk. Morgan knew only one way to check, but he was not about to open that bedroom door. It really did not matter. Either way, he could get some sleep. He had an idea how to deal with the morning.

So clearly, Barton had stayed out, gotten drunk and now, just seconds before daybreak, he was trying to slip in. Morgan's reliable sixth sense registered no danger, so it had to be him.

Then the door swung open, and in dawn's half light, Morgan found himself facing a wide round woman with udders where her breasts should be, wearing a sun dress in a yellow print. The woman drew breath for a scream, but it could not seem to come out.

Then a man stepped around her. He was her height, about five foot six, Mexican, whipcord thin with a mousy face and slicked back hair. "Who the hell are you?" he bellowed.

"Just visiting Mister Barton, the man who's renting this place." As Morgan said it, the woman's scream finally broke free. Felicity appeared in the bedroom doorway in a tee shirt and shorts she must have slept in.

"Your friend," the thin man said. "Your friend. He's, Jesus, he's out here. The police. Madre de Dios."

Morgan burst through the couple at the door with Felicity close behind. He ran toward the street, stepping through sea oats and morning glories, toward a flashing light and the ambulance under it. As sunlight played over the street at a sharp angle, he saw two tall blond men crouching to lift a body. Moving as if he saw a stranger walking out with some property he owned, Morgan stepped up to the corpse just as the two blondes placed it onto a black body bag.

Chuck Barton's face reflected neither pain nor fear. Those brown eyes flashed rage. His muscles were already rigid, increasing the effect of anger. Morgan stopped the men from closing the bag long enough to scan Barton's entire form. He was dressed as Morgan had last seen him, except for the five projections.

One small knife handle stood out from each thigh. One was in his right forearm and another in his left biceps. The one in his throat hung to the right. There was little blood, only deep brown stains on his clothing. Most of Barton's blood would still be where he died.

"For God's sake, would you close his eyes?" It was Felicity. Morgan had forgotten she was there until it was too late. He looked over his shoulder at her shattered expression, then reached down and brushed Barton's eyes shut.

When Morgan stepped out the door, his focus had narrowed to Barton's body. Now he slowly expanded his perceptions. Felicity stood shaking, barefoot on the wet grass, her fists pressed into her face. The woman in the print dress tried to comfort her. Then he noticed the two quiet men carrying the zippered bag into the back of the ambulance. Passers-by and curious neighbors clustered around the white panel van in a small, tight group, wanting to see but not wanting to get too close to death, as if it might be contagious. When Morgan finally took in the plain clothed detective and two uniformed officers, they approached him.

"Marcell," the detective said, flashing a badge. "I understand you were sharing a beach house with the deceased. I'm sorry for your loss." He had a big square jaw and shoulders so wide they made him look triangular. He had a lot to say, but Morgan cut him off.

"I'm Stark. The guy in the bag is Chuck Barton. That's O'Brien." Morgan hooked a thumb at Felicity. "She and the deceased were going to be married soon. I think he's involved in police work too, FBI or something. Sure looks like a gang execution, eh?"

"What do you know about it?" Marcell asked, pulling out a note book.

"Not much," Morgan said. "I'm in the security business in California, but this was a pleasure trip. Look, let me find the girl a hotel room and I promise we'll come down to the station house in a couple hours and give you a statement, okay?"

"I'm not an insensitive man, Mister Stark," Marcell said, although his voice said exactly the opposite. "In fact, I'll be glad to have one of these officers escort you and your friend to a hotel. Before you go, could you just give me Mister Barton's home address?"

Morgan could not. Barton was neither in deep cover nor in an agency office job. He maintained a free-lance relationship with the CIA and after several years as a mercenary, he might not have a home of record at all. Before he could stammer out an answer, Felicity fell into his arms.

"Morgan, get me away from here," she said. Then, to Marcell she said "Chuck lived alone, but I can give you a number to call. His office was near his home."

Less than an hour later Morgan and Felicity walked into the blue brick and glass palace known as The Sheraton Marina Inn, on North Shoreline just across the street from the Bay. They registered at the desk in separate rooms. Their police escort left. They went to the elevator with their luggage. Once inside, they went to the basement and from there out a rear exit.

"Abandon the Bronco," Morgan said as they stepped into the morning sunshine.

"And we need to be getting to a hotel with a lower profile," Felicity said. Her eyes were hooded, and Morgan knew she hurt. Later, they would deal with it. Right now, he had to hail a cab.

Felicity stared out the window during the entire ride. Morgan sneered his best snicker and told the driver to get him to a small, cheap motel. With thirty minutes they checked into a place with flowered wallpaper, a plastic clock radio on the headboard, and a color television mounted in the corner. For a fee they could get erotic movies.

"Hungry?" Morgan asked as soon as he set the luggage down.

"We lost the boy," Felicity said, staring out the window. "Now Chuck's dead. Why is he dead?"

"Right," Morgan said. "I'm going after some breakfast. When I get back, you tell me why."

The nearest fast food restaurant was three blocks away. Morgan returned with ham and egg sandwiches, hash brown potatoes, orange juice and pastries which bore no resemblance to Danishes, but still carried that name. He sat on the edge of one of the twin beds with his legs between them and laid his treasures out on the thin blanket. Felicity sat cross legged in the middle of the other bed, facing him. She ignored the food, but Morgan started on a sandwich right away. While he chewed, he turned on the radio, twisting the knob until he found something symphonic. Public radio, he assumed. The sound was tinny, but somewhat soothing nonetheless.

"What was the phone number you gave the police?" Morgan asked.

"CIA headquarters," Felicity said. "It's in Langley, so if he checks, the cop'll think it's FBI, backing up your quick story. Whoever answers will know what to do and say to make the police investigation go away."

"Right. So, why is Chuck dead?" Morgan said between mouthfuls. Felicity looked up at him, but he kept his eyes off her. He had been in this spot before with fellow warriors. He knew Felicity had pain, grief and guilt to unload, and Morgan knew she had to start talking to get it done.

Morgan pressed again. "Tell me why."

"How should I know?"

"You know," Morgan insisted. "Think. Then tell me."

After a moment, Felicity said, "I see. I drove him out. Because I wouldn't sleep with him he went back to the warehouse..."

"Try again," Morgan said.

"He went to the warehouse to get back at me..."

"No," Morgan said. "Not you. He loved you. Try me." This idea seemed to push Felicity's thoughts in a whole new direction. She considered, and then started talking while she put new thoughts together.

"Loved me? Frederico said he loved me. But I wasn't in love, Morgan. I mean, I liked him but I didn't...he was a good friend. A good lover."

"Why did he die?" Morgan asked again.

"He was jealous. Can you believe it? Jealous of you, of our relationship. I guess I see why. Nobody's as good as you, Morgan, not at the rough stuff, at the tricky stuff. He wanted to prove himself to me." At this point Morgan nodded, but continued eating. "He went to that warehouse to prove himself to me." Felicity's voice rose. "He wanted to beat that Tomas guy and find the drugs and prove he was as good as you." Then her voice dropped to a whisper. "I did kill him."

"Nope, he killed himself," Morgan said, finishing his juice. "Listen, Red, you're not God and you don't run people. Chuck used to be one of the best. I know. I've fought side by side with him. But hanging with the CIA too long hurt him. He lost his edge. Slept wrong. Drank too much. Just lost his edge. He got mad and headed out drunk or almost drunk to confront that Tomas guy. That was suicide."

"Is it wrong to want revenge?"

"Not where I come from," Morgan said. "I think we ought to take about a dozen of my best guys, catch the next plane to Colombia, find out where this Anaconda bitch lives and blow the place up." He did not smile. He was dead serious.

"You know, I don't think I've ever wanted anyone dead so badly," Felicity said. "But we can't just go. Chuck got sent here to find the ice she's shipping into Texas. We can't leave until we finish that job for him."

"Just how do we do that?"

"Not sure yet," Felicity said, pulling her legs up into a proper lotus posture. "I just know Chuck's death is for nothing if we don't. I need some time, Morgan. Time alone, to think." She did not necessarily mean he had to leave. Her hands rested on her knees and she focused on a point in space.

Morgan recognized it. She was in a mild trance state, like his wharangdo instructors had tried to make him attain back in Vietnam. He never quite mastered it, mostly because it did not seem like a manly practice to him. He was a boy then.

Then he quietly stood up and left the room, locking the door behind him. He doubted anyone was looking for him or Felicity in that city. The bad guys had hunted for Frederico, and now that search was over. If they wanted revenge on Morgan or Felicity they could just wait for them to return home where they would be easy to find.

Morgan thought he understood Felicity's problem. she felt guilty because Frederico counted on them for salvation and they failed him. Piled on top of that, she felt guilty because she had not returned Barton's love. He died thinking he had a chance to win her heart. Any woman would have trouble dealing with that. She would need a lot of time to get it all in perspective. That was all right. A long walk would help him relax. First, though, he needed to make a phone call and he didn't want it traced back to his cell.

It took a bit of searching but Morgan found a pay telephone outside a drug store. He was pleased to see it accepted a credit card, since he hadn't thought to load up on change. He dialed a number in Panama City. After an unexpectedly quick connection, a mechanical voice answered.

"Hello. Put me through to Mark Roberts please. Tell him it's Morgan Stark. I think he's expecting my call."

Morgan waited through a silence that was just long enough for the receptionist to find his name on Roberts' list of contacts. When she returned she spoke in a slightly warmer tone.

"Sir, I'm afraid that Mr. Roberts is on vacation this week. Can I take a message?"

"No, this is rather urgent. Do you have a number where I can reach him today?"

After another brief pause the girl gave him a phone number. Another extensive dialing session gave an exchange in Colombia.

Morgan met Mark Roberts in the Congo years ago. Roberts was undercover then, and Morgan helped in his mission. They lost contact, but last year Roberts had remembered him and gotten him involved in an assignment involving the aborted Piranha submarine project. Now Roberts was the Central Intelligence Agency regional director for Central America, a prestigious if ulcer-ridden assignment.

"Yes?"

"Mark, it's Stark," Morgan said. "Unsecured line. Flash priority. L and D." It was a very simple pass code, Morgan thought, indicating important news, of a life and death nature.

"It's okay, Morgan. Incoming is scrambled and a phone booth's good enough. What's going on? Did you hook up with Barton in Texas?"

"Roger that," Morgan said. "We got here safe. But Mark, we hit some opposition."

"How heavy?"

"Mark, Chuck Barton's dead." A long silence came over the line, followed by a deep sigh. They had not really been friends, and Roberts had lost men before, but Morgan knew it always hurt.

"I copy. I.D. the hitter?" Roberts asked, trying to keep it business. Morgan decided to follow his lead.

"That's a roger. Also located probable ice drop."

"Can you gather evidence?"

"Check," Morgan said. He was certain Felicity would find a way.

"You know Company policy when rival organizations

drain our manpower. Can you?" Morgan knew that Roberts did not really want to ask, but he had to. And Morgan was very glad he did.

"A free sample, if available."

"Okay, Morgan." Roberts sounded tired. "Get me that evidence if accessible without excessive risk. And request hitter be dismissed with extreme prejudice. I'll cover legal." No qualifier. Just get him.

"Wilco," Morgan said. "*Thank you*." he did not say.

"Give my condolences to Felicity, will you? I understand they were pretty close. And call when you've got something."

"That's a big roger all around. Stark out." Now, thought Morgan, time for that long walk.

Born a New Yorker, Morgan never really adjusted to how streets look in California, and Texas was not much different. Palm trees lined broad avenues, sidewalks were wide, and pedestrians, not cars, ruled the road. Back in The Bronx, stepping off the curb made you a target if you were not directly under a traffic light. In Corpus Christi, a transplanted West Coast city, jumping out into traffic suddenly could cause a twenty-car pile up as all the drivers locked up their brakes.

Morgan did not know how long he had walked, but the sun was almost directly overhead when the increased salt in the air caught his attention. He had wandered into the docks area. Oh, well, he was a man who lived by his instincts. He walked a long loop which brought him to the corner across the street from the main door of Golden Heart's warehouse.

This building had an exterior fire escape. Morgan pulled down the bottom ladder, and climbed to the flat roof. Standing with his hands in his pockets, he surveyed the area. While he watched, Tomas stepped outside for a little knife practice. Morgan knew the knives in Barton's body would show no fingerprints, but he had no doubt they came from that bandoleer around Tomas' waist.

It would be so easy. A drive by shooting, like they did it so often in L.A. Tomas would be history. Barton would be avenged.

Yeah, Morgan thought, and cops would descend on that warehouse and there would be no getting at any drugs inside before the rightful owners moved them away. First, he and Felicity had to get inside and find the poisonous evidence. Only then would he have the privilege of sending this particular man to hell.

When Morgan reached his motel again the sun was long down and a slight breeze cooled the city. No one followed him or even noticed him all day. He turned the key in the lock, not really sure what he would find.

Felicity sat in a chair eating from a white carton using chopsticks. Similar boxes were lined up on the low chest of drawers. She wore a plain gray sweat suit, indicating she must have gone out for a while to buy it. Somehow Morgan could sense she was in control. Not quite her old confident self, but much closer.

"Hi, partner," Felicity said with a smile. "Found a place with pretty good Chinese food. They wouldn't give up any forks, so I hope you know how to work these things."

"No problem," Morgan said, returning her smile and picking up one of the cartons. Shrimps and fried rice. Good choice. "You look a lot better than when I left, Red. Got your balance back?"

"Want to hear it all?"

"Of course," Morgan said, plopping on one of the beds.

"First, I didn't let Frederico down. He'd still be safe if he'd stayed in the cottage like he was told. Boy was a little slow, he was, and he got himself in the fix he's in."

"Very good," Morgan said, shoving rice into his mouth. About two thirds of it reached its destination on each trip.

"Second, I won't take the blame that Chuck fell for me.

Besides that, he made a stupid mistake, he did, in a business that doesn't allow for stupid mistakes. I'll mourn him and I'll miss him, I really will, but I can't take the blame for his death."

"You had to see that for yourself," Morgan said, gathering rice from his bed and dumping it into an ashtray.

"And third, Anaconda hasn't locked all the right doors," Felicity said, smiling into Morgan's face. "I can get in the warehouse. I checked it out and I can do it tomorrow, but we will have to leave here before dawn to make it work."

"No special gear or prep?" Morgan asked, going to the chest of drawers and fishing an egg roll out of another carton.

"Got everything we need in that bag," she said. While he was standing, Morgan opened the large black vinyl purse Felicity must have bought while she was out. He saw a claw hammer, a small plastic mallet, a few big nails, a short crowbar, two chamois cloths, a tiny flashlight, a small hand drill and a box of drinking straws.

He chose not to ask.

-30-

The target clicked across the street half a block away on snake skin cowboy boots. Paul leaned back into the doorway to avoid the light drizzle. He was not worried about losing his target.

His name was Eduardo Salazar. Paul had learned his name from the young drug user with the dislocated shoulder. Paul thought this was the easiest surveillance job he had ever had. The man was loud, in every way imaginable. His voice of course, and his manner. And his clothes as well. He wore a yellow silk shirt and a collection of gold chains which must have weighed heavily around his neck.

Even without all that, he would be hard to miss. He carried a scar on the side of his face from a knife or broken bottle that had just missed his right eye. Aside from that, Paul saw the evidence of serious burns on his chin and left cheek.

Edwardo went into a bar called El Noches. Paul stepped out into the night, barely aware of the rain. He had been following Edwardo for the better part of three days, and he had an idea of his motion pattern. He was a small time dealer, who stopped at four places in the neighborhood to take care of his customers, but always ended the evening here. Paul thought he might meet his supplier in this place. He seldom came out that door until noon the next day. He eventually crashed in a small apartment two floors above the bar.

Paul strolled around the end of the building. Out of the glare of street lights, he stared up the side of the blood colored brick wall at the rusting fire escape.

It took Edwardo a couple of minutes to get his key into the lock. He had consumed more than his usual share of rum that night, but he had put every other man under the table. While he no longer did flaming shots, he shared more and more drinking games. He was still as much a man as he was before the red headed black dude caught his shirt on fire.

Finally the door swung open. Total silence. Complete darkness. Home. Thank God he had sense enough to never use the shit he sold to his customers on the street. A simple thing like a dark, quiet room could be terrifying to a guy on the ice. Edwardo, he walked right in. He knew where everything was by now. Sofa on the right, television console on the left with a low slung chair. He headed up the center, over his antique Turkish carpet which he owned just because it was expensive.

Then something dropped over his head and slipped around his throat, and he was bent backward. Edwardo dropped to his knees, feeling another knee in his back. His left hand went to his throat. What felt like a light cord was cutting into him under his chin. His right hand went to the holster inside his waistband and the thirty-eight it held.

Then something like a blackjack or sap thumped into a certain spot on his back, and the strength went out of his arms. He could barely breathe, let alone speak. But he tried.

"Top drawer," he squeaked out hoarsely. "Stash."

That drew a chilling, whispered laugh. "I don't want your drugs, or your money. I want information."

"What?" Edwardo croaked out. The tension on his spine kept him weak, helpless.

"I understand you've seen a couple of my friends." The

voice behind him was like cracked ice. "I want to know what happened to them."

Edwardo tried to ask who but all that came out was a long hiss. The strain of the cord was drawing his burned skin tight, covering his face with a raw, burning pain.

"A man and a woman." The voice was at his left ear. "The man is black, the woman is not. They would have been asking about the drug business, maybe about getting into it."

Edwardo's panicked brain cast about, sifting through every face he had seen in the last week. The pain in his face stirred the memory of the man who caused his most recent injuries. That man was black, and he had come into the bar with a Mexican woman. They had spoken to Rico, his supplier, and then the trouble had started.

Edwardo vigorously nodded his head when he realized he had the answer. The cord around his neck wasn't as tight as before. He swallowed and said, "You mean the redhead."

"Yes." The man behind Edwardo tensed, but the cord did not cut into his neck like before. "Where?"

"Anaconda took them. I heard she intended to hurt them, then turn them loose. They said they wanted to make a buy, but she said they were fakes. She took them out to..."

The sound of three heavy blows came through the door. "Edwardo, what's the hold up man? We waiting for you. Can't party without the stuff, you know."

Edwardo managed a strangled cry of "help" before he was spun around. A large, heavy fist smashed into him. He felt a short flash of pain just before oblivion took him.

Paul flexed his fingers to stretch them. He wore a black leather glove. The front of the knuckles were padded and filled with lead. He felt with his left to check the damage. Edwardo's nose was broken, and blood was running down his face to the floor.

"You do seem to have a lot of trouble with your face," Paul said. Shouts in Spanish were coming through the door and something heavy crashed into it. Paul leaped to his feet. There was no back door, so he ran back to the window he had come in through. A second thump shook the door and Paul knew the lock would not resist much longer. He jerked the window open, seeing no need for stealth this time. A stiff wind shoved a sheet of cold rain into his face. The window sill, like the fire escape, was rain-slicked and slippery.

A broad shoulder hit the door a third time and it slammed open. The first man in slapped the wall switch. Even before light flooded the room, three men were filling the air in the room with flying bullets.

-31-

After seventeen hours in darkness Felicity decided it was time to move. She reached behind herself, awkwardly lifting her plastic mallet. She needed it in her hand to free herself from the crate she was nestled in. Even with it in her hand, this might not be easy.

At four o'clock that morning, Morgan was still telling her it was a crazy plan. They were standing behind Gold Heart Limited's headquarters. It was a moonless night, and they were miles from the night clubs just closing down. The business district was as silent as any ghost town. Only a tall link fence separated them from the loading dock. Several wooden crates sat on it, probably filled with something nourishing but not palatable.

Security inside the office looked pretty efficient. Outside, well, no one expected serious thieves to make off with any baby food. Besides, where could you go with a crate of the stuff? A fence topped with barbed wire did not intimidate Morgan or Felicity. In heavy leather jackets and gloves they simply climbed and rolled over it. Moving in the shadows, they made their way to the loading dock.

Felicity took a quick accounting and found the least popular crate type. Once crouched behind her chosen large packing crate, Felicity pulled tools from her big black purse. She handed Morgan the crow bar. He shook his head in protest one last time, but she was determined.

Felicity held the light while Morgan applied the bar. In silent slow motion, he fitted it under the head of one of the big nails holding the crate together. Gritting his teeth, Morgan pulled the nail, so slowly it made no squeak sound as it came away from the green pine board. While he handled this boring chore, Felicity used the drill with no more haste and no more noise than her partner.

It took most of an hour, but the two managed to get the crate's top completely loose. Then they waited, relaxed but attentive, making sure no curious guard had been attracted by their noise. After five full minutes they decided no such people worked there. When they lifted the crate's top off, they did not disturb the silence.

The chosen crate contained powdered milk. They counted twelve cardboard cases in two levels, twelve boxes to a case. Despite all the packaging, powder breathed out, tickling their noses. Morgan lifted out three middle cases from the top layer, starting at one end. Then he reached in to pull out the case beneath the last one he had removed.

As if it were a new revelation, Morgan leaned toward Felicity and whispered "This is nuts."

"The only way," she whispered back. "Nothing I haven't done before." That was only an exaggeration, after all, not a lie. She smiled at him and gave a mock salute. After shaking his head in frustration, Morgan gave her a boost into the crate. With her feet where the bottom layer case had been, she lay back into the space the other missing boxes now left empty. She was grateful for a fairly tight fit. It made her less likely to get battered by moving cases.

"How you can do this is beyond me," Morgan said.

"You're kidding, right? Aren't you the man who crawled through narrow tunnels in Vietnam?"

"That ain't like being nailed into a box for almost an whole day."

The last thing Felicity saw before Morgan set the lid in place was his face, as grim and sorrowful as a reluctant executioner. Then she heard the muted hammer blows.

Morgan was holding the nails in place with a wadded chamois the way she had told him. Getting them in this way took a couple dozen modest taps, but it minimized the sound. He had to get the lid on as solid as it was when they arrived.

While Morgan hammered, Felicity fitted straws into the two holes she had drilled. The holes would go unnoticed by a casual observer because they just widened the existing cracks between the boards above her. The straws would make her breathing easier, as long as she kept it shallow. That should prove easy enough, since she would use little energy just lying still. Once the straws were in place, she pushed her purse under her head.

Now, seventeen hours and fourteen minutes later, Felicity reflected that her job had ended right then. Morgan was left with the heavy work, lugging the powdered milk cases to the gate, stacking them there and leaving a note saying they were "an anonymous donation for our brothers and sisters". And of course, he had to get out of the area undetected.

For Felicity, nothing remained but lying still with her eyes closed. She heard the day begin outside, and played a game with herself, following the activity in the area, picturing how many people were around and what they were doing. In her mind's eye she could see the activity at the docks, much like a bee hive with every worker going about his assigned tasks with the mechanical efficiency of habit.

In time she heard gears grinding, and endured the eerie weightless feeling of being raised on a forklift. She rode on a truck for a brief time, then it stopped and the forklift returned. She heard Tomas' voice directing workers, and soon she was shoved into a corner and forgotten.

For the next few hours her only enemy was boredom. She took occasional drinks from a water bottle and ate sporadically from a bag of dried fruit and sausage. Primarily, she meditated in a shallow trance state, while her internal alarm clock ticked away the hours.

In the screen in her head she saw Anaconda, her diminutive form dressed to attract attention to her feminine proportions. Felicity saw her sitting like a huge spider at the center of the world, her long, glossy tresses fanned out behind her like some obscene web. So distant, so untouchable, she sent her orders down the lines of her web commanding dozens, maybe hundreds of men around the western hemisphere. Directing them to smuggle and distribute drugs, to steal, to kill on command.

In her mind, Felicity could see those silver eyes shining, hypnotizing and terrorizing anyone who might stand against her. Felicity and Morgan might cut off one or two of her extended limbs, but how could they hurt her as long as she controlled it all long distance?

Then her internal clock told her it was time to move. No light filtered into her tiny temporary home, and no sound squeezed in between the cracks. She tapped against one corner of her "roof". It moved an inch, and Felicity sighed with relief. They had chosen a powdered milk crate because there were only four that day. They put her in the one positioned to most likely get picked up first, loaded into the truck first, unloaded last. Despite their logical planning, they had no guarantee against something being stacked on top of her for some reason. Thankfully, they had played the odds correctly.

With the hammer, Felicity loosened the two corners she could reach. Next, she raised her numb legs. Her right leg was mostly asleep, and painful invisible needles jabbed it as she pulled her knees up. Twisting, straining, she managed to get her knees against her chest. Then, one good push with her feet raised the top like a coffin lid mounted sideways.

Felicity slipped out of the crate into the still deeper blackness in the warehouse. She used five more minutes sitting still, massaging her legs while she listened. Surely no one else was in the building. As long as she did not turn on a light or make any noise, there was practically no chance of interference.

Felicity's small flashlight could be dialed down to a laser pointer beam or up to a wide cone of light. This time she chose a fairly narrow setting. Using it in two second bursts, Felicity explored the warehouse, looking for anything that was not on its way out. Things were more orderly than she expected, with each product grouped for easy inventory. She moved across pallets covered with canned goods, flour, dried beans, sugar, and powdered eggs. Most were name brand items, corporate donations, but many were government surplus. Felicity marveled at the depth of Anaconda's cover operation, realizing it must be doing quite a bit of genuine good. Was drug traffic financing an actual humanitarian objective?

No. She had met the woman. No driving force existed there but greed and a hunger for power. Any positive by-product had to be incidental.

After exploring the entire huge warehouse Felicity found seventeen crates that could be returning from South America. Unlike everything else in the building, they had no stencils on the outside describing their contents. She was about to try to open one when her internal alarm reminded her of the time. She had arranged to meet Morgan at midnight, but first she had to find the building's burglar alarms. She had noticed an office on the far side of the warehouse. She went to it now, and found an array of controls.

Across the street, on the roof he had looked down from the day before, Morgan sweated in the cool night. He checked his watch, noticing that only four minutes had passed since the last time he could not resist checking. Had someone discovered her? Was she trapped under four other crates? Had some incompetent forklift driver dropped her Trojan horse, spilling her out in full view of the warehouse's murderous guard?

As a mercenary, Morgan had never worried about his men this way. Every job had calculated risks and they accepted them. They celebrated their victories and avenged their losses, but rarely mourned.

Of course, none of his men had ever become real friends.

Then he saw it. A tiny dot of light at the door's edge. Without it, no one could tell the door was open a crack. It lasted about half a second. It was enough.

It took a few minutes for Morgan to reach the door. Once on the ground, he walked a block away before crossing the street. As he strolled toward the building he watched the spaces between the shadows cast by street lights. His instincts revealed no danger present. When he reached the warehouse door, he simply sidestepped and slipped inside.

"Somebody thinks there's something valuable here," Felicity said in hushed tones, leading Morgan across the cement floor. "Considering the lack of security at the headquarters building, you can bet they're not worried about losing any of the food. But I had to cut electric eye beams at the doors, motion sensors across the front and rear of the building, sonic sensors crisscrossing the whole place, and infrared beams between the street lamps all around."

"No cameras?" Morgan asked, pulling a slightly larger flashlight from his jacket pocket.

"Probably didn't want to pay anybody to watch them all night," Felicity answered. "But what they had was plenty. Now, look here."

They had reached the unmarked crates. Morgan pulled out his big fighting knife, chose a crate, and began prying the lid off. It was tough, but so was the knife. The seven inch bladed weapon was more a sharpened pry bar than a surgical instrument. Morgan put both hands under the handle, crouched, and surged upward with a subtle grunt. Felicity smiled in the dim reflected light as the top wrenched free.

And up in the high vaulted ceiling, a row of powerful incandescent lights suddenly came on.

-32-

Blinded, Morgan and Felicity scattered in opposite directions. Ten seconds after the lights came on, Morgan huddled behind a series of food crates, his gun in his right fist, cursing himself for leaving his knife behind. He knew Felicity would seek high ground while he stayed at floor level. They had discussed situations like this and planned their response. They would try to crossfire an enemy force, if their number was small. Felicity provided the distraction, Morgan the firepower. They knew exactly how many opponents they faced when the voice rang out.

"I never thought anyone would break in here," Tomas said. "You got past alarms and stuff I can't even understand. You just didn't know about the last line of defense, huh? I sleep in a back room, over behind the office."

Just one man? Morgan's vision had nearly returned to normal. He could simply spin, stand, squeeze the trigger and remove Tomas' head. Problem solved.

"I know who you are, you know," Tomas said. "Saw you with the Anglo I killed couple days ago. Bet you got a gun too. That's why I turned the sound sensors back on. Talking won't kick it on, but a shot, that'd have a ton of cops here in thirty seconds. We gon' do this my way."

Felicity crouched behind the top crate in a stack six crates high. She was almost behind Tomas and could see him from her vantage point, stepping forward from the front door in a sleeveless undershirt with his knife bandoleer around his waist. She thought she could maybe shove the crates over, start a landslide of canned vegetables which would bury him. But that would make as much noise as a gun. For now, it was Tomas' play.

"I wonder did you bring the girl in with you," Tomas said. "Hope so. She can watch me kill you, just like the Anglo. Know how he died? Maybe you do. Listen, slide your gun out where I can see it. Do it, or I push the button and the cops come anyway."

After considering every option, Morgan pulled off his leather jacket, and pulled his throwing knife up from his right boot. The seed of an idea was forming.

From above, Felicity saw a small object skitter across the cement floor toward Tomas. He bent and picked it up. Tomas looked at Morgan's Browning Hi-power and laughed.

"Very funny, boy. You give me the gun, but keep the clip. That's okay. I don't want the bullets anyway. You'll get what the Anglo got. Know how he got it?" Morgan slid around the crate so he could see Tomas, whose left hand held a short throwing knife. Morgan showed only his face. He looked first at a shadowy stain on the cement floor. He knew that pale red blot marked Barton's fall. Then he looked up at Tomas and their eyes met.

"He pulled a gun on me. Then he said something about showing some girl. Yeah, like, `I'll show her who the real man is', or something like that. So I put a knife in his right arm. He dropped the gun. Then I put one in his left leg so he couldn't run. Then I hit his left arm. Then his right leg. Then..."

"Then, when he was immobilized and helpless, you killed him." It was Morgan's voice. Felicity saw him step out into the open with his hands behind his head like a prisoner of war. The posture showed the two empty holsters under his arms. He had rolled his new leather jacket around his right arm. Tension showed on his face but not at all in his body. Felicity knew it then. Tomas would soon die.

"You killed him in pieces," Morgan continued, stepping forward. "I guess you like that stuff. Makes you feel muy macho, eh?"

"I didn't think you'd give up, man," Tomas said when Morgan stopped about fifteen feet away. "I figured you'd die the same way. But, since you got no cojones, maybe I just call the cops and let them take you away, eh? Or, maybe not."

Just kill him. Felicity thought. *Kill him now. Please.*

Tomas' left hand moved. It was a casual movement, as if no effort was involved, but the small knife shot through the air. The throw might have surprised someone else. It beat Morgan by about a tenth of a second. As the blade left Tomas' hand, Morgan's left arm arced down. Tomas dropped the gun, his right hand reaching for another blade at his waist. Too late.

Tomas' first knife bit into Morgan's right forearm. His second thudded into the floor about halfway between the two men.

Morgan's black throwing blade glanced off Tomas' collarbone, angling upward into his throat. Paralysis came instantly. Death followed in seconds.

Felicity hit the floor almost as soon as Tomas did, racing toward Morgan. He sat down on a wooden crate and yanked Tomas' knife out of his arm.

"I'm still shaking," Felicity said. "God that was scary. Saw the whole thing, I did. He was faster than you."

"He kept talking about it," Morgan said. "How he killed, I mean. One limb, then another. I realized he forgot a basic rule. Never do your enemy a minor injury."

"So you counted on him hitting your arm, while you, er, went for the throat." It seemed so simple to verbalize, but the thought of doing it was beyond her. "You planned to take a knife in your arm. That's why the jacket. To reduce the penetration."

"A fact of life, Red," Morgan said with a weak smile. "Sometimes they hurt you. Wounds heal. What he got, don't."

Felicity felt a deeper understanding of her partner and considered all it meant before she snapped back to reality.

"Got to get you out of here, and get that tended to," she said.

"Not before we get what we came for," Morgan said. "And my fighting knife's over there."

"I'll get it," Felicity said. "Then we grab up your other knife and get the hell out of this place."

-33-

Under harsh bathroom lights, Felicity helped her partner clean out his wound. It was little more than an inch wide and less than two inches deep. It bled freely, but a few months in this man's company had accustomed her to blood.

"You ought to get stitches," Felicity said, blotting his arm with a towel.

"A pressure dressing'll do fine," Morgan replied.

"Are you daft? Would any injury make you admit it's more than just another flesh wound?"

"Of course. And this one was pretty close. If not for that jacket, that little blade would have gone through to the other side. Then we'd have a problem. I know it looks pretty bad, but in a couple of weeks, it'll be just one more scar."

Just one more scar. Those words echoed in Felicity's head while she lathered herself with a torrent of hot water beating against her back. Why was it so easy for men? Maybe because scars looked rugged. Scars are masculine things. What is for a woman a disfigurement is on a man a badge of action.

She remembered how Morgan had collapsed on his bed as soon as they finished bandaging his arm.

"Not a bad cut," he had said, kicking off his boots. "Certainly an acceptable amount of blood loss. Think I'll stretch out for a minute."

"Go ahead," Felicity had told him. "After spending a day in a wooden box, I need me a shower more than anything."

Now she stepped out of the stall, reaching for a towel. She dried herself facing away from the mirror. Her mind focused on the surprise she had found in the unmarked crate, and all Raoul had said about smuggling, and whether they left any clues to their identities in the warehouse where, in a few hours, someone would find yet another of Anaconda's men dead. She and Morgan may not have stopped her operation, but they were certainly being hard on her manpower.

At first she heard a low moan. Then it became a choked gasp, and finally a strangled scream. Without thinking, Felicity ran out of the bathroom. After all, Morgan had seen everything she had before.

He was sitting straight up in bed in the dark, covered with sweat, staring at some point a mile ahead of him. He was not quite panting. These were more like short, separate breaths of fear. Felicity pressed his head against her chest and wrapped her other arm around his massive shoulders.

"What is it, Morgan?" she asked. "Are you all right? Is it your arm?"

"They always come back," he muttered.

"They who?" Felicity asked, pulling back just enough so she could see his eyes. They seemed out of focus at first.

"I've killed a lot of men," Morgan said after spending a moment catching his breath. "Most in war. Some in self defense. One or two for revenge. People think it's all over after a fight. But at night, some times, they come back. You could never..."

Four seconds later, Felicity realized why he stopped. He was staring at her. He was staring at her body. It was too late to cover up, to turn away, or even to raise her hands. She gritted her teeth, frozen still in the soft glow from the street lights coming in the window. She could feel tears coming but refused to let them fall.

Morgan reached out gingerly, as if he could not believe the evidence his eyes offered; lightly tracing her scar from three inches below her collarbone to just above her left nipple where it ended. It felt rough as new scars often are.

"When?" he asked. "In the truck? Anaconda's office?"

Felicity stood and the tears hung just inside her eyelids. Morgan stood beside her and reached for her but she stepped away.

"Don't," she said, barely above a whisper

"Red, when did this happen….why didn't…" Morgan reached for her again but she took two more steps away from him.

"Morgan you don't understand." Felicity could no longer stop the tears from dropping but she would not sob or weep. She turned away from him and the tears slid down her cheeks onto her bare breasts.

"Help me understand."

"Don't you see what that bitch did to me?"

"Red, you are…."

"Don't say it."

"Say what?" he asked with a confused look on his face.

"Don't say that I'm beautiful…because that bitch took that from me." She said breathlessly.

"Not in my eyes."

"When I take my clothes off the first thing a man will…" her voice trailed off as the tears flowed more freely. "They will see this." She pointed but couldn't bring herself to touch it.

Morgan stepped in front of her and let his fingers trace the scar again. "Not true. All I see is a beautiful, green eyed, Irish, redhead." His head dipped lower and he heard her breath catch as his tongue joined his finger.

"Morgan…you don't have…"

"I know I don't, but I want you to see. If it wasn't for

our weird mental connection I would be all over you."

When they first met, Morgan and Felicity felt a strong attraction for each other. Their first and only attempt at sexual intimacy proved their minds were too close for such a relationship. They actually felt what was happening to each other. Morgan found it terrifying but he never stopped admiring her body.

He continued to lick her softly and finally garnered a small almost inaudible moan from her lips. She suddenly pulled away from him and grabbed a shirt from the back of the chair. Her voice was harsh, "No woman is beautiful with a deformity."

"You're not just another beautiful woman. You are the most beautiful woman I know."

"Don't patronize—"

"And don't you dare take that tone with me." He reached for the shirt that she was holding against her. "Felicity, I don't say anything that I don't mean, and you should know that by now. Besides I have plenty of scars…"

"We aren't talking about scars that you can't see, we are talking about something that defines me as a woman."

"But…"

"But nothing. The scars you have are, are sexy in the worlds eyes. My scar is a hideous reminder that I let…"

"No, you didn't let anyone…"

"That I let someone get the jump on me. Besides your scars are on your arms and chest and body. This is my breast… my breast." the tears started again.

"So?"

"So…women don't look at you for your arms, "Felicity said, pacing back and forth. " Women don't judge you by the look of your arms. No man will want to look at me with this. I used to be so beautiful."

"And you still are."

Felicity braced her hands on the dresser, leaned forward

and swallowed hard. "Oh Morgan, to be disfigured here…you can't understand."

"You're right. I don't understand. But listen to me, Red. You've still got the best damn tits in the hemisphere. "

She smiled and leaned into him. "This is why we have got to get her."

"Absolutely. She's going to pay for this."

After an eternal silence that may have lasted two minutes, Morgan stood and hugged his friend to him. Maybe he didn't know what else to do. They were both haunted, and they both knew it, but his ghosts were chased away for now. Her demon was present and real.

Then his body froze in mid-breath. His head snapped up and he was staring into her widening eyes.

"Did you feel that?"

"Oh, yeah!" Felicity said.

Morgan grasped her arm and flung her through the bedroom door. He dived, hitting the floor at the same instant she did, and a tenth of a second before a bullet punched through the bedroom window and passed within an inch of Morgan's head.

-34-

The cheap carpet smelled of cigarette smoke and scratched Morgan's cheek as he clung to the floor, cursing himself for his carelessness. What made him think he could eliminate one of the Escorpionista's killers and just walk away? The thrill of victory had made them miss being followed home. And now the opposition, a little more careful after seeing what Morgan could do, was moving to eliminate him and his partner.

A pro would expect their targets to lay low, and would aim low to compensate. Knowing that, Morgan flipped up onto the bed, staying flat while easing his pistol out of its holster hanging at the corner of the bed. He heard another shot but this time a bullet zipped across the living room. The first shooter couldn't have gotten to the other side of the house that fast, so there must be a second. A crossfire could be an issue, but he had to deal with one problem at a time.

Then another rifle bullet raced across the bedroom, punching into the wall no more than two inches from the first. Morgan stared at the entry hole and a slow smile spread across his face.

Felicity squirmed into her tee shirt and rolled across the floor a second before the shot raced across the living room. She didn't waste much time wondering how the shooters had found them, who they were or why they were firing into the bungalow. At least two people were out there right now who wanted her and her partner dead. This kind of situation was in Morgan's wheelhouse. Her job was to stay alive, and see if there was any way to help him.

She moved quickly along the floor, pushing into the bathroom where she had dropped most of her clothes and gear. Another rifle shot rang out just as she reached her tool belt. These killers clearly weren't worried about neighbors interfering with their work. Even with silencers rifles make a lot of noise. But she knew they would have limited time before someone called the police. She had an idea of how she might distract them for a while. Grabbing her little flashlight she got to her feet and sprinted for the kitchen area. A glass exploded on the counter, a victim of another rifle shot. She judged the delay between shots to be a good four or five seconds which was plenty of time.

Felicity sprang across the room, one bare foot slapping on the counter beside the sink, her leg driving her upward. Outstretched hands slapped against the hatch over the sink, covering the attic access. Her strong fingers clamped onto the edge of the opening and for a moment she hung, vulnerable, a long vertical target naked from the waist down. After one deep breath she heaved, pulling herself up through the port and into the attic space.

The darkness was even deeper there, but darkness had always been Felicity's friend. What she hated was the dust, the heat, the stale air, and cobwebs clinging to her hair. She wished she had had time to pull on a pair of shorts. Fear tried to press itself on her but she forced the thought of unknown insects out of her mind. This was where she needed to be, and she had things she needed to do.

Unfinished wood abraded her legs as she moved on hands and knees across the boards. Pressing upward periodically it didn't take her long to find a hinged door that pivoted upward and opened to the sky. She flipped it up and stood to her full height which put her head and shoulders outdoors. She took a deep breath of the fresh, salt-flavored air and looked around. The moonless night would pose no challenge to her navigating on the flat tar roof, but she would still have a use for her flashlight.

Morgan lay on the bed with arms extended toward the outer wall. Somewhere beyond that wall someone sat with what Morgan guessed was a bolt action .308 caliber rifle. The caliber he guessed from the bullet holes. The action he guessed from the time between shots. He didn't know how far away his attacker was, but he knew the general direction. That would be enough to reach out and touch him if he didn't move. The risk, of course, was that if the shooter did move, Morgan returning fire would allow the shooter to pin down his location in the house. A good sniper would then be able to blow a hole in Morgan a second later.

But Morgan lay still and soon his patience was rewarded. A third shot tore through the wall right on top of the first two, to impact the opposite wall an inch away from the first two shots. That was all Morgan needed.

Twisting his shoulders allowed Morgan to roll off the bed, holding his body straight as he did. He landed hard on the floor on his right side. Ignoring the pain in his hip and elbow he rolled another quarter turn. That aligned his body with the incoming bullets' trajectory, his arms outstretched toward the source of the shots. In the darkened room he could just see the entry holes. He adjusted his pistol so that one of those holes appeared to rest on top of his gun's front blade sight, and right between the glowing blades of its tritium rear sight.

He was sitting on the bull's-eye now. The sniper could take another shot at any time. But Morgan could not be hasty. He exhaled and held his breath out. He slowly squeezed his trigger until his gun jumped in his hand. Then he rolled under the bed, ears still ringing from his own shot.

Felicity was scampering around the roof, looking for the shooters. She knew there were at least two, and maybe more. Her night vision was exceptional, and her eyes had adjusted to the scant starlight. She moved along the edge of the roof, ignoring both the smell of the tar and the feel of it clinging to her skin and fine hairs that were seldom exposed outdoors.

There! A man brazenly leaning back against a car parked in the lot about twenty-five yards away. He was seated with his knees up, holding a rifle whose barrel rested on what looked like extra long bipod legs. He was focused on their bungalow, but had not looked up to see her peeping over the edge of the roof.

"Comfortable, you bleeding bastard?" Felicity whispered. "I hope you…"

She was interrupted by the sound of gunfire but there was no muzzle flash from the sniper's rifle. The man's head jerked forward, then back against the car. Then his hands slipped from his weapon and he slowly tipped over. He landed on his right side and lay still.

"Morgan," she thought. "How the hell did you do that?" She grinned, shaking her head at her partner's abilities, and then scurried across the roof to the other side. That side of the building faced a small but lush park, thick with trees, bushes and lower vegetation. She didn't know how Morgan targeted the first shooter, but was pretty sure the second would be harder to spot. She wanted to get into position to help if she could.

With a quick dash across the floor Morgan slid into place behind the sofa in the living room. Peering over the couch's back Morgan tried to mentally picture the other shooter. He'd have no way to know his partner was down, and no reason to retreat until the police appeared. If Morgan could get the man in his sights he could leave without fear of being hunted down, at least for a while.

An instinctive jolt of danger made Morgan drop down behind the couch just before another heavy bullet tore through the furniture. This stuff was getting old. Morgan pushed up onto hands and knees and scurried to the wall facing the source of the rifle fire. He just needed one chance at the killer outside. He crouched beside the window, held his pistol muzzle up in front of him, and waited.

A slow, deep breath. A second. A third. During his fourth breath a bullet poked through the wall on the other side of the window. Morgan quickly turned so that his outstretched arms held his gun's muzzle against the glass. He was prepared to guess the vector and empty his gun, hoping for a hit. What he saw made him pause, but only for a second. A pencil thin beam of red light shone down from the roof to a spot at the edge of the park.

"Felicity," he said. "It has to be." With a grin he squeezed his trigger to place a single bullet on the spot where the flashlight pointer beam ended. He couldn't see the impact point, but his trust in his partner made him pretty confident. Still, he waited one long minute for some response. He felt no further danger warning, but he needed to be sure. Morgan was still frozen in place, aiming out the now empty window casing, when Felicity dropped down out of the ceiling.

"You can relax," she said behind him. "You put that bullet right in the center of his chest. He dropped the rifle, but didn't move again after that."

"Were there only two?"

"There were," Felicity called from the bedroom. She was squirming into a pair of skinny jeans. "I'm not sure how you got the first one, but he won't be getting up to follow us either."

"Well that's good," Morgan said, "because we need to get moving."

"Way ahead of you," Felicity said. "Everything I need to take is in this little duffel, and nothing I'm leaving can identify us."

Morgan pulled a few things together and within three minutes of firing his last shot they sprinted across the parking lot to disappear into the woods that so recently concealed one of their attackers. They moved with a practiced economy of movement, not speaking, knowing there would be plenty of time to exchange stories when they were safe.

Ten minutes later they turned and emerged onto a city street. Felicity looked around for a few seconds, choosing her target.

"There. That Chevy van." Morgan moved toward the blue van without protest. Transportation was her responsibility. Felicity walked up to the van as if she had parked it there. With casual confidence she handed Morgan her duffel bag and pulled what looked like a silver bobby pin from her hair. In the time it took Morgan to walk around to the other side of the vehicle she had opened the driver's door and slipped behind the wheel.

"Good choice," Morgan said, dropping into the passenger's seat. "This thing's got to be more than ten years old. No one would notice it."

"And these older vehicles are easier to steal." Felicity's hands went under the dash and two minutes later the light blue vehicle roared to life. She pulled into traffic and pointed herself at the greatest amount of traffic.

"Where to, partner?" she asked.

"Downtown. We want to park in the nearest garage."

Ten blocks of Corpus Christi's night life passed before Morgan spotted a tall parking garage. Felicity pulled the ticket that allowed the gate to rise and pulled into the garage far enough to park in front of the exit stairs. Morgan gathered their things and dropped a couple of twenty dollar bills on the seat for the owner's trouble.

On the street they strolled slowly for three blocks, assuring themselves that they were not followed. Then Morgan stepped off the sidewalk and hailed a taxi. When the cab stopped, Morgan opened the rear door, shoved Felicity inside and climbed in after her. He wrapped an arm around her and turned an impatient face onto the driver.

"Get me to a hotel, my man," Morgan said. "Not a dive, this one don't belong in a dive," then he lowered his voice and said, "but not the Omni either, you feel me?" The compromise turned out to be a Hampton Inn. Morgan wasted no time in getting them inside and registered. He held Felicity's arm on the way up in the elevator. He guided her down the hall and held the door open for her to enter the room.

Morgan headed straight for the bedroom. He felt better once free of shoes and socks. What a ragged night it had turned out to be, he thought. He stood when Felicity returned to the room and to his surprise wrapped her arms around him.

After a few seconds she said, "That wasn't fair. Can't expect a body to function while she's dealing with this kind of shite. I'm all frazzled and frayed now. What the hell?"

Wrapped in his arms, squeezing him like a security blanket, she felt just like she had one minute before some idiot took a shot at them. Morgan shook his head at her, the strongest and most vulnerable woman he had ever known.

"Nothing wrong a shower and a night's sleep won't cure," he said. "Go freshen. I'm beat."

Morgan watched Felicity stagger off toward the bathroom, then stripped and got into one of the two full size beds in their generic motel room. His eyes closed, but his senses tuned to the sound of the shower. He mentally followed her actions in the bathroom, and her movements when she stepped out. With zombie-like stiffness she wandered over between the two beds, then lifted the covers and slid under them beside Morgan. He should have been surprised, but he was not.

Again he was reminded of how much he wanted her when they met, until that frightening night he learned what it feels like to be a woman having sex. That was a life altering scare, but didn't prevent him from appreciating her obvious gifts.

Now they cuddled in his bed, sharing physical and emotional warmth. Soon Felicity slept, still as an infant, with her head on Morgan's shoulder.

After their talk in what was Barton's bungalow, Morgan now understood the change in his partner, the shift in her self-confidence and ego strength. And more now became clear. She rejected Barton's advances because she could not bear to let him see what Morgan saw earlier that evening. She could not even talk about it. That rejection had driven Barton to confront Tomas. Felicity had tried to take the blame but in a very real sense Anaconda had killed Barton.

That's one more on her list, Morgan thought. And, with one casual sadistic act, she had damaged his partner. Not just superficially, but inside. There would have to be a reckoning soon.

-35-

When Morgan awoke, the sun was in his eyes. He faced outward, perched on the bed's edge. He turned to find Felicity lying on her back with her head propped up on a pillow. She had her knees up, her chin holding the sheet in place. She stared straight ahead, poring over a thick, black-covered book.

"If anybody had told me I'd find you with your nose in a Bible..." Morgan said, turning to face her.

"This is what was in the unmarked crate," Felicity said. "Boxes and boxes of these Bibles."

"Great," Morgan said, standing. "No drugs, just free literature. Salvation those South American handout takers didn't want."

"I think you're wrong," Felicity called to Morgan as he walked into the bathroom. "Remember what Raoul said. Misdirection. Change the form."

"Right," he called back, over the sound of running water. "Whatever's being smuggled is right where you thought. That means in the bible?"

"These books are the only things coming back on that ship," Felicity said. Morgan heard a binding cracking. When he left the bathroom, Felicity was sitting on the bed dressed in shorts and a tee shirt, staring into the bible's binding down its edge.

"The covers are vinyl," Morgan said. "I don't see how anything could be hidden in there." While he dressed, Morgan watched Felicity shake the book, then begin flipping pages absently. Her mind was wandering around the problem, probing for possibilities. as she flipped it, one page tore loudly.

"Watch it, Red," Morgan smiled. "You may not remember, but the pages on those things are like onion skin. They rip pretty easy."

"I don't know," Felicity said, holding the torn page. "That didn't sound like a rip. More like it broke, or cracked. Something isn't right here. I don't know what." She pulled open a drawer in the table between the beds and pulled out the Gideon bible there. She opened both books, rubbing individual pages.

"I think I've got them," Felicity said. Then a broad smile spread across her face. "Boy, were we stupid."

"I'm still stupid," Morgan said. "Where's the ice?"

"The whole thing comes down to this," Felicity said, getting up and going into the bathroom. "DEA and Customs both searched the ship. They looked at the crates, the cases and the books, but they never picked one up and handled it. This book's a bit heavier than the one that was here in the nightstand. If I'm right, Raoul was right, and Anaconda came up with one hell of a good plan."

Morgan stood up when he heard the water come on. He followed Felicity, and looked over her shoulder into the slowly filling basin. After turning the water off, she held her arms up like a magician, tugging at invisible sleeves. Then she lifted the bible and tore out a page. Morgan's reaction to that was stronger than he thought it would be. He was surprised that Felicity, raised by her priest uncle, could do it at all. She handed him the book, and pressed the single sheet of paper into the sink full of warm water. When nothing changed she shook the page. A look of doubt just had time to cross her face before they saw sediment rising.

"Well I'll be damned," Morgan said, slapping his partner

on the back. "Look at those crystals."

"There, my dear Doctor Watson, is the ice." She was beaming. "For the first time since they shoved me into Anaconda's tractor trailer office, I feel like I've done something positive."

"If you've figured the smuggling angle, that'll put this end of her operation out of business," Morgan said, pulling on his shoulder holster rig. "We're done here, right? Because now, I want to head south. I say we put that book in Mark Roberts' hand, then we can scope out the area. Do a thorough survey of Anaconda's home and drug factory. Then I'll get some boys together and go in and get her."

"That's sounding like a fine plan," Felicity said, tipping her head toward him. "First, of course, we'll be needing to get out of here alive."

-36-

As the door burst open four men rushed into Edwardo's living room. The first man tripped over Edwardo, then scrambled to his feet. Two of them ran to the open window, to stare down into the darkness. The fourth man hung back nearer the door.

The first man stuck his head out into the rain and fired twice down the fire escape. After his eyes recovered from the muzzle flashes, he turned, his bull neck barely contained by the collar of his striped shirt.

"Damn it, Rico, I don't see nobody." The second man, wearing a thin mustache under a crooked nose, put one foot up on the window sill, about to climb out after whoever had been in the room. Number three pulled a gun from under his plaid jacket, prepared to follow.

"Hold up." Back at the door, Rico was licking his lower lip. His face was gaunt, his hair short cropped, his mustache pencil thin. One heavy gold chain looped under his lapels, hanging down to the edge of his sternum. He filled his lungs with smoke from a Chesterfield while the others stared at him.

"Only Charlie goes down the fire escape," Rico said. "Just in case. But I don't think anybody could have got to the bottom that fast."

"He's right." Paul rose from behind the sofa, firing his pistol. A bullet went down the silencer with a sound like a child clearing its throat. It slapped Charlie in the back of the head, shoving him out the window. Paul took a step to his left as he shot Crooked Nose in the throat. Then his hand brushed the wall and the lights went out.

Plaid Jacket dived to the floor and sent three loud shots in the stranger's general direction. Then he hugged the silence, waiting for return fire that never came. When he could finally hear over his heart's thumping, he figured the other man might be dead. Still, as slowly and quietly as he could, he slid his body left. There was a table there, at the end of the sofa, and there was a lamp on it.

Plaid Jacket turned the light switch while he held his gun forward, looking for a target. His eyes snapped left and right, until he accepted he was the only man in the room. The only man alive, anyway. His shoulders had just dropped to their normal, relaxed level when a moan drew his aim. Then he whistled, and lowered his gun.

"Edwardo, man I thought you was dead and I almost killed you just now myself." He walked toward his dazed friend, helping him to his feet. "Oh wow, man. What happened to your face?"

"Where are they?" Paul slammed the weighted glove into Rico's gut, and drug dealer crumpled like a crashed paper airplane.

"Madre de Dios, I don't know," he rasped out.

"You better get smart fast, you bastard, or you're going to get dead." Paul swung his gloved fist back hand, and Rico's head snapped into the wall. "You said this Anaconda took them?"

"Yes, but they got away from her," Rico said, squeezing his eyes shut, hiding from another blow.

"She had to know they were trouble," Paul said, staring down at his captive. "She must have tracked them."

Rico's head bobbed up and down. "They went to Texas. She sent men for them. Some didn't come back. She wanted to send more, but we lost them. I swear to God. We been looking, but they just disappeared."

Paul considered this news from a man far too scared to lie. He turned away for a second, then turned back, whipping his automatic forward. He rested the gun's muzzle in the notch of Rico's collar bone.

"This Anaconda woman is bad news," Paul said. "And she's made some bad enemies. Like me. Now, you can live if you swear to me that you're out of the drug business."

"I can't," Rico said, more pleading than defiant. "She'll kill me. She has eyes everywhere."

Paul thumb cocked his Sig Sauer. "Scared of her? Or scared of me?"

Rico's mouth hung open. He swallowed hard, which jerked the gun barrel up and down. "Okay," he finally said.

"Nobody does business with this Anaconda's organization anymore. I'll be watching. Anybody deals with her, I'll be back. Comprende?"

"Si," Rico said. Paul pulled the gun away and snapped it forward, not too hard, but it would put a bruise on Rico's temple. Rico dropped to the floor and lay still. Paul holstered his gun and walked out, brushing dust off his sport coat.

So they had gone to ground, perhaps left the country. Paul's search had led him nowhere. It would be pointless to leave for Texas if Morgan and Felicity had already moved on. And he had no idea where they might turn up next. As much as he wished it otherwise, they were on their own.

As he stepped into the night rain, Paul's telephone vibrated, alerting him to a message. He pulled the phone out of his inside jacket pocket and pushed a speed dial button. When the connection was made, he said, "It's Paul."

"Paul, thank God. It's Sandy. I just heard from Mister Stark and Ms. O'Brien. They're okay and they're coming home."

-37-

Heat haze made the asphalt shimmer in front of them as the taxi pulled to a stop in front of a long, flat dun-colored building. Morgan opened the back door and stepped out first, scanning the area for possible trouble. Then he shouldered his duffle bag and held a hand down to help Felicity out of the vehicle. It was more humid than before, but his mind was not on how hard it was to breathe.

"Do you feel at home?" Felicity asked.

"Sort of. Hard to describe. The atmosphere is familiar, even though I've never been here before. A military landing strip has its own feel to it."

"Hey, it was your idea," she said, "And it was a good one. Let's go get on with it."

Walking toward the control building Morgan reran the conversation that got them there.

It had been one of those conversations that highlighted their different thinking styles. Morgan had fished out a notebook because he did his best planning with a pencil in his hand. Felicity paced the small motel room, barefoot with arms folded. She didn't appear to be watching where she was going, yet she never stumbled or bumped into anything.

"So we need to get back to base," Morgan said. "How do you want to travel? Steal another car? If we haul ass at nightfall, with no kid to slow us down with rest stops…"

"That doesn't work," Felicity said. "Once Roberts gets

things moving to crash their smuggling ship they'll be too distracted to bother with us. But for now they'll be watching every road out of town I'm betting."

"They ain't as good as they think they are. Anybody comes after us on the road it won't be like rolling up on poor Mary Carter. They come at us I know I can take them out."

Felicity nodded and stopped to lean back against the dresser. "Of course, you can, Morgan, but think about that last attack. These bastards don't care about getting innocents caught up in their wars. You really want to find yourself in a gun battle in a populated area again? Want to risk a stray bullet hitting a civilian? No, I know you better than that."

"Mark could probably swing a protective escort for us."

"CIA?" Felicity snorted. "Or maybe local police? That just means a bigger gun battle with more undisciplined shooters."

"Fair enough. Driving might put a lot of people at risk that got no reason to be. But then what? If they're on the roads you know they'll be on the airports too."

"No doubt," Felicity said, beginning to wander the room again. "And the ports are even easier to watch. I don't fancy trying to get out of here by boat."

"Hmmm… I suppose we could walk out. Hitchhike?"

Felicity slowed her pacing and knit her brow. Then she gave a definitive shake of her head.

"Tempting, lad, because of a low chance of being spotted, especially if we split up. But if they did spot us, well, that's a death sentence for whoever was kind enough to pick us up."

"Yeah." Morgan stood, crossed the room, and stared out the window at a city that probably seemed perfectly safe to everyone else out there. "How in God's name do we get out without risk of collateral damage?"

"Well, let's go back to your idea about CIA support. A motorcade out of here might be too dangerous, but do you suppose they could take over a port for us to sail out of?"

"Sounds a little public for them," Morgan said.

"All right then, how about commandeering a small airport for a while? That could be pretty discreet. I'm betting you can fly any kind of aircraft they come up with. And little airstrips don't have many people on them at any one time, so not much danger to them if something pops off, eh?"

Now it was Morgan's turn to mull over an idea. It almost seemed like a winner until he began to try to piece the details together.

"Pretty good, Red," he said, still facing the window, "but I doubt they could give us a private plane on such short notice. I don't think they'd be willing to just bogart somebody's jet… but…"

Morgan suddenly spun to face her, his face alight. "Hold on. There is a way for the government to put us on a plane that's totally safe and under the good guys' control. Let me get back down to that payphone. Mark's going to love this."

That call to Mark Roberts had led them to the edge of that airstrip on Naval Air Station Corpus Christi. Just a six mile cab ride from the city, NAS Corpus Christi was the home of Naval pilot training since before World War II. Uniformed men and women hurried here and there without sparing Morgan and Felicity a glance. The odor of jet fuel competed with the smell of sun baked asphalt. The tarmac was littered with small training aircraft but Morgan didn't see the transport he was looking for.

Within two minutes of them stepping out of their cab a tall black man in fatigues marched up to them. He made eye contact with both of them before speaking.

"Mr. Stark? Ms. O'Brien? Master Sergeant Kevin Buckler. I've been instructed to escort you to your hop."

"Lead on, Master Sergeant," Morgan said. He suspected this man had more important things to do, but orders had come down and he would follow them. Morgan wanted to be as small an interruption to the NCO's day as possible. Buckler turned and walked toward one of the low buildings with Morgan and Felicity in his wake. Morgan fell into step with their escort, while Felicity looked around.

"A lot of uniforms," she said. "Similar, but not the same. Now why would your Air Force have so many variations? Not exactly uniform in their uniforms."

Before Morgan could respond, Buckler spoke over his shoulder. "Not all Air Force, ma'am. This is a Navy facility, but Navy, Marine Corps, Air Force and even foreign student pilots earn their wings here. There's also an Army Depot on base and the aviation component of Coast Guard Sector Corpus Christi. This is one of the most purple military installations in the world."

She stepped closer to Morgan and asked, "Purple?" in a low voice.

"Just what we call it when all the services' uniform colors are combined," Morgan replied.

Buckler walked them into a barely air conditioned waiting area, handed them each a sack lunch, collected their bags and walked off toward the runway.

"Well, he's kind of intense," Felicity said.

"He's a senior NCO tasked with babysitting a pair of civilians with no good reason to be here as far as he knows. He's really being pretty good about this. Trust me, nobody in uniform likes the way the CIA does business."

Buckler was back within five minutes and with a wave guided them to the runway. As soon as they were on the other side of the building Morgan saw what he had been waiting for.

"Yeah, this is the way you do a military hop, Red. You'll never forget your first ride on the big bird. And yeah, the C-5 Galaxy is one of the biggest planes in the world. "

Felicity stared up at the plane that seemed to get bigger as they got closer to it. Her green eyes took in the high T-shaped tail, the sharply angled sweep of the wings, and the four goliath turbofan engines hanging under those wings. Buckler turned to face them and almost smiled.

"First military hop?"

"Hers, not mine," Morgan said. "But most of my flights on a C-5 were as part of a fully equipped combat-ready Army unit. It was me, about 35 pallets of gear and 80 of my closest friends."

"I get that it's a giant transport plane," Felicity said, "But what's this about a hop? You've said it a couple of times."

"A military hop is what they call space available travel," Buckler said. "If there's a military plane going where you need to be, and if there's an empty seat, you can hop on and fly for just a couple bucks. It's a perk for military folks and their families, retirees, and, er... special guests."

Buckler stopped at the edge of the aft door, which was dropped open. Morgan and Felicity thanked him for his time and walked up the ramp into the belly of the gray steel whale. Morgan quickly got comfortable in a seat but Felicity was slow to settle in next to him.

"Well this is a bit of a surprise. Whose idea was it for the seats to face the back of the plane? That's going to feel a bit odd."

"Just strap yourself in, Red," Morgan said with a grin. "And pop in these ear plugs. Even with them, the noise of the flight will distract you from the weird seats."

A dun colored Humvee stopped just outside the main

gate of Travis Air Force Base. Morgan stepped out first, thanked the driver, and offered his seatmate a hand. Felicity's legs were shaky but she moved quickly away from the military vehicle.

"Lord, that thing rides almost as rough as the bloody plane we just got out of."

Four hours in the C-5 had rattled Felicity's brain but it had also given her plenty of time to think. During the ride from the landing strip to the gate she had filled Morgan in on her thoughts and he had agreed with all she told him.

As soon as the Humvee had disappeared back into the base a Mercedes limousine pulled up in front of the two travelers. Felicity broke into a huge grin as Paul popped out of the front passenger door.

"Sure and you're a sight for sore eyes," she said. "Are you holding things together in the office?"

"Hopefully we've handled the business well," Paul said. "It is good to see you both uninjured. I imagine you have quite a story to tell." His face betrayed little emotion, but his ice blue eyes spoke volumes.

"Well we'll have plenty of time to catch up," Morgan said, pulling the back door open. "I'm glad the time zones bought us a couple hours, because we're probably more than six hours from home."

"A long drive for sure," Felicity said, "But I still want to talk to senior staff tonight. It's a little after one o'clock here, so let's plan for a late supper around the conference table."

Felicity thought that if anyone had been able to look in on their conference room at 8:15 that evening they would have learned a great deal about their company and the people who run it.

First, the table was cluttered with Chinese food take out containers. Five people sat around the table, side by side despite the wealth of empty chairs, all using chopsticks to fish food out of cartons. Morgan, like Felicity, wore jeans and a tee shirt. Sandy Fox was still in her office skirt suit. Paul wore something from his seemingly endless collection of blue suits. The other three men, Paul's hand-picked lieutenants, wore ties but no jackets and had rolled up their shirt sleeves. Neither Paul nor Morgan seemed to mind the differences.

"Let's keep this brief," Felicity said, pacing at the front of the room, occasionally seizing a piece of bourbon chicken. "We had plenty of time on the drive up from Travis Air Force Base, down by Fairfield to fill Paul in on where we've been and what's happened in the last few days. He can back-brief you later."

She recalled how little reaction they saw on Paul's face as they recounted their running conflict with the Escorpionistas. Even without any reference to Felicity's knife wound it was a harrowing tale which he simply took in. His reaction stood in sharp contrast to her responses hearing how Paul had single-handedly hurt the criminal organization there in California.

Morgan cleared his throat, glanced at Felicity, then turned to the others. "The bottom line of what you guys all need to know is that you're going to have to run your divisions on your own for the next three weeks or so. Ms. O'Brien and I will be out of the net entirely during that time. We got faith in you guys to run the business in our absence."

"I would submit that you could use some backup on that mission," Paul said. Morgan smiled.

"Yeah, I know you want to get in it, buddy, but I need you here to make the tough decisions while we're gone."

"You are going into battle against serious opposition," Paul said.

Morgan's smile dropped. "We're going to war against a

huge, well organized criminal enterprise in a foreign country. I know what that means. We're ready, and we need to keep the element of surprise on our side, but we can't be distracted wondering what's going on back here. That's why you stay here."

Paul nodded and sat back. That was the end of that, Felicity thought.

"Before we go we'll need your help, Sandy," Felicity said. "Don't book flights, but we need an itinerary that will get us where we need to be without the chance of being noticed or tracked. And we'll need cash drawn from different accounts that will get us the distance."

Fox looked up from her notes. "Ma'am, please don't take this the wrong way, but might you be biting off a bit more than you can chew?"

Felicity allowed ten seconds of silence and when she answered she was addressing the room.

"We've got a score to settle that simply cannot be set aside. You deserve to know that we have very good support on this from the U.S. government. And trust me, they won't even see us coming."

-38-

"When I was a child, we made rock candy just like this," Felicity said. Brushing long brown hair out of her temporarily brown eyes, she watched the white crystal grow in a beaker filled with liquid. The atmosphere was not of a warm family kitchen, but rather the cold, technical ambiance of a chemistry lab. The little man in a white lab coat removed safety goggles, looking at Felicity with an odd tilt to his head.

"Smoking this rock would keep you awake for forty-eight hours," he said.

"So that's all there is to it?" Morgan asked. "A few simple, commonly found chemicals?"

"Ingenious in its simplicity isn't it?" the chemist asked. "This simple process turns the rock into liquid. The Filipinos call it `batu', their word for rock. Anyway, then they just open up the books and soak the pages. When they dry, they pack them and ship them. At the other end, they just soak the books in the same chemicals, and when they add this stuff, the crystals re-form and distill out."

"It's so simple," Morgan said.

"Yeah, but nobody ever thought of it before," Roberts said from across the room. He was a very dark black man, six feet tall and wiry. He wore a lightweight suit and tie. Felicity had had to wait until they reached his, actually the CIA's, laboratory in Colombia to test her theory. It turned out to be correct.

"How do you know?" Felicity asked. She and Morgan

wore identical corduroy pants and nylon jackets. "There's no telling how much of this crap is coming into your country. Could be others doing the same thing."

"I just care about this Anaconda bitch's operation," Morgan said, staring out a window at the tropical growth outside. "So, armed with this knowledge, you can grab that ship and shut down the import at Corpus Christi, right?"

"Well, we'll stop the ship and raid the warehouse, but it's probably pointless," Roberts answered. "Once they found their man dead inside, I'll bet the Escorpionistas folded that operation anyway. The good news is, they'll lose millions of dollars while they're setting up a new system for getting that shit into the country."

"The time lapse," Felicity said, shaking her head.

"Was necessary," Morgan added.

Roberts thanked his chemist and ushered his visitors out of the hangar. They filed into his Volvo and strapped in for the long drive in from Bogota's outskirts to the city's center where Roberts kept his office, on a floor above the American embassy. The highway carried them between dense tropical forests. Just outside the city, they passed a loading point for one of the cable cars that haul sightseers up into the steep Andes Mountains. The view, Felicity reflected, must be spectacular.

"I guess you guys are serious about this blood feud with Anaconda, but I'm not really sure why, you know." Roberts spoke as if he did not require an answer, but would very much like one.

"I owe her something personal," Felicity said, unzipping her windbreaker now that the heat was coming on. "And there's Chuck, of course. Morgan has his own reasons."

"Unnecessary roughness," Morgan said, watching the jungle phase into a modern city.

"We play rough games," Roberts said.

"Sure, guys like you and me, we get what we get. Chuck

was a player. Frederico was probably a volunteer. But there's a forgotten girl named Mary Carter. I want the boys who did her. But if I just took them down, then it'd be hit for hit with Anaconda, not exactly a safe position to be in. So we take her down first. Then I can take the hitters."

"Well, I guess you know what you want," Roberts said. "I can't stop you. You're just a pair of private citizens. But if I can help, after all you've done, you know I will."

"Come on, Mark," Felicity said, "We're not stupid. You've got to see us as a gift from heaven. Nothing we do can come back on the CIA, but you know we're as good as anybody you've got."

"And we're happy to take your help. To start, we need maps and surveys," Morgan said. "After so much careful preparation it's like a little too much foreplay. I want to get started."

Sitting back, Felicity reflected on how much planning had already gone into this mission. Their long drive back to California, making only food, fuel and rest stops. Staff meetings at their security company for their projected three week absence. Clearance, thanks to Roberts, for equipment and weapons no tourist would carry. Packing for the cooler climate in Colombia's higher elevation. Reservations made in false names. And for Felicity, hair dye and contact lenses to conceal her most obvious identifying characteristics.

"I know you want to spy on the Escorpionistas," Roberts said as they approached their hotel. "But are you sure they're not following you?"

"No chance," Morgan said. "They lost interest in us when they got Frederico. Even if they figured us for the Texas problem, they had to track us down again. We were in and out of L.A. in forty-eight hours."

"Besides, we drove up to Seattle to fly out," Felicity added. "I doubt they keep anybody on that airport. We flew to New York, to Brussels, down to Dakar, Senegal, then over to Natal, Brazil and then to Panama City before finally landing in Colombia. Nobody could have followed. Cash all the way, so no paper trail." She did not say it, but any loyal Escorpionista would present a clear danger at this point, surely setting off their highly developed danger senses.

"Well, I think I got everything you need," Roberts said when he pulled up in front of the hotel. "That attache case in the back is the total of our intelligence, and some other things you might find interesting."

"Right," Morgan said, opening his door. "And thanks. We'll keep contact to a minimum until we're ready to move." Morgan picked up the case and headed for his room. Roberts drove around the block before letting Felicity out. She entered ten minutes after Morgan, through a different door.

Thirty minutes later they were on the floor in Morgan's room, staring at a four foot square map and several 8 X 10 photographs.

"I can't believe how much these satellite photos have improved," Morgan said, sitting at one edge of the map, holding a cup of coffee. "Here's Anaconda's base, in this little basin about a hundred and fifty miles south west of here."

"I can't believe she's still there," Felicity said, on her stomach at the map's opposite edge. "Lord, the Escorpionistas have practically declared war on the States, and the CIA knows exactly where she is. Why haven't they just dropped a bomb or something?"

"You know the political B.S. they have to deal with. Look here, they've got the primary production facility marked off. Jesus, it looks like a regular Dupont chemical plant. And look at these barracks huts. Must be close to fifty guys living on site."

"Her house is almost a mansion. Two stories, nearly flat roof. Perched right on top of this steep hill, between the helicopter landing circle and, what's that? A satellite television dish. Can you get to her house, here, without dealing with those guys?"

"I can see a probable access right through these mountains, here. With a good squad of men we can slip in and make the snatch without facing a serious firefight."

"You sure you just want to pull her out?" Felicity asked.

Despite some other opinions, I ain't no hired killer," Morgan said. "I've killed a lot of commies, and a healthy handful of terrorists, but that was war. Besides, if she goes on trial in the U.S. it'll have more of an impact than if she just disappears. Now all we need to do is survey the area in person. I can pin down the assault path and have the rest of my team down here in a week, ready to go."

"Okay, partner," Felicity said, smiling. "Before we head for this great camping trip, there're a couple of snapshots here that Mark threw in. I think you'll want to take a good close look."

-39-

A hearty aroma bubbling up from a unique stew pulled Felicity's head out of her sleeping bag. It meant good and bad news. A hot meal after two days eating packaged Army rations would be a pleasure. Morgan called them MRE's, for Meals Ready to Eat. Felicity suspected this bland fare would be Meals Rejected by starving Ethiopians. It was filling and nutritious, but what did that have to do with dining?

The down side was, Morgan would not start a fire unless there was a strong enough breeze to quickly disperse any smoke, masking their presence.

Climbing out of her bag, Felicity had to admit the last two days had been relaxing, alone with Morgan away from civilization. True, the hike into the mountains had been a killer, even though he carried most of the gear. Living in a tent would be better if everything was not always wet, and at this elevation the temperature hovered around fifty degrees year round. Yet it was so peaceful in this unspoiled mountainous countryside she found a peculiar sort of tranquility.

"What is that delicious smell?" Felicity asked, crawling across their narrow landing. Their tent stood against a cliff face. The landing, twelve feet across, had tall bushes rising at its edge, obscuring them from below. Morgan sat on a folded blanket, stirring a potful of something.

"Morning, Red. This is ajiaco. Just a kind of a thick soup. Potatoes, corn, cassava and some chicken I brought.

Get a couple of bowls."

"Anything new?" Felicity asked, as Morgan poured their breakfast.

"Their routine is rock solid," Morgan said.

"So, you can do it?"

"No doubt," Morgan said, flashing a big smile. "And there's more. I spotted both Marta and Quesada. They stick close to Anaconda's house."

"Mansion, actually. Ooh, this is so good. Are you sure they're the ones?"

"Roberts' people tracked them all at the airports. When Anaconda's travel team returned from the states, they left four heavy hitters behind." Morgan pulled a set of photographs from under his Gore-tex camouflage jacket. "They got some excellent pictures at the airport. Roberts' people confirmed which ones never came home. I left two of these guys in my room at the Wagon Wheel Inn. I'm sure the other two, Marta and Quesada, pushed Mary off the road. When they got back in country, they had Frederico in tow. They're dangerous characters. Real pros."

Their faces were already burned into his memory. Marta, the darker one, had sharp pronounced teeth and a weasel's face. Quesada's hair hung straight down his forehead and a scar on the right side of his face suggested some earlier attacker had just missed costing him an eye. They both had the look. Casual killers.

"Any sign of Frederico?" Felicity asked, finishing her soup.

"Sorry, Red. Only glimpses of Anaconda and not even a hint of the boy. He might already be history."

Felicity hugged herself against the cold, feeling the rough sweater under her jungle camouflage jacket scratch against her new scar. This was Morgan's operation, a military strike, but she wanted to stay as close to it as she could. She regarded Anaconda as a dangerous animal, and

Morgan as the hunter who would get her into a snare. So she had hiked along, and watched as Morgan observed Escorpionista activity and took notes. She could see his notebook, within reach while he finished his food, but she knew what was written there was a shorthand that only Morgan understood.

"So, based on what we've seen so far, can you do this thing?"

"Don't worry Red," Morgan said. "Now that I've walked it I got a clear plan for access through the jungle and up the mountainside to Anaconda's house. I can get a team in and we can grab her, just like that, and haul her ass out of here to face what she's done."

"Shouldn't you wait a bit, till she's forgotten about us? Seems like that would make it easier to take her by surprise."

Can't wait," Morgan said. "Time is critical. Think about it, Red. It's losing Frederico that has left her vulnerable to surprise. It will take her a while to get used to not having him. Everything we know says the other boy's not as good, but given time, he might anticipate our attack."

"I was just thinking of the least risky approach…"

"Red, I need just a little more intelligence," Morgan said, breaking her concentration. "I think I'll slip in for a little up close surveillance."

"Sounds like an excellent way to break the boredom," Felicity said, standing and stretching. "Lead the way."

"Just me this time, partner."

"Why?" Felicity asked. "Afraid I'll give you away?"

"Red, I never met anybody quieter than you on the move, you know that. It's just, I might get into something you don't want to see. You know, like a target of opportunity."

"Uh-huh," Felicity said. "Like if you see one of those bent noses, you might want to kill him on the spot. Well, we're in this together, we are, and it's time I grew up a little. I promise to turn my head while you do what you got to do." She met his eyes in a way that told him there was no turning her away. With a sigh, he began clearing away his cooking gear. Felicity fell in, dousing the fire and helping to erase its evidence.

Minutes later they were sliding slowly and carefully down the slope from their landing. Felicity looked back, amazed at how quickly their tent disappeared from sight. Just a few feet away it was invisible. Years ago, she thought camouflage was a myth, just as some people believe knife throwing and ESP are. Now she knew better. Like so many other things, Morgan was a genius at this.

A clear stream trickled through the deep crevice at the bottom of the hill. They crossed, Morgan leading, and started up the slope toward Anaconda's hidden estate. Felicity found their route a little ironic. Anaconda had put in an excellent road for truck transport of needed chemicals, but of course it was watched too well.

Morgan slipped through the dense, bright green vegetation like some verdant ghost. Felicity followed almost in his footsteps. The ground was soft, and each step raised the sweet smell of rotting vegetation. As always, it seemed perpetual twilight to Felicity in the deep woods. Actually, the sun, unseen, seemed irrelevant. Light was diffused, coming from all directions or none at all. How else could it be this dark with no shadows being cast?

When Morgan froze, Felicity froze. She did not see or hear anyone, but she recognized that tilt to Morgan's head. It was an unconscious move he made when he encountered something he did not understand. She moved forward silently, until she could see what had stopped him.

The fence was only about three feet high, and looked like chicken wire from back home. The space on the other side looked just like where they were, wildly overgrown with long grass. The fence was invisible from their observation post, embedded in the trees and bushes.

"Why?" Felicity asked.

"Got me," Morgan whispered. "Not strong enough or high enough to keep anything out. Motion sensor? Some kind of infrared alarm?"

"Not likely," Felicity said, moving close so she could keep her voice down. "Every small animal or bird would set it off. Or trees waving in the breeze. It'd go off every five minutes."

"Then, what?" Morgan asked. He reached out, touched the fence, and snapped his hand back. "It's hot," he said, shaking his hand.

"Clearly not enough to do any damage," Felicity whispered. "Think she just wants to keep animals out?"

Morgan shrugged and stepped left. They would skirt this fencing to see how far it went. They kept their movements slow but steady, disturbing their environment as little as possible.

Forty-five minutes later, Morgan and Felicity had moved nearly a quarter of a mile through the woods. The fence curved around Anaconda's house, separating it from the chemical plant. Morgan assumed they would find a gate further on. They paralleled a dirt road the fence cut across. The road led to the drug factory. This was a low, flat roofed cinder block building, about twice as big as an ordinary ranch style house.

The ground dropped off steeply at the road's edge. Morgan and Felicity looked up over that edge, clinging to the soft earth. After a few more minutes side stepping brought them even with one side of the factory. The narrow road, about one car wide, wound around behind the building. Hanging onto the edge, Morgan and Felicity were barely a dozen feet from the cinder block wall across the road.

"I'll be right back," a voice said in Spanish. A man with a light tread approached. Morgan and Felicity hung lower over the edge, gripping it with their fingertips.

As they watched, a short, dark man in jungle fatigue pants and an olive drab shirt walked toward them. A machete hung at his side. Morgan froze, and Felicity slid down the hill a few inches. The man walked with excessive confidence, staring out into the jungle as if he expected to see an old friend. Then he turned away. Morgan stole a glance over the road's edge, catching a glimpse of a weasel faced profile.

Marta.

Morgan had told Felicity about "targets of opportunity." Here was one of the men he wanted, straight ahead, just six feet away, turning to face the wall and reaching for his fly. He was too vulnerable to ignore, but a pistol shot would bring a horde of Escorpionistas down on them. Still, he was right there.

Felicity knew he would go for it. She knew before Morgan did. She scanned for other watchers but she knew it would not really matter.

Limbs scrambling wildly, Morgan launched himself forward. Hands, knees, feet hit the narrow dirt road. Morgan's right hand hooked into Marta's belt just as he heard a button come open. One good yank sent both men tumbling backward down the slope into the jungle.

Felicity's alarm went off full blast, and she stared around in all directions. Behind her, Morgan and Marta tumbled toward the valley floor, until a poorly placed tree halted their progress. A sound like a dog barking snapped her head back up.

An animal stared at her through the fence. It looked like...well she was not quite sure. A yellowish German shepherd perhaps, about four feet long, whose legs were stretched out to almost cartoon proportions, with a horse's mane growing down its neck and back. Breath froze in her chest and she dropped to her arms' full length. Her body was stretched along the steep incline with her face pressed against the fetid ground.

Only then did she hear the man. He trotted over to the road's edge, probably thinking his friend had slipped and fallen over. He was laughing gently when he looked over, missing Felicity completely. She saw a flat, broad nose in the middle of a flat, olive skinned face. The man's laugh vanished when he saw the big black man wrestling with Marta. The short, muscular Escorpionista had managed to get his machete in hand, but Morgan had his wrist. They struggled on the ground, their heads pointing down the steep hill.

The watcher stepped carefully to the very edge of the drop off and pulled a gun from a waistband holster. Felicity clutched a root and a rock in the dirt surface, pulling herself up very slowly. She knew a shot would stop the fight even if he missed Morgan, and it would also certainly bring help. She could allow no shot.

Halfway down the slope, Morgan transferred both hands to Marta's machete arm. The other man grabbed Morgan's collar and used it to bang Morgan's head against the tree that had halted their fall. Morgan pushed the captive arm, then pulled it hard, getting the machete blade embedded in the tree trunk. A hard twist broke Marta's grip. Marta's legs locked around Morgan as they slid slowly downward, pushing stones and dirt into a small avalanche.

"Are you crazy coming here?" Marta asked, putting pressure on Morgan's ribs.

"I come a long way for you," Morgan said through clenched teeth. Almost black soil rolled up under Morgan's jacket and shirt. He slammed an elbow down into Marta's leg, just above the knee, and the pressure eased. Then he pushed out with his feet, forcing the pair toward the bottom of the slope.

Felicity looked up as Flat Nose took aim at Morgan. Reaching up with her left hand, she managed to grab his bloused trouser leg. When he looked down she released her right hand's grip on the ledge. Her weight dragged the man over the rim. He rolled forward past her, the gun sailing into the air. Twisting, Felicity got her feet under herself in a deep crouch. Flat Nose rolled to a stop not far ahead. He looked up at the girl, then down at the two fighters.

Morgan and Marta had almost reached the bottom, nearly fifty yards away. Flat Nose started down the hill, moving carefully, sliding as much as stepping. When he reached the machete, he freed it from the tree.

Inches from the bottom of the hill, Morgan finally freed his knife from its scabbard. Marta reached behind him to the narrow stream bed for a rock. He swung it at Morgan's head, but Morgan blocked it. The blow landed on his left hand, numbing his fingers and sending his fighting knife spinning away. An edge of hand blow from Morgan made Marta release the stone. His fingers switched to Morgan's throat. Damp soil clung to their faces and rolled down their necks as they wrestled for control. The loose, uneven ground made any kind of controlled motion almost impossible.

Felicity watched the Escorpionista receding ahead of her. Morgan had gained the top in his private battle, but he might not have noticed the approaching attacker. If he did, he might be unable do anything about it. She wondered what she could do. Reaching the bottom safely would take her a long time, and Morgan might die before then. She had no weapons or tools to slow the man down with.

Finally, she slid forward just far enough to reach a young but solid tree. She pulled herself up its narrow trunk a few feet, and reached a low hanging branch, maybe seven feet above the ground. Gripping the branch with both hands she swung twice, and let go at her third swing's apex.

The sensation was frightening and thrilling. She flew perhaps thirty-five yards, dropping through space, while never being more than seven feet from the ground. Blurred fern trees flew past as she twisted her body, weaving between them. Leaves of a bewildering variety of trees slapped at her during her long seconds in flight. Then her knees smacked against Flat Nose's back. The impact thrust him to his feet, then forward onto his face. A dull thud told her his head had found a stone. He continued to slide forward, out of control. Felicity leaned back on her haunches, pushing him ahead of her.

Morgan and Marta were on their knees on the narrow creek bed's mud floor like high school wrestlers. Morgan had one arm around Marta's waist, while the other controlled his support arm. As Felicity watched, Morgan drove forward, forcing Marta into the ground. Marta's face splashed into the shallow creek, and he struggled like a landed fish. Now Morgan had Marta's right arm behind him. He held Marta's collar in his left fist, with his forearm across the man's neck. Marta was making a bubbling, gurgling sound with his face pressed into the shallow stream. Morgan was gasping in the crisp mountain air, apparently not feeling the cold cutting into his sodden clothes.

"You killed her just to be snotty, didn't you?" he said through clenched teeth. "Well you'll die for a reason, asshole. To make the world smell better."

Felicity had seen men shot, knifed, and killed with

various other weapons, but watching Morgan kill a man with his hands, this was something very different. The act's personal nature made her shudder, but she forced herself to watch. She reminded herself that this man was a purveyor of deadly drugs, that he was a killer who murdered without remorse, that the world would be a better place after he left it. She watched Marta's final throes, heard his death gurgle, telling herself Morgan was an avenging angel, delivering fair retribution for the death of an innocent.

It didn't help.

When Marta lay still Morgan stood up, mud dripped from his knees. He drew several deep breaths, trying to regain some self control. He offered Felicity a half smile, and took a few steps uphill to regain his knife. Only then did he see the man with the flat nose, lying spread eagled on the slope. Dead leaves, palm fronds and black dirt were banked up in front of him, indicating a long slide. Morgan turned back to Felicity with new respect.

"Somebody will come looking for these two before too long," Felicity said. "Shouldn't we be gone?" Morgan nodded, drawing his pistol. Felicity's eyes cut to the second man, fear showing on her face.

"Relax, Red," Morgan said, approaching the prone man. "I'm not looking to finish him off. This is a perfect source of intelligence." He knelt and slapped the man hard across the face. His eyes snapped open, sagged, then widened again as his brain registered the gun hovering inches from his nose. His gaze quickly left the pistol, focusing on the face of the man holding it.

Another seasoned pro, Morgan thought. His attention is on the man, not the gun. That should make this easier.

"Habla ingles?" Morgan asked. Flat Nose nodded. "Good. Look left." Flat Nose twisted his head around. The dead man was just in his field of vision. "Marta's dead," Morgan continued. "You don't have to be. If you come with me and tell me a little about your job with Anaconda, I guarantee you'll get out of this with a whole skin. Now, can you walk?"

Before answering, Flat Nose moved his limbs experimentally. Not enough to make Morgan nervous, just enough to make sure his joints all functioned. Then he nodded.

"Good," Morgan said, easing the gun back from the man's face. "What's your name?"

"Jorge," Flat Nose replied.

"Well, Jorge, do you believe I'll kill you if you give me any shit?"

"Yes," Jorge answered. His tone was respectful but calm. Morgan helped him stand. Jorge looked quite surprised to find a woman watching all this. Then realization popped onto his face.

"You hit me from behind while I was sliding down the hill." His face changed to something approximating a smile.

With Felicity behind Morgan and Jorge six feet ahead of him at gunpoint, they moved off toward camp and, Felicity hoped, some more of that ajiaco.

-40-

It was two o'clock before Morgan and Felicity were invited in. Morgan rankled at being separated from a prisoner he felt was his but CIA interrogators wanted him first, and Roberts had been pretty insistent.

The room was warm when they entered. On their left, large square windows offered a panoramic view of downtown Bogota, but the city's grand setting overshadowed it. Bogota sits on a plateau surrounded by the towering Andes Mountains. The city's many high rise buildings are all dwarfed by the height of those peaks. And the mountains host some impressive adornments. Felicity stared up at the huge figure of Christ atop the mountain directly ahead of her. She knew from another room she would see the giant cross on a different peak, or the lovely white convent on yet another mountain at the city's edge. It was a struggle to force her attention to events inside the room.

Roberts sat at one end of a long table, his hands folded before him. Jorge sat at the other end. A wire trailed from a microphone which sat up, like a begging dog, in front of Jorge. The wire disappeared into a hole in the table. Felicity guessed the wire would go to some sort of recording device and maybe machinery designed to judge from the man's tone of voice whether or not he was telling the truth. Beside the mike sat a water pitcher with four paper cups, three of which remained unused. Two men in short haircuts and identical gray suits stood as Morgan and Felicity entered.

After one replaced a syringe in a black leather attaché case, they both left without a word. Morgan looked a question at Roberts.

"Gave him something to relax him," Roberts said with a smile.

"Right," Morgan said. Then he walked over to face Jorge. His pupils were dilated, his stare a bit vacant, but Morgan saw no signs indicating physical abuse. "You okay?" he asked.

"As you promised," Jorge said. "With a whole skin."

"I know your interests aren't the same as ours," Felicity said, pulling a chair out from the table and dropping into it, "but did you get a layout of the grounds?"

"Our resident artist is putting it into scale right now, based on topographic landmarks," Roberts said. "We have the shape and size of all buildings, guard positions, roads, the works."

"I thought these people were so tough."

"Felicity, we couldn't have gotten anything out of this guy in three weeks of physical persuasion," Roberts said. "Water boarding is for the military. We're a little more sophisticated than that."

"These new pentothol derivatives are amazing," Morgan said, pulling off his suit coat. His gun and knife were in full view, over a white dress shirt which somehow accented the weapons. "If you can keep the subject alive, you can coax him into telling you things he didn't know he knew." Then he turned to Roberts "Get all you wanted?"

"Well, this guy's pretty low on the totem pole," Roberts said. "He doesn't know that much we didn't already have. It's just an exercise anyway. You know we can't take any legal action. And the president doesn't want any real action taken down here anyway."

"No big surprise there," Morgan said. "They hate the drugs, but not enough to take action to fix the problem."

"Let's not get into a political thing," Felicity said. "Mark, do you mind if we ask him a few questions?" Roberts waved a hand as if to say "help yourself."

"Thanks. First thing, I'm wanting to know about the mutant dogs." Morgan and Roberts looked at her dubiously. "Really. I saw them behind the fence, Morgan. Big dogs, but with horses' manes and giraffes' legs."

"Oh, you mean the maned wolves," Jorge said.

Morgan chuckled. "They're not mutations, Red, just one of the unusual animals that grow in South America, although I didn't know they had them in Colombia."

"We don't," Jorge said. "We chased all over to get them: Brazil, Argentina, Paraguay, Bolivia, even down to Peru. Just because Anaconda thinks weird animals look dangerous."

"That's a laugh," Morgan said. "They eat small animals, like guinea pigs and such. "They may look funny, but not particularly dangerous."

"That's what you think," Jorge said, listing a bit to the right. "Anaconda, she's conditioned them. That electrified fence keeps them in, even with their long legs. By controlling their food and feeding them drugs, she's made them all really vicious."

"Why are they there?" Felicity asked.

Jorge chuckled. "Don't you see? They are her last line of defense. See, Anaconda's house sits in the middle of about an acre and a half of rolling grass land up in those mountains. That fence surrounds the whole area, and those wolves live in there. They make a hell of a racket if anybody gets inside, and they'd probably eat up an intruder anyway."

"How does she get in and out?" Morgan asked.

"Oh, they're too skittish to attack you if you're in a crowd.," Jorge said. "Now, one or two men they might jump, especially if they got spooked."

"You said last line of defense," Felicity said. "What else? I mean, infrared beams, motion sensors, pressure alarms?"

"You Anglos. You just don't get it," Jorge said, reaching for water. "Out where we are, all the power's from a generator. Anaconda, she likes her television, her DVD movies, her stereo music, her computer. There's not much electricity left for alarms and such. She figures a couple dozen trigger men and the maned wolves ought to protect her."

"I see," Felicity said. She stood and crossed to the window, her mind wandering to the task ahead, entering this mountain fortress. "And no sign of Frederico, eh?"

"That boy has a spirit inside him," Jorge said with a sudden shiver. "Anaconda has not let him step out of the house since he returned." A curtain of silence settled over the room, its inhabitants paralyzed. Felicity's stomach turned to ice and breathing became difficult. She moved first, turning slowly from the window to stare into Jorge's wide, vacant eyes.

"He's there?" she croaked out. "Alive?"

"Not for long," Jorge answered. "Anaconda's anger, it was great. For days she's insulted and abused the boy, shaming him publicly, not allowing him to see the sun. Some of us, we thought it was a bad idea. Spirits commune with the boy. If she angers them enough, they might decide to take action against the Escorpionistas. I think she's started to see the fear in her followers. She might not be able to keep control if it keeps up. So, she's going to kill him. It will be a spectacular death, to prove her power's greater than any spirit."

"Kill him?" Felicity said, snapping forward, stopping inches away from Jorge's face. "When?" She put her hands flat on the table and held her breath.

"When? Well, let's see. What's today? Wednesday?

Yeah, well she's going to do him Sunday morning. Death at dawn. Drop him from a copter, I think."

"Four days," Morgan whispered. "No, three, really, if she's talking about dawn. Jesus." Felicity could see his mind was running down a predetermined past. It seemed that Roberts' mind was on the same path, but unhampered by excessive imagination, his reached the road's end faster.

"No way to stop it," Mark said. "You couldn't possibly get a team here and together in that time. And the political repercussions of getting anybody CIA involved would be excessive."

"Excessive? What's excessive is letting him die," Felicity said, straightening. "Saved our skin, he did. That's how he got in this mess. He's counting on us to get him out of it."

"Felicity, how can we..."

"I don't know," she said. "I don't know, but we will. I'll just figure out how I'd rob the place, and substitute Frederico for a set of Van Gogh's. You just be ready to go in there and get him." When the door closed behind Felicity, Roberts looked at Morgan, mystified.

"What'll she do?" he asked.

"Well, I'll tell you," Morgan answered. "She'll go for a long walk. She'll go to the hotel and do some writing, maybe make some drawings. Then she'll come up with a plan. It'll be impractical, maybe impossible. And you and I won't be able to see any way it can work. But it will work and we'll do it."

"Why do I get the feeling if that woman asked you to walk into hell through the front door..."

"I'd go get me some fireproof boots," Morgan said.

At the table, Jorge went on staring straight ahead while his body slowly chased the synthetic drugs out of his system.

-41-

Agent Isaacs pushed the small Robin Dr 400 Regent down through the last cloud layer, turning away from the approaching sunset. He had flown this four-seater propeller plane for the agency before, but never with passengers as intense as those two behind him. Even with their breathing apparatus off, they spoke little, and when they did, it was in a kind of shorthand he seldom completely understood. He was used to flying missions he knew nothing about, and he clearly did not have a need to know this time.

Over Anaconda's estate, Morgan had examined the area carefully through borrowed binoculars. Mostly, he was judging distances between landmarks and comparing likely wind directions with topographic factors. He was about to hand off the glasses when he saw movement below.

A group of human figures was leaving the house, and he was just close enough to distinguish Anaconda among them. They walked past the helicopter, attracting the attention of several maned wolves. Growling, baring their teeth, these animals circled the group. When they got too close, Anaconda and her escorts pulled out cattle prods. Morgan watched as they jabbed at the wolves, and then pitched what looked like steaks into the woods. The wolves ran off after the easy food. He lowered the glasses as the plane pulled away from the mountain estate.

"Pick out a good drop zone?" Felicity asked.

"Looks pretty level just south of the copter pad," Morgan replied. "There's a pretty good dead zone in case the wind picks up. It's still a dumb idea. No reception committee to sterilize the area. No easy place to hide a parachute."

Agent Isaacs brought the small single engine plane in for a smooth landing, coasting down the runway toward the farthest hangar. Morgan liked this minor private airfield, and wished he had known about it on previous South American missions. When the plane eased to a stop, Mark Roberts stood at the hangar door.

"See what you wanted to see?" Roberts asked while helping Felicity down from the plane.

"Morgan says there's a decent drop zone. Been over the plan a dozen times, we have, debugging it. An `insertion' Morgan calls it, but I'm not too comfortable with that term as I guess you can understand."

"Actually it's an extraction," Morgan said, stepping down to the tarmac, "but that always makes me think of pulling teeth. I hope that's not what this is like."

"What do you think of Isaacs?" Roberts asked, ushering them to his car.

"Damn good pilot," Morgan said, settling into Roberts' back seat. "He's not happy about what he's got to do, but I think he'll do as he's told."

"Hey, can we continue this over some dinner?" Felicity asked, as Roberts started the car. "It's going to be a long night, and I'm needing some sustenance."

Since they were casually dressed they settled on a small local restaurant. Besides, Felicity wanted to try ajiaco prepared by a local cook. She found it even better, although she did not say so. Lighting was pleasingly low, and the trio sat in low wooden chairs at a round table adorned with a natural color tablecloth. The aroma of the soups and stews so popular in Colombia filled the dining room. It was a dense mixture of onions, garlic, cumin, bay leaves, chile peppers, and cilantro that tickled the nose and augmented the appetite.

"I know it was only yesterday we planned this deal, but were you able to get everything on our equipment list?" Morgan asked between mouthfuls.

"Either got it, or got it lined up," Roberts replied. "I still don't see it. I mean, a night HALO jump into an unfamiliar LZ?"

"Morgan doesn't get it either but really, we've got no choice," Felicity said. "There's no walking in undetected, and hang time in a normal jump practically guarantees our being spotted. And we'll have to fly in high enough so the plane won't be seen or heard from the ground."

"Not the point," Roberts said. "It's just too dangerous, even with these rectangular aerofoil canopies."

"Not for us. We've jumped together before. It's just a matter of popping the silk at the right altitude, right? Morgan watches the wrist altimeter, and when he reaches for his cord, I'll know it. You know how close we are."

"Indeed," Roberts replied. Just months ago, he had stood in their private underground gun range and seen Morgan shoot at targets blindfolded. As long as Felicity could see them, Morgan could hit them. Their psychic rapport was that strong. "Okay, let's say you make the jump, within spitting distance of a densely wooded area, and come up with no broken bones. How you going to get at this kid?"

"If you get us the guns before we take off day after tomorrow, it'll be easy," Felicity said, switching from her soup to a rice dish she did not recognize. It was spicy and sweet in a way foreign to her tongue, but good. "We stop the wolves with tranquilizer darts, break into the house, knock out the guards, grab the boy and get out of the house. Then we just steal her bird and scamper. We ditch the copter a couple of miles from town and hike on in."

"Yeah," Roberts said grimly, "real simple. You been

awful quiet here, Morgan."

"I'm eating," Morgan replied.

"Think it can work?"

"If everything goes right," Morgan said. "If it don't, I think I can fight my way out and level the place with the C4. With a fire like that to deal with, they'll be too busy to go chasing after us."

"You guys do understand it'll just be the two of you, right?" Mark repeated for the umpteenth time. "I can't give you any support if it all goes tits up. Oh, Sorry Felicity." Despite Roberts' natural darkness, Felicity could detect a definite blush.

"No offense taken," she said with a smile. "I know that military phrase from hanging out with this animal. Besides, this particular plan starts with just that situation, eh? Mine will be up about twenty-four thousand feet."

-42-

Twenty-four hours after that dinner, Morgan and Felicity were walking down one of the less tourist-friendly streets of Bogota, Colombia. Felicity was familiar with the trendier sections of the city with their nightclubs and cafes haunted by Bogota's jet set. She had found abundant targets for her special skills there, back when she made her living as a thief.

But this was San Victorino, a neighborhood right in the middle of Bogota not recommended by the guide books. They were crossing a plaza surrounded by pastel colored buildings reminiscent of Miami. She saw all kinds of cheap stores selling a variety of goods, everything from clothes to food and pets, but none of it aimed at tourists. She thought this might be the most colorful part of the city, and maybe the most characteristically Colombian as well. It was Times Square with llamas, where break dancers seemed right at home but the one McDonalds seemed completely out of place.

Felicity's instincts told her that gringos were not well received there, but she was confident that Morgan's darker skin and broad shoulders would keep petty thieves and muggers at a distance. Bigger fish might be a different story. Felicity took Morgan's arm, cuddled close and whispered.

"You still feel them back there?"

"Oh, yeah," he said softly, smiling down at her as if she were his date. "And I'm still not getting a real danger zing off them."

Felicity stopped them in front of a shop to admire the hand woven blankets and check out their followers in the window pane reflection.

"They can't be Escorpionistas. Think the Agency put a tail on us?"

"They wouldn't dare," Morgan said. "Local hustlers?"

"Unlikely," Felicity said, resuming their walk across a brick street. "To good at tailing, they are. These aren't the boys who do the rough stuff. Or if they are, they're part of an elite group."

Morgan nodded. "Just wish they'd make their move, whatever it is. I'm getting bored."

"You know, Mark would say we're crazy for staying out here. As soon as we picked up the tail we should have gone back to the hotel and called in reinforcements."

"And then we'd never know who they were or why they're on us," Morgan said. "I figured if we just walked on a predictable trajectory they'd make contact or tip their hands some kind of way."

They turned down a narrower street, too close for motor traffic. Felicity looked up to enjoy the glow of the stars she so missed back in California. Bogota was nearly as big as New York or Mexico City, and yet it managed to keep its skies clear. Drug manufacture was not an industry with a large carbon footprint.

Her thoughts were interrupted by two men approaching. Their shoulders were so broad that walking side by side they cut off the breeze blowing up the street. Morgan stopped and eased Felicity behind him.

"Okay, I think these are the boys who do the rough stuff," he said. "At least they sent the A team."

From behind him a voice said, "We would not insult you by underestimating you, Mr. Stark."

Morgan made a slow ninety degree turn and checked out

the speaker. Of the two men who had been following them he was the shorter, but also the better dressed.

"You know me?" Morgan asked.

"By reputation," the shorter Colombian said. "And we don't want any trouble with you. I was just told to ask you to come with us to meet my chief, Senor Pulido."

Morgan's eyes returned to the men in front of him. "And what if we don't want to meet your chief?"

"Then we will go on our way."

"And we never know what this was about," Felicity said. "He's being safe, but respectful. We should be equally polite."

Morgan checked Felicity's eyes, nodded and turned back to the group's spokesman. "Walking distance?"

"We have a car." As he spoke the two larger men flattened against opposite walls to allow an ancient but well maintained white Mercedes Benz enter the street.

As they pulled up in front of the tan brick house Felicity turned to Morgan and said, "Rather a dump, eh?"

"Yeah, won't win any Home and Garden awards."
The house could have been mistaken for any middle class urban home in American, with an enclosed front garden tucked inside a gated community. Of course, American gated communities don't generally have armed guards and if they do, they aren't armed with Uzis. Still, the air of familiarity relaxed Felicity. This didn't figure to be the home of some high ranking master criminal.

As they climbed the outside stairs to the front door, white security bars on the front window came into full view. They were rusted at the points where they disappeared into the bricks but they were still holding fast when Morgan reached out to yank on one.

Their lead escort knocked on the door. It swung inward, and another edgy sentinel eyed them suspiciously before letting them pass. They stepped into a small hallway that opened into a massive living space, forcing an audible gasp from Felicity's lips.

"What bloody hell?" she said in a hoarse whisper.

A life-sized statue of the Colombian president dominated what she could only assume was the living room. Granted it was a plaster figure, but it moved her to see it standing in a room filled with the most expensive furniture money could buy, especially knowing where that money came from.

The windows were draped in the finest ivory silk and the hardwood floor was white ash showing a beautiful prominent grain. The mantle of the massive fireplace spanned the entire wall to their left. The opening to the right showed off a cherry oak formal dining room set but they were ushered forward through a back door and onto a brick patio. There they found a short, pecan-colored man fussing over a barbecue grill. When he looked up at them Felicity saw graying hair and the relax smile of a man who is in total control of his universe.

"You like the house?" he asked in almost accent-free English.

"Impressive," Felicity said. "Nicely appointed, and bigger inside than it looks from the outside."

The older man paused to seize a steak with a pair of tongs and turn it carefully. Then his eyes moved across Morgan and Felicity in turn, as if trying to decide something.

"I see. You speak. He observes. And you do not ask."

"You'll tell me," she said. Felicity maintained a casual, relaxed attitude. Morgan was tense and ready. That was enough.

Their host nodded. "I am Diego Pulido. I consider myself a successful businessman, and I am successful in part because I am curious. And you two have piqued my curiosity."

Felicity closed her eyes for just a moment to take in the aroma of the sizzling steaks. When she opened them she matched Pulido's smile.

"Senor Pulido, I would be pleased to satisfy your curiosity about anything that is my information to share. I'm sure you will understand if I refrain from sharing anyone else's secrets."

"Of course, senorita. I am aware that you consort with the American Central Intelligence people, but they are of no interest to me. What I do find interesting is that you managed to enter my country without my knowledge."

"Now why is that so interesting?" Felicity asked. "Do you observe all tourists?"

Pulido chuckled and shook his head. "Let us be open with one another, eh? I earn my living in the trade of coca and its derivatives. It is my business to know who comes and goes. You are a thief whose reputation leads me to believe that only a high value target would earn your attention. Your friend here is a soldier for hire. It is only because one of my men recognized him from a prior visit to our land that I am aware of your visit. During that visit, Senor Stark was part of a team who executed a number of men in my business. I am in the position that I am in now in part because of the damage he and his team did to the Medellin and Norte del Valle Cartel."

Now Pulido turned back to the grill, turning each of the seven steaks, raising a loud sizzling sound as the juices reached down to the ash-covered coals. Felicity gave a slow nod. "I now see your concern. Your question is really…"

Pulido looked up and locked eyes with Felicity. "I would simply like to know why you are here. Need I prepare for conflict?"

Felicity looked to Morgan, registered his small nod, and turned back to Pulido.

"If I understand the situation, sir, our visit here has nothing to do with you. I can assure you that we are not here on government business. We are merely accepting a little government assistance. We are here on personal business. We have a score to settle with the woman known as Anaconda."

"You are here because of a conflict with the leader of the Escorpionistas?"

"Yes," Morgan said. "Is that a problem?" Felicity was the only person in the room who was not surprised when Morgan spoke for the first time. "Does that put us in conflict with you?"

All eyes were on Morgan, but he kept his gaze locked on Pulido. Felicity felt the tension in the air and in her partner, even though he made no threatening gesture. If anything was going to happen it would be at this moment. Pulido had abandoned the steaks for a moment, and her nose told her that at least one of them was getting a little too dark on one side.

After ten long seconds a slow smile crept over his face.

"You ask is it a problem? That a warrior such as yourself is moving against my competition? Mr. Stark, I make my living from the coca plant. I do not believe in these new chemical products. They are more harmful, and more addictive, than traditional drugs. This attracts the attention of our northern neighbors. I am like the neighbor's yapping dog. You get used to it and after a while you stop complaining so much about the noise. But then, if he gets a new, noisier dog, you get annoyed all over again and go back to trying to get rid of the dogs. All the dogs."

Morgan nodded. "Anaconda's ice is the new dog. And she is drawing too much attention from my country."

"Just so," Pulido said, pointing the tongs at Morgan for emphasis. "If you want to reduce my competition, by quieting the new dog, well… If your sights do not wander to me or my business afterward, then you and I, we are not in conflict. Do you agree?"

Morgan said, "I do," and Felicity could feel the group heave a collective sigh of relief. Then Pulido turned to her.

"And you?"

"Sir, I follow my partner in this area. If he says we're all good, then we're all good."

"Excellent," Pulido said, breaking into a broad smile. "Then will you stay for a steak? This is excellent, locally raised beef."

-43-

Forty-eight hours after dinner with Mark Roberts, a knock on Morgan's hotel room door roused him. His response was slow and gradual. He lay on his bed, face up, only half aware. Felicity sat on the floor beside the bed, in a full lotus position. She was in a deep trance. Morgan stirred slowly and answered the door. Roberts stepped in, glanced at Felicity, and gave Morgan a questioning look.

"We're preparing for tonight's fun. We take off in about seven hours, you know."

"Yeah, well I've got some bad news," Roberts said. "I'm afraid the mission's a scrub."

"What? Why?" Felicity looked up, uncrossing her legs. She wore a leotard, and was unconsciously demonstrating why the other garment was called tights.

"Well, a couple of wrinkles," Roberts said. "First, the latest weather report indicates a pretty healthy increase in the cross winds by one o'clock."

"So, we move the timetable up a bit," Felicity told him, stretching her arms over her head to restore full circulation.

"And then there's the equipment snafu,"

"Okay, Mark, what couldn't you get?" Morgan asked. He was already adjusting their plan to work with no darts, inferior helmets or even lacking the requested explosives. In such a case, he could mix up a substitute himself.

"Wrist altimeters," Roberts said. "Not just the kind you wanted, we couldn't get any at all. Just a bizarre coincidence. With the amount of diving they do on the coast, the whole country seems to be bought out."

"Damn," Felicity said. "If you'd told us sooner, I'd just gone out and stolen one. This won't wait until morning, Mark. Poor Frederico'll be cooling in his grave by sunup."

After a silent moment in which Felicity paced across the room five times, Morgan said "That's it, Red. I can't judge that distance. Not in the dark. We can't do it blind."

"Sure we can." Felicity stared into Morgan's face with that Irish look that dared anyone to gainsay her. "I can. It's just time, after all. Once we're free of the plane we fall at a constant rate right? What do they call it?"

"Terminal velocity, and why do you think they call it that? No. Sorry, Red. Too many variables. We just can't. Out of the question."

"Bull. We can, and we will. Or fly it by meself, I will." Green eyes flashed their personal fire and Morgan had to know she meant it. When he finally released a long held breath, she knew she had won.

Felicity's first touch of doubt came while the Regent taxied down the runway. As it lifted off into the blackness, she considered the possible damage to her partner, or herself, if she was wrong.

"Final mike check," Morgan whispered.

"Loud and clear, partner," Felicity answered. Throat mikes gave their voices a deeper, more guttural tone, but they could still understand each other.

They had all they could ask for, a cloudy, moonless night with moderate winds, and an excellent pilot who knew the area. Tuned in to the steady thrum of the twin engines up ahead, Felicity did a mental inventory.

They crouched in the plane's rear compartment dressed entirely in black: jumpsuits over warm jeans and sweaters, soft boots, helmets, gloves. Even their sport parachutes were black, inside and out. Felicity wore a black carpenter's belt filled with burglary tools and several drug darts for her silent pneumatic dart gun. Morgan also had one, plus a crossbow and bolts for longer distance shots. He carried his two boot knives, plus his pistol and fighting knife. In squeeze pockets on his jumpsuit he stored a half pound of C4 high explosive wrapped in paper and several varied pencil-sized time fuses.

They were as prepared as possible, assuming they reached the ground intact. Morgan had a pretty good idea from experience how long they would fall. Because he said "about", Roberts had given the problem to a professional mathematician on the CIA payroll. He had confirmed Morgan's estimate.

At the pilot's signal they would slide out the door, nearly twenty-five thousand feet above a tiny, one and a half acre landing zone. Four and a half seconds later and three hundred twenty five feet lower, their downward velocity would go from zero to one hundred forty-six feet per second. "Round about a hundred miles an hour straight down," as Morgan would say.

Two minutes and thirty-eight seconds later they would be five hundred feet from the earth. Low enough to minimize their hang time and make it very unlikely even an alert guard would see them. Also minimizing the amount of time the growing wind could blow their parachutes off course. Two minutes and thirty-eight seconds.

Two minutes and thirty-nine seconds after jumping, they would be a hundred and forty-six feet lower, too low for their canopies to fully develop before the soft, fertile black earth of the Andes Mountains rushed up and crushed their bones into powder.

When she looked down, Felicity saw her hand tracing the scar on her breast under her jumpsuit. Morgan saw it too. She had never doubted herself before. But in all her life, no one had ever managed to hurt her. That was Morgan's advantage. He had been hurt before and always come up a winner.

"Sure wish you could do this," Felicity whispered. Her voice seemed throaty, but it could have been the microphone.

"And you know I can't," Morgan answered. "I can judge distances perfectly, but not in this situation. Tall trees would throw me off by dozens of feet, even if I could see the ground. If we pop too soon we'll end up in the trees, and probably be spotted by the bad guys. If you're not sure, Red, we can still just turn around and nobody will call you chicken. If you are sure, I'm right next to you." He kept facing straight ahead.

"No," Felicity said, biting her lip. "We go or he dies. I made a commitment. Besides, that bitch can't win." That bitch can't hurt me again, she did not say. "Morgan, one other thing. Taking the boy a second time is going to hurt her."

"Yeah."

"Remember what you said?" she asked. "Never do your enemy a minor injury."

"Yeah?"

"I think if we're in there, you should finish it," Felicity said.

"Red, are you asking me to kill her?" He paused, letting it sink in. "I don't know. You've never killed and I don't want to be your gun."

"Don't be silly," Felicity said. "Of course I've killed. Since I've known you."

"Accidents," he responded. "Or indirectly helping me kill to save my life. This is different. This is cold blood. Can you handle that? Inside?"

"I know you're trying to protect me but I got past it before," Felicity said, her voice strengthening. "Remember

Monk? O'Ryan? And there was Herrera just a few months ago."

"All of whom were actively involved in trying to kill me," Morgan reminded her.

"I got past it each time because I saw that they weren't people at that moment. They were animals, wild animals, rabid creatures that you dispose of before they can do any more damage. Well, Anaconda, cold, calculating, hands-off Anaconda is an animal too. A vicious deadly animal that needs to die."

"Coming up on drop time," Isaacs said from up front. The new voice coming into their ears startled them, until they remembered he had no earphone, just a microphone.

"Red, think about it some more," Morgan said, standing. "It's impractical right now. We'll be pushing our luck as it is. Dwell time in the house needs to be minimum and we'll be running a search pattern if Jorge was wrong about what room Frederico's in. We get the boy and get. That's final. When we come back if you want to be in on Anaconda's finish, well, we'll talk about it some more."

"Pop the door," Isaacs said, and Morgan did. "I'll take one circle at exactly twenty-four thousand feet. I'll give you a countdown and on go, hit it. And good luck."

Morgan stood in the doorway, his left hand on the plane's wall, his right gripping Felicity's arm. She held the plane's wall on the other side. A sharp wind slashed across them, curling under their helmets. Small rebreather devices allowed them to take deep, slow, comfortable breaths. The helmets and breathing masks combined to cover their entire faces. They could not even see each other's eyes. Felicity slid her hand up onto Morgan's back. Somehow, she knew he was smiling. It was two minutes to midnight.

The plane leveled off. A voice in Felicity's ear said, "Five, four, three, two, one, go!" Two bodies launched themselves into the void. They separated, and there was the weightless feeling of free fall. Felicity spread her arms and legs, ticking off seconds in her mind.

Ten seconds. The wind was coming up sooner than expected. Subjectively, in the dark, she felt as if she was holding still. What if the wind became a downdraft, reducing the air's resistance? They would fall faster. A steel ball, not subject to air resistance, would reach nine hundred feet per second before it hit the ground. How much could the wind speed their bodies up?

Twenty seconds. Where was Morgan in the darkness? Was he in position? Above her? Below her? Either way could spell disaster.

Morgan's hand was pulling on his rip cord exactly as Felicity's voice said "Now!" in his ear. From her, he had felt the time was right but it was comforting to hear her say it as well. He felt the pack open and his pilot chute leap out - heard the deployment sleeve yank the rectangular sport canopy out into full deployment - felt a jarring shock as the nylon raft above him grabbed air and his speed suddenly dropped to a little over ten feet per second.

Morgan's hands slid up the risers to grasp his steering lines. He was farther south than he wanted and pulled the lines to slip some air, drifting himself north again. He wondered if Felicity was similarly off course. He had no way to tell her which direction to drift herself. He could not know which way she was facing, and a compass direction would not help her with no landmarks visible.

Then, thirty seconds after he pulled his rip cord, Morgan's feet folded under him and he rolled comfortably across the tall grass. As he came up on one knee he pulled his canopy release and the black parachute drifted away like some land-bound jelly fish. He had a tranquilizer gun in his hand within five seconds of hitting the ground.

"Felicity," he called, standing. "You okay?"

"I'm not hurt," her voice came back. "I'm also not on the ground."

Morgan did a slow half turn and centered on his partner's location. He began an easy jog across the grass and forty yards later reached the base of a tall cigar box cedar.

"I can free myself from the chute," Felicity said, "but I've got nothing to grab onto."

"You're only about thirty feet up," Morgan said into the darkness. "Go ahead and pull your harness release. I've got you."

Three seconds later Morgan heard a subtle click, and Felicity's weight slammed into his waiting arms from three stories up, slapping him back onto the ground.

Felicity just had time to say, "Thanks," before her head snapped up. Morgan sensed it too. Something was coming their way, something unfriendly. He pointed his dart pistol toward the danger signal's source. The world showed bright green in the night scope mounted on the gun's top rib.

Into his sights loped a peculiar animal. A green glowing fox-like beast on stilts, easily clearing the tall grass which would slow down and hang up a shorter animal. Morgan saw long wavy hair ranging down its back. Before the maned wolf could pinpoint the human intruders, Morgan's air gun made a coughing sound and, forty feet away, a dart stabbed into the wolf's neck. It stopped, looked around, and decided to lie down.

"He knew we were here, but that neutral scent soap of yours seems to keep them from pinpointing us," Felicity said.

"Told you," Morgan replied, pulling off his helmet. "If it lets you get closer to deer, it'll work against anything on feet."

After a minute to think and orient himself, Morgan pointed them toward the house. Without helmets, breathing gear or their parachute seat packs, they moved smoothly and silently, slipping through tall grass like two stalking leopards. They found it relaxing and almost fun, knowing they were undetected, in fact unexpected, due mostly to Anaconda's incredible confidence in her fearsome reputation and her political protection. While no nation would risk an international incident, no local person would dare risk the Escorpionistas' wrath.

During their slow trek to Anaconda's house they put seven maned wolves to sleep. Felicity had prepared the drugs and assured Morgan the animals would awake, healthy and strong, in five or six hours.

One hundred yards from the house they made their first infrared contact with human guards. One patrolled in front of the helicopter with an Uzi submachine gun. Three others walked a perimeter around the house, under lights directed so they bathed the house, but left darkness fifteen feet from it. It was token security. They counted on the wolves to raise an alarm if intruders approached. With the radios on their belts they could summon help from the barracks in seconds.

Morgan and Felicity crept in to within sixty yards of the helicopter. Felicity lay prone in front of Morgan, who stretched out, forming a "T" with her body. He placed the small crossbow on her back, cranked the string back and nocked a quarrel. His left forearm rested in the small of her back as he focused on the bow's four power night scope. Now they waited.

Twenty minutes later, the copter guard picked up his radio. Morgan whispered "Reporting in."

"About time," she answered. "The grass is tickling me something fierce." She did not mention the chill from the ground creeping up into her body because she knew Morgan felt it too. The night sounds also annoyed her. She had learned few things were universal in the world, but one of them seemed to be crickets. With her head on the ground, the noise was nerve wracking and chilling.

Sixty yards away, the guard put his radio away. Framed in a green luminous circle, he never even knew about the cross hairs leaning across him until a crossbow bolt punched him in the neck and his life blew out the hole and he crumpled like a deflated balloon.

He does it so easily, Felicity thought. To him, this is a war.

Crouching, the two intruders jogged to the helicopter. Morgan dropped to one knee. When a second guard rounded the corner of the house, he fired another bolt. Another corpse hit the ground. A thirty yard sprint brought Morgan to the house, setting himself prone behind the dead man. Guard number three stepped around into his sights. A second later he dropped from sight with a quarrel in his throat. Number four, shining a flashlight ahead of himself, spotted a dead friend and had reached for his radio when Morgan's next bolt made a crease between his eyes.

As quickly as possible, Morgan returned to the copter, climbed in and checked out its controls. It was a Eurocopter Ecureuil, a light six-seater he had flown a dozen times before. The fuel gauge read full and he saw no signs of unusual modifications. He could take off and fly this thing in his sleep. Something was going his way.

With men down, time was ticking away, so they headed for the house. The back of the house faced east. There, a long glass wall separated them from a large sitting room. A sliding glass door anchored one end of the glass. Felicity drew a small electronic device from her belt and clipped it magnetically to the metal tape running up the door near its edge. That would continue the current through the alarm, keeping the circuit from being broken. She spent three minutes picking the lock. The door slid open easily on whisper quiet tracks. Like that, they were in.

A fireplace covered the room's left wall, with two huge sofas facing each other in its center. Felicity entered first, moving across the large cold tiles, probing for a trap. She found nothing. With Morgan behind her, she went down the short hall, stopping at the first door on her left. This door had no alarm. Its simple slam lock yielded to her talents in seconds. The door opened without a sound on well maintained hinges. They found Frederico inside, and he had company.

If the room was divided in half diagonally, one side could be the mirror image of the other. A wooden chest of drawers stood against the wall to their left, followed by a twin bed. The wall ahead of them held identical furniture, placed so that the beds were head to head. them. Frederico lay face up and snoring on one of the beds, but it almost looked like he was on both.

Felicity hesitated at first, greeted by this double vision. Of course, only one face in the night scope belonged to Frederico. The boy snoring in the other bed had to be his brother. Morgan stepped forward quickly and jabbed an anesthetic dart into his shoulder. The boy started up, but Morgan slapped a hand down over his mouth, holding him in place until the drug took effect. Felicity went to the other side of the small room.

"Wake up," Felicity whispered, kneeling beside Frederico's bed. "It's Felicity. We're here to get you out of here." No response. She shook him gently. Then she gave him a rougher shake. Then she pinched his earlobe hard. Nothing. A peek under an eyelid with a penlight on his pupil told the story.

"He's drugged too," she said. Morgan stepped forward.

"So this is where the wrinkle comes in," he said. "He can't walk on his own. Damn. You know, if we're spotted, it's over." Felicity nodded. Morgan handed her his dart gun, bent and lifted Frederico onto his shoulder. The boy wore only the familiar shorts. Morgan pointed Felicity ahead of him and followed her out of the room. Preparing for his mission's final goal, Morgan pulled the paper wrapped lump of C4 high explosive out of one squeeze pocket, the fuses from another.

Still they heard no sound, sensed no danger in the vast house. Navigating the darkness with extreme care, they slowly made their way to the sitting room. Morgan eased around the couches.

That's when Frederico jerked, as if a seizure was starting. His weight shifted radically and Morgan, caught off guard, lost his balance. He pitched forward under the weight of a full grown six foot tall man they had called a boy since they met him. Morgan's knees cracked painfully on the hard tile floor. Thrust out full length on top of him, Frederico's heels hit the open sliding door. The impact was not enough to break the glass, but it started the barest crack.

"Shit!" Morgan's oath was loud in Felicity's earphone, almost simultaneous with the clanging alarm. Before Morgan could stand, lights started coming on in the house. He managed to get Frederico onto his shoulder again, and ran out the door with Felicity close behind. Three steps from the house powerful flashlights supplemented the outside lights.

A harsh voice shouted "Halto." Morgan transferred the fuses to his left hand with the C4, drew his pistol, spun, and dropped one of the light carriers. A burst of automatic weapons fire answered his challenge. He gritted his teeth and ran, as well as he could with his burden, toward the helicopter.

Felicity fired both dart guns blindly behind her. She heard yelps of pain when she connected and wondered how many men pursued them. She moved on an evasive course, hearing bullets hitting the ground around her. She always knew when one was targeted on her and so far had managed to jog left or right to avoid them. Long black shadows stretched before them over the long grass through which they frantically fled.

Morgan charged into those shadows as quickly as he could. Ear-splitting as it was, he knew the volume of fire came from only four guns. Felicity must have dropped several with tranquilizer darts. He was within reach of the copter. He figured he had a fifty-fifty shot at getting it airborne before some idiot put a bullet in the right place and brought it down. Good enough odds to run with.

Morgan planned to throw the boy ahead of himself into the cockpit and count on Felicity to get in on the other side while he fired up the engine. Anaconda's men fired from the house, but seemed reluctant to give chase. It was a bit of luck Morgan hadn't counted on. Unprepared for such a daring invasion, the guards could not know how many armed intruders might await them in the dark. By the time they decided to pursue, Morgan and Felicity could be lifting off. Three steps from the helicopter it was looking like a fair shot.

Morgan felt it coming, but with Frederico on his shoulder he could not move fast enough to avoid it. Like a cigar's glowing tip, a nine millimeter bullet dug into the back of Morgan's left calf. He fell forward, sliding on his knees, dropping Frederico to the left. When he pitched forward, Morgan's forearms slammed over the helicopter's left runner stunning his hands open and empty. Explosives could not help him now anyway, but he searched frantically in the grass for his pistol. When he had it he rolled over, prepared to exact an awful price for his life.

But he froze, not squeezing his trigger for lack of a target. All incoming fire had stopped, cut off as if a switch had been thrown. On his back on the grass, Morgan found the silence more frightening than the gunfire had been. His world was a wall of light lancing into his face, except for one black vertical band in its center. As his eyes slowly adjusted, the black blot resolved itself into Felicity's form. She stood in front of the sliding glass door, facing him, with a CAR-15's muzzle pointed at her head. The pain on her face overmatched what he felt in his leg. He let out a long breath, stood straight and slowly holstered his gun.

"Oh well, it was a hell of a shot," he said into the light.

From behind the lights, Anaconda's voice said "I hope I can make your death as exciting."

-44-

Morgan and Felicity had both been strip searched before. Morgan knew it was part of the price you paid for getting caught. Far worse for him was lying on the floor with a gun at his temple watching it happen to Felicity. She wore an expression he would expect if she had to search through raw sewage to find a dead fish. When the searchers were satisfied, they dragged Felicity out. Morgan stood helpless with two guns trained on him. He heard the sound of running water but no screams.

When Felicity was brought back, she was once again a green eyed redhead. After pushing the girl in through the doorway, both gunmen backed to the door, and Anaconda stepped into the sitting room. Morgan expected a round of gloating, which he knew was another part of the price of being captured.

"How could you be so stupid as to think you could come right into my home and take what is mine?" Anaconda stood with her fists on her hips, barely waist high to the three gunmen behind her. Her tightly belted purple silk robe highlighted the curves of her diminutive form. Frederico was stretched out on a sofa, still in the shorts, still unmoving. Morgan and Felicity stood side by side, naked.

"Oh, I don't know," Morgan answered. "Seems to me we did pretty good. Your security's kind of sloppy, lady. Maybe you should hire us."

"You may joke about it, but your bravado does not

239

change the facts. You are my prisoner, are you not?"

"You got lucky," Felicity said, her right hand on her left shoulder, her left over her crotch. "I tripped. That clown couldn't have run me down if I wasn't blinded by those damned lights in me face."

"All talk," Anaconda said, waving her men to push Morgan and Felicity onto one of the sofas. Morgan gritted his teeth when his leg hit the leather. Anaconda padded across the room toward them on tiny bare feet. Stopping just out of reach, she signaled to one man, who knelt to examine the wound.

"The bullet isn't here," the gunman said. "It creased across the muscle, here, and went on. A lot of blood, but no real injury."

"Bind it," Anaconda commanded. "I want him healthy at dawn when I kill them. I want him to die knowing I bested him."

"You're kidding, right?" Morgan said, flashing his most annoying smile. "You may be a big fish in this little pond, I'll give you that, but normally I step over people your size to get into fights."

"You do not understand, do you?" Anaconda asked, crossing her arms. For just a moment, Morgan saw more than a small time drug dealer. "Your Al Capone was a big fish in the pond of Chicago until he became the name identified with a generation of criminals."

"Wait a minute," Felicity said. "What are you saying? Aspire to greatness, do you?" Was the late hour making Anaconda talk? She was confident of their helplessness. Would she reveal a weakness?

"There have been women in crime since it was invented," Anaconda said. Here gaze when to the ceiling as she paced slowly. One might say that women, physically weaker, had to invent crime. But since Eve, no woman has ever been given credit for her own brilliance. Men would not follow women, even the most daring, because they did not think them strong enough to hold power. I have broken that pattern. I am as ruthless, as deadly as any man. A fortunate set of coincidences, my height, my eyes, this culture, has positioned me to be the first great woman of crime."

"Oh I don't know," Felicity said. "Anne Bonny and Lady Killigrew made names for themselves as pirates. And I made a pretty good living at it myself before I gave it up."
"You, Miss O'Brien, I respect. You succeeded in a man's world, but your thefts only earned you money and a reputation for ingenuity. You never gained any power. But I. I will build a financial empire on the backs of America's drug hungry citizens. Unlike cocaine or heroin or LSD, the ice is amazingly addictive but rarely is its use fatal. I can maintain my clients without using them up. Like the bootleggers of America in the 1920's, I can gather power filling the need I create for this drug. And because it is synthetic, it is a resource which cannot run out."

"A nice theory," Felicity said, "But you must know there's a limit to how many Americans will be stupid enough to use this hateful drug of yours. The market's not as big as Capone's market for liquor was."

Anaconda nodded, and held up a hand. One of her men filled it with a drink. "Of course I know this. Like your rap stars who call themselves gangsters, I am diversifying. Your Jay-Z used drug money only as seed money, and he did not build his half-billion dollar fortune writing rhymes. He invested wisely and ruthlessly. I will follow that pattern. And when I have enough money, enough influence, I will commandeer the political power in this country."

"Wait a minute," Morgan said, ignoring the man bandaging his leg. "Colombia's the longest running democracy in South America. Damned near the only country in this part of the world I never found work in as a mercenary. You'll never get into power here."

"Fool." Anaconda brushed her hair back, letting it sway across her buttocks. "I will soon have the largest payroll in the country. As the Yakuza support Japan's power structure, the Escorpionistas will support mine. Power by intimidation is always possible in a democracy. I'll even get your government's support once I'm in place. Any fascist state is preferable to communism in the eyes of your small minded leaders. Soon, I will be the greatest female criminal on earth, and unstoppable, because I will make the law."

"You truly are an ice woman," Felicity said quietly. "Not just the drugs, I mean. Your heart."

"It is the only way a woman or a person my size can succeed in this world of machismo giants."

"You're wrong," Felicity said, standing. She dropped her arms, gaining the immediate attention of every man in the room. "Wrong, because you have no respect for the people you command. Even these superstitious and bloodthirsty killers won't follow you for long. Being around Morgan has taught me that even the worst terrorist has some kind of ideology or purpose. Gang members in the streets of L.A. have a warped sense of loyalty and pride. Yes, even the Chicago gangsters you talked about had some sort of code of honor. That's why we had to come down here after Frederico. A matter of honor, it was. Honor. You're completely without it. Not worth respecting, or following, or fearing. You're nothing. I didn't see it before but now I do. You know, you scarred me." Felicity pointed out the line on her left breast. "But it's healed now."

Anaconda stepped forward and looked up, cocking her hand back to slap the other girl. To Morgan's surprise, Felicity stood her ground, her hands balling into fists.

"Come on then, girl," Felicity said, in the strongest Irish Brogue accent Morgan had ever heard from her. "Do your worst. Give me a fair shot at you, and I'll kick your little

Spanish arse."

Silver eyes flashed hatred, and were met by pale fire from the deep green orbs staring down into them. Anaconda hesitated, and then stepped back. "Bind them well," she said at last. "We'll shred them in the trees with the boy in a couple of hours. Two guards at all times. Don't get close enough to touch them, they're too tricky. At dawn, we shall enjoy the last laugh."

-45-

Felicity's voice, small and pale, crawled out of the shadows. "I'm sorry," she said. She sat on the sofa, shivering. She and Morgan had been allowed to put their nylon shell jumpsuits back on, but with nothing underneath them. Wire held her hands together in her lap, and her ankles were bound the same way. Morgan, in the same condition, leaned against the sofa's other arm. Between them, Frederico tossed in restless sleep.

Two men stood at the other end of the room. They had stood there since Anaconda left. At any time, one of them was always facing the captives. A table lamp kept them well lit, but was positioned to leave Morgan and Felicity in partial darkness.

The guards wore semiautomatic pistols, and held Uzi submachine guns. One of them looked like any Mexican you might see in Southern California. The other had straight hair hanging over his forehead and a scar just outside his right eye. An hour ago, Morgan called to one of them in a voice so friendly, Felicity had shivered.

"Yo, mirar. Habla Ingles?" Morgan's call got a simple shake of the head. No.

"You're Quesada, aren't you?" Morgan asked, switching to English.

"Why?"

"I've heard about you," Morgan continued. "I hear you're one of the best. Too good for this crowd."

"So?"

"So, look, you can do better up north," Morgan said, trying to make eye contact with the killer. "It's worth a million pesos to turn us loose and get us out of here on that helicopter outside. Think about it. A million pesos."

"Not much more than ten thousand American dollars," Quesada observed, waving his Uzi in Morgan's direction.

"I can give you that in Bogota, and double it in Los Angeles," Morgan said. He paused for a moment, then added "She doesn't deserve your loyalty."

"I am an Escorpionista," Quesada said, in a low, grating voice. "Since I was a boy, I would die for the Escorpionistas. Through them, I am much man. Even if I was not loyal, it is death to betray Anaconda."

That closed the conversation. Morgan turned to Felicity, unable to really see her face.

"Got anything useful, like a weapon?"

"Afraid I wasn't able to hide anything in this outfit," said Felicity, putting on her brave voice.

"Can you get loose?"

"Sure, but to what end?" Felicity answered. "There's no getting you free. And there's no getting out of the room. Even if I could get out, or get to a weapon, you'd die instantly." She paused, and Morgan heard her voice soften. "Maybe I can get invited out."

"Quesada," Felicity called in Spanish. "Could you come over here, please?"

"No closer. You are too tricky. I can hear, and see you, fine from here."

"Well, you can't see enough," she said, seduction oozing from her voice. "Look, you did a pretty thorough strip search, so I've got nothing left to hide from you. But I don't want to die like this. Just a room away, we could have...some fun, one last time before I die."

"You think me fool enough to untie you, just for sex?"

"You...you wouldn't have to," Felicity said. Her face

showed this was harder than she expected. Mostly, her embarrassment probably stemmed from Morgan's presence. But she continued. "A creative man like you can see a way. I could, well, I can be on my knees and elbows, still tied. A lot of men like to do it that way. And in my experience, many men like their women tied."

"Getting that close to a captive, physically or emotionally, is the mark of an amateur," Quesada said. "I am not an amateur."

That closed that conversation. Their other guard, under Quesada's eye, was unapproachable. Morgan wished Felicity would bolt, even if he died for it, but where could she go? Flight in the jungle, at night, barefoot, in just a thin nylon shell, would be painful at best, dangerous at worst.

Morgan was deep in thought, exploring the situation, looking for an undiscovered winning option when Felicity's voice sneaked up on him in the darkness. "I'm sorry," was an unexpected remark.

"Yeah, me too," he said. "But we gave it one hell of a good run, didn't we?"

"No," Felicity said. "I mean for this whole mess. We'd never gotten into this if I hadn't insisted we go undercover against an unknown enemy. It's all..."

"If I hear the phrase `it's all my fault', I swear..."

"But it is," Felicity said. "Not just the start. You had better sense than to pick up the kid here and carry him with us. That's what really pissed Anaconda off. If I hadn't made you take us to Texas the girl wouldn't have died. Chuck, dear sweet Chuck wouldn't have died, and we wouldn't be about to die." Morgan did not think he had ever heard an actual sob, but he was sure he heard one now.

"I'm glad you're willing to take all the blame, Red, but you're wrong," Morgan said, sitting back in the deep cushions. He was not sure if both their guards understood English, and right then he did not care.

"First of all, we're partners," he continued, forcing calm into his voice. "We decided to take the job, for money, and to help a friend. Nothing wrong with that. Besides, if you recall, Anaconda fired the first shot in this war with that scorpion gag in your car. No way I'd have ducked out after that. And something else you maybe didn't understand. I didn't want to take Fred here under our wing, but I would have anyway. It was the only honorable option."

Morgan paused and wet his lips, because the next bit made him uncomfortable. "Now, remember, when those two killers tried to hit us in our hotel rooms, Mary called and warned me. She was the only person who saw them. If they'd got us, they'd have killed her anyway. Standard operating procedure. We didn't cause her death, we just adjusted the place." He heard her breathing slowing, and knew he was getting through.

"And, for the last time, you didn't kill Chuck Barton," Morgan said. "He got sloppy, lost his edge and committed suicide by throwing knife. Yeah, I might not be here now if you hadn't pushed me, but I wouldn't like me as much. And while we're on the subject, we ain't dead yet!"

Morgan stopped for breath.

"Red, when you said what you did to Anaconda, when you stood up to her like that, I was cheering for you. You gained a lot of face in the eyes of her followers, and what you gained, she lost." He chuckled here, drawing stares from their guards. "For a minute there, I thought you really were going to kick her ass. I've never been prouder of anyone I've been to war with, and if it comes to that, I'll be proud to die with you, Felicity O'Brien."

"I'd hug you if I could, Morgan Stark," Felicity said. "And you're right about one thing. We're not dead yet."

-46-

Anaconda entered the sitting room with the sun's first rays, accompanied by two men. One was a gunman, the other, Frederico's brother, Anthony. Two guards roughly yanked Morgan and Felicity to their feet. Frederico's eyes fluttered open, but he looked around in horror and kept silent.

While Quesada held his gun on the captives, his partner tied a heavy hemp rope around Morgan's waist, then around Frederico's and Felicity's. They all faced the same way, with Felicity behind Morgan and Frederico behind her. About two inches of slack rope separated them from each other. A guard used wire cutters to free their ankles and pointed them to the sliding glass door. It was dawn in Colombia and the somber mood felt appropriate. They were, after all, going to an execution.

After a slight false start the prisoners fell into step, marching at gunpoint across tall, damp grass. Climbing into a very clear sky, the morning sun warmed them despite a gentle breeze. Morgan heard parrots and, he thought, toucans discussing their day's plans. When Felicity stumbled, he could not help but catch the impression of her nipples, stiffened by morning's coolness, pressed into his back.

Their short walk ended beside Anaconda's helicopter. Morgan could see those controls he had expected to be sitting at by now. Quesada dropped a much longer length of rope at his feet, picking up the end. Before any further action could take place, a howl got everyone's attention. A lone maned wolf staggered forward, wobbling like a newborn colt on its stilt like legs.

"What is this?" Quesada asked. "It looks like the wolf's been drinking."

"The drug in the darts must just now be wearing off," Felicity said. "They'll be groggy for a few minutes after they wake up."

Laughing, Quesada stepped forward, swinging a booted foot into the wolf's side. The animal fell over, rolled, and scampered away. Then Quesada turned to his prisoners, wrapping the rope around all three of them. He stepped in close to make a knot in the middle of Morgan's chest. He cinched it tight, grinning into Morgan's face.

"You did run Mary off the road, didn't you?" Morgan asked. "Remember? The Mexican girl?" Quesada looked at Morgan, twice bound with his wrists wired together.

"The Mexican girl?" Quesada rubbed at the scar next to his eye. "You mean on the highway in New Mexico. Si, I was driving. That cheap car, it rolled easy. So?"

"It's just nice to be sure," Morgan replied. Quesada stepped back, and never saw the naked foot snap upward into his crotch. The crunching sound was nearly as loud as Quesada's strangled cry. The killer dropped to his knees, his face to the ground.

Morgan's attack, born of frustration and rage, tipped the tethered group off balance. Morgan fell backward onto Felicity and Frederico, who landed face down on a helicopter runner. Morgan knew his rash attack had probably hurt his allies as much as the enemy. He heard the click of hammers being pulled back and Anaconda shouting "No!" to stop bullets from flying.

"Stand them up," Anaconda shouted. Rough hands grasped their arms, hauling them forward. Felicity's head smacked the helicopter's frame on her way up.

"That was your final act of defiance," Anaconda said, red faced. Then, to one of the gunmen, "Get Quesada into the copter. You! Get the rope around the tail. Now!"

A chill rolled down Morgan's spine as he realized what came next. He looked at the knot on his chest, the wire around his wrists, the helicopter, looking for a way out of what seemed a trap too simple to break. Anaconda walked to within a foot of him, then stepped back until she was out of reach.

"Touch me and they will shoot to wound," she said. "I will decide how you die. I will lift you into the sky, so that all my men can see how helpless you are. Then, we will cruise by, over there." She pointed a thumb behind herself. "See those tall tree ferns. We will fly over them, very fast. You three will hit the trees. Hard! Again and again, until there is nothing left of you but bloody skeletons. What, no final words of resistance, Miss O'Brien?"

Felicity stood behind Morgan with her head down, her hair obscuring her face, as if she was hiding behind her partner.

"And you, Mister Stark?"

Morgan responded to her question, staring at his captor. His gaze seemed to glance off those silver orbs but he held her eyes anyway.

"If this is it, bitch, I'll be waiting for you in hell," he said.

Anaconda looked around. This was a perceptive woman, and Morgan, following her gaze, could guess what was happening in her mind. She was noting the subtle shifts in body language and less aggressive facial expressions. She would note how gun barrels swayed away from their intended targets. For a moment she seemed uneasy, aware of her men regarding Morgan with respect. Too much respect. Morgan started a small smile. Then Frederico, ignored until now, faced his brother who stood just behind

Anaconda. His eyes were sad.

"You will die with her, you know," he said. Frederico's pronouncement made all her men nervous. The situation would become critical if they stayed on the ground any longer. Anaconda quickly boarded her helicopter, along with Quesada and her pilot. Anthony climbed in last, just as Anaconda ordered the pilot to lift off.

While the big rotor slowly started turning, Morgan was cataloging the situation. The rope, now tied to the helicopter's tail, had a good forty feet of slack. If he managed to somehow free himself quickly, he would get a bullet in the head. If it took him more than a minute, he'd face a long fall to an unpleasant death. He had run out of good options at last. Feeling the biting wind the rotor sent down, Morgan tried to twist his head around.

"Time for an idea," he said to Felicity.

"Do not worry," Frederico said. For the first time, Morgan became aware of him, and the confident look on his face. "You are the puma, and she, the hawk. Together you will pull the flying serpent from the sky."

Morgan's response was jerked out of him when the rope suddenly snapped taut and dragged them into the air. At first it was a dizzying ride. They were swaying under the rising helicopter, spinning as the twined rope uncoiled. The cold cut into Morgan right through the thin jumpsuit, and two ropes bit into his skin. The earth twisted below in all directions. The continuous helicopter sound from above quickly became the meaningless drone of white noise.

Soon the twisting stopped and they were hanging straight, a few hundred feet in the air. Morgan pulled his stomach in, trying to turn. If he could face Felicity, his body and Frederico's would protect her, hopefully until the rope frayed and broke from impact with the trees. He was half turned when he saw tears flowing freely from Felicity's eyes.

"God damn it!" Felicity swore, startling Morgan as much as Frederico. She looked up at Morgan through tortured eyes he did not understand. "I was going to do it, but I can't figure out how the damn thing works."

"What?" Morgan never finished his question because Felicity held her hands up as far as she could. Her left held the small paper package that held C4, and her right had a single pencil fuse.

"When we fell, I was over the helicopter runner and I felt this stuff in the tall grass. I grabbed them, but only got one of the fuse things. Sure and I would have set it off too, so you'd never know what happened. No time for fear. But I can't figure out how to get the fuse to go off."

A rush of thoughts, facts, and ideas flashed through Morgan's mind, first and foremost being "Thank God."

"Red, you're brave as hell, but it wouldn't have worked. The blast wouldn't have reached the copter. But maybe, maybe I can. Shit, the boy could turn out to be right." *If I really can climb like a puma,* he thought.

"Can you get this damn wire off my wrists?" Morgan asked. Felicity bent her neck, Morgan raised his hands, and the girl applied her teeth to twisting wire. It seemed agonizingly slow under the circumstances, but in fact she freed Morgan's hands within two minutes. Then she worked at the inner rope, separating him from herself and Frederico.

"Look out!" Frederico called out and Felicity's eyes grew wide. Morgan half turned and saw the top of a huge fern rushing at him. He had almost forgotten they were moving. He hugged Felicity, gritting his teeth.

The sharp edges of fronds and branches heightened the jarring impact. Morgan felt his back getting warm and wet, and knew why. The crash had shredded the nylon shell away, leaving his back covered with only blood. The helicopter turned. Positioning for another pass, Morgan assumed. He placed the pencil fuse in his mouth like a cigar, and clutched the plastique under his chin.

"You two hold tight to the outer rope, and we'll see if we can go out with a bang." With a forced smile toward Felicity he squirmed free and started climbing.

In difficult situations, you thank the Lord for any help that appears. Morgan appreciated the thick, rough hemp rope because he could easily grip it and climb. He moved upward slowly, trying to ignore the raw wounds on his back, the grating on his hands, the rough cord scraping across his crotch with each move upward.

Twenty feet up the rope, Morgan felt a directional shift. They were making another run for the ferns. He looked down at Felicity who nodded her head stoically and began to swing. Despite their forward momentum, she managed to get a good swing going, side to side. Morgan, halfway up the rope, pulled in rhythm with her. Their swing became pronounced as they approached the next tree. As they came even with it, Felicity and Frederico reached the end of a lateral swing. Long fronds lashed Felicity's limbs but that had to be much better than hitting the springy trunk.

Morgan kept moving up the rope, but his progress was slowing. Damage done during their private war with Anaconda was taking its toll. A lancing pain in his right forearm from a knife wound was being echoed by his left calf, thanks to a bullet hole. Pain sapped the strength in those muscles, making a difficult climb impossible. The downdraft from the rotor shoved against him, forcing him to close his eyes. The noise was ear-splitting. Vibrations travelling down from the copter tail made his grip less dependable each second.

Just two meters from the helicopter's body Morgan realized he could not push himself any higher. His grip was failing and he had no desire to become part of the beautiful rain forest landscape he now flew over. Instead, he wrapped his right arm in the rope, looping it three times. He held the explosive plastic in his left hand.

The fuses were so simple, it was no wonder Felicity had not figured out how they worked. You had to look at one to see how the mechanism did its explosive job. Inside each detonator was a thin metal band, like you find in electrical fuses. Squeezing the pencil rod ruptured a squib of powerful acid. Fuse delay time depended on how long it took the acid to eat through the metal band. When the band snapped, it would release the plunger which, he hoped, would trigger the explosion. Felicity had only grabbed one, a fairly short one, but it would have to do.

One handed, Morgan pulled the paper wrapping from the plastic lump and squeezed off half. He bit down on the detonator, releasing the acid and beginning the countdown. It was a one minute fuse. He swung the small wad of putty up toward his mouth, jamming it onto the detonator. Then he swung his arm back and tossed his explosive ball straight up into the powerful wind.

Fire shot through Morgan's upper arm where a knife had so recently been, but the lump of plastique hit and stuck to the helicopter's belly. Sucking in a deep breath, Morgan slid back down the rope, a bit more quickly than he wanted.

"And?" Felicity asked when Morgan reached her. Her hair was scattered in all directions and he thought he could see goosebumps on her flesh where the wind pressed her jumpsuit tight against her arms and shoulders.

"We'll know in a few seconds," Morgan replied. Over Felicity, he could see Frederico's mouth gape open and this time he did not wait to be told. He wrapped himself around Felicity anticipating another impact. They were driving in at another tall tree fern, faster this time. Morgan clenched his teeth and clamped his eyes shut. It would be close.

The world's sound track was cut, and a tangible silence surrounded Morgan. A shock wave instantly deafened him, followed by a wave of searing heat that swept him from above. The rope went slack. His eyes opened a crack but the world was spinning so wildly it did not help. The feeling of weightlessness spurred the vertigo.

When the impact came it was on his side, and Morgan clutched wildly at fronds that broke off in his hands. He managed to grasp the woody stem that imitated a trunk for the tree fern. The outer rope's large, loose loop dragged on him, threatening to tear his grip loose. In a burst of panic he struggled to free himself from it but before he could, he realized he was holding up the other two captives. In a moment that weight eased. Frederico was holding the stem below him and Felicity was pulling herself up to Morgan's level.

Morgan could taste last night's dinner, his last meal, again. Felicity did not look as if she enjoyed the ride any better. Most of her jumpsuit's top half had been torn away. Shaking his head to clear it, Morgan spotted the helicopter listing in a wide circle away from them. It was losing altitude unevenly, as if the pilot were somehow trying to keep his ruptured aircraft flying. The tail boom was almost completely disconnected, and without a tail rotor, the copter gyrated wildly. Two bodies flew from it just before it landed with a heavy thump next to the drug production plant and erupted in flames.

Felicity stared long and hard into Morgan's eyes before saying, with dramatic understatement, "Well, you did it."

"We did it," he answered. "I was out of ideas until you came up with the plastique."

"Okay, we did it," Felicity said through a giggle. "Now, how do we get down?"

Hands moving stiffly, Morgan pulled in the rope they so recently dangled from and tied its end to the treetop. Frederico and Morgan then gripped it and lowered the three of them to the ground.

"Now what?" Morgan asked the sky. He leaned back against the tree fern's stem, then snapped forward, wincing with pain. His sleeves slid off, having nothing to hold them up.

"Well, I figure the house is only about fifty meters away, and everybody just ran out of it toward the wreck," Felicity said. "I'm thinking that's the place to be."

"They are not running to the crash," Frederico said. "They are running in all directions, disappearing into the jungle. They fear Anaconda's death, and without a clear leader, the Escorpionistas will begin fighting each other for dominance. No one wants to be in that battle until they know which way it may go."

Morgan nodded, and struck out for the house. The grass was wet and sharp against his toes and it felt good. The sun had risen a bit and its warm rays felt good too. He was not sure he deserved to be alive, but he sure appreciated it.

Felicity gripped Morgan's arm. He staggered and almost fell over. When he looked at her with a question in his eyes she pointed off to their right. At first he saw nothing, but he soon focused on a figure in the grass. He was propped up on one arm, holding a gun with the other but unable to aim it. Oily hair hung straight down his forehead to a scar stretching out from next to his right eye.

"I'm thinking that's unfinished business," Felicity said, and Morgan nodded. He left Felicity behind and walked toward Quesada. He stopped when he stood five feet away. The Colombian's gun hand wavered aimlessly. Morgan looked down at the helpless figure and smiled a crooked smile.

"Rough landing," Morgan said. "Break your leg?" Quesada looked up at Morgan and dropped his gun, trying to sit straighter. "No, it's your hip that's broken, isn't it?" Morgan knelt beside him. "They left you behind, didn't they? And you can't walk, can't even crawl, can't defend yourself. You don't want to lay here and wait for blood loss or thirst or the wolves to come for you."

Quesada looked up at Morgan, his eyes pleading. Morgan leaned toward him and wrapped an arm around Quesada's head. "By the way, the girl's name was Mary. Mary Carter. Got it?" Quesada nodded. "Good. When you get there, make sure you tell Marta. He doesn't know why I killed him."

Morgan looked toward Felicity. Although she was facing away from him, he saw her jump when she heard Quesada's spine crack. A moment later, he rejoined her, handing Frederico a torn jacket, which he wrapped gently around Felicity's shoulders.

Numbed by all that happened in the last half hour, it was a moment before Morgan felt the eyes on him. He turned to face a snarling maned wolf. They had not looked this big before. Morgan and the wolf locked eyes. As long as he faced the animal, it hesitated.

"Frederico, get Felicity to the house," Morgan said. "Slow and easy." Why didn't you pick up Quesada's gun, he asked himself.

Morgan felt danger from another source and glanced quickly behind himself. Felicity had almost reached the back of the house, and she was face to face with evil. She was staring at Anaconda who, impossibly, was standing almost unhurt, pointing a pistol at Morgan.

"I cannot be destroyed so easily," Anaconda said, her silver eyes wide with madness. "Don't you understand? I will always come back. I have power. I have a destiny."

Frederico opened the sliding glass door and thrust Felicity inside before turning toward his former mistress. "I am sorry," he said. "Your story ends here."

Uncertainty crossed Anaconda's face as she waved her small pistol from Frederico to Morgan and back. Morgan watched her closely, gauging distances and timing, knowing full well that in his present condition he could never reach her before she shot him.

Then a growl made Anaconda turn. A maned wolf was racing toward her. He stopped when she spun on him, but she panicked and shot him. Four others stepped toward her. While the animals focused their attention on Anaconda, Morgan sprinted for the house. He heard a second shot behind him, then the nerve shattering clack of a hammer falling on an empty chamber. Tiny footsteps followed him toward the door, falling hopelessly behind.

Cowering, intimidated animals had become a pack of ferocious predators and the sound from those slavering maws drove Morgan forward. He dived through the door and Frederico slid it into place behind him. Anaconda never got closer than fifteen feet from the glass wall. Felicity dropped her head, but Morgan and Frederico, for different reasons, felt drawn to watch the grisly scene. When she fell forward, Anaconda's mirror eyes held Morgan's for an instant, before predatory jaws closed on her face. She never got a chance to scream. The slavering sounds mingled with occasional short growls as the beasts fought over their prey. In two minutes, nothing recognizable as a woman remained.

On her knees at Morgan's side, Felicity said "Sure and she won't be coming back from that."

"She'll come back," Morgan said somberly. "They always come back."

-47-

"We must look a sight," Felicity said, climbing down from a Ford Ranger they "borrowed" from Anaconda's retreat.

"Well, they look okay," Roberts said, nodding toward the men. "You look like a little kid in her father's clothes."

"After we phoned you, I scouted the house," Felicity said. "There weren't any women's clothes that came close to fitting me, so I had to take men's stuff."

"Well the reports are already coming in," Roberts said, ushering his three guests into his office building. "At least I never have to wonder where you've been."

"Just what do you mean by that," Morgan asked. He regretted snapping at his old friend, but he was as tired as he could imagine being. Plus, he hated wearing someone else's clothes, especially since the man he took them from did not seem particularly clean.

"Well, for one thing, I mean you leave a trail of unconscious and dead men. And women."

"So what are they...wow. Mark, you're my hero." Felicity had just stepped into the conference room. The table was laden to overflowing with food. She sat and began filling a plate with whatever her hand fell on. Morgan and Frederico followed suit. Roberts sat smiling, watching his guests filling themselves. It was all basic breakfast fare and pretty bland, but it was hot and fresh and filling. After six or seven scrambled eggs, Morgan slowed down.

"Just what are your reports saying?" he asked.

"You'll be pleased to know that the Escorpionistas are in chaos," Roberts answered. "The sudden leadership vacuum has them sniping at each other in a massive power struggle. The locals don't generally like to get involved in that stuff but after talking to you, I made a couple of calls. I got the Colombian National Guard to investigate this report of a helicopter crash in the mountains. In the process a number of small time gangsters were gathered up."

"So, all the deaths and injuries get chalked up to infighting?" Felicity asked, using fingers as a comb to keep her hair out of her food.

"Roger that! And the bonus is, with production shut down for now and no real leadership, it looks like The Escorpionistas won't be exporting any ice to the States for a while."

Morgan stopped eating and opened his mouth to say something, but reconsidered. He looked at his partner and saw that she had followed the same thought pattern.

"You're right," Felicity said with a weary sigh. "It wasn't worth it. Nothing could be." She stopped with a fork halfway to her mouth, and lowered it as if her appetite had faded. She rose from her place and went to one of the windows. Morgan was about to ask about her pensive mood, but he had a feeling she wanted to be out of their conversation for a while.

"Do you need a ride home, Frederico?" Roberts asked.

"Home?" The question seemed to surprise Frederico. "My mistress is gone. My brother is gone. I have nothing here but parents who sold me for money. There is nothing for me here. I hope to go to America and get a new start."

"I'm sure we can find you a place to stay," Morgan said. "There's got to be a job for a guy with your talents. Maybe in Las Vegas, or at a race track, eh?"

Away from the group, Felicity stared at the mountains dwarfing the city below and slowly shook her head. She had lied to Anaconda after all. The scars, physical and emotional, did not go away. She had always been proud of her body. Now she realized that was where the real damage was. Not to her body, but to her pride.

"I'll deal with it," Felicity whispered to herself. "I'll just have to be as strong as Morgan." She said it, even as she realized she would be leaning on him more than ever. Forcing herself to stand straighter, she turned to face the group.

Behind her, Morgan was looking at Roberts, only half listening to him. "By the way," Roberts was saying to Morgan, "not all the calls I made last night were local. I managed to get in touch with..."

Before he could finish the sentence, the door banged open against the wall and Claudette Christophe blew into the room. She was dressed casually and her eyes sagged from sleeplessness. Morgan leaped from his chair and rushed into her embrace.

"God, it's good to see you," he said into her jacket collar. Her face and body felt cold, but she clung to Morgan as a nursing baby would its mother. "This assignment has been one snafu after another from the get go. Chuck Barton is dead. And I...I got a girl killed."

"Do not worry, mon cher. Mister Roberts has told me more about what happened than I really should know. I can make you whole again, my love."

"Maybe later," Morgan said, pushing a hand through her straightened black hair. "I need to be by myself for a while. I'm going away."

"Merde," Claudette snapped. "This running off to lick your wounds is for children. I am here for you. And I can heal you."

"You don't understand." Morgan pulled away just enough to see her sharp, dark eyes. "The girl and I, we..."

"I can guess." Claudette's face was stern but not hurt. "I don't expect to own you, but when the time comes for caring, I want it to be me."

Morgan stared out the window at the giant cross standing at the crest of one of the mountains surrounding the city of Bogota. He considered that perhaps he would try healing after a mission without the solitude he had grown accustomed to. It was not like a lifetime commitment, after all. He was not yet ready for that. Or was he?

So much of his life had changed since he met Felicity. He was a businessman now, with responsibilities and a permanent address. In some ways he had committed to his partner. After their years as lovers, did he not owe Claudette a certain commitment as well? Maybe, just maybe, he would try to tell her he really cared.

That thought reminded him they were in a rather public area for this conversation. When he looked over his shoulder he found Roberts staring, Felicity smiling, and Frederico pointedly looking away.

"Say yes, partner," Felicity said, "and give yourself a real vacation. You deserve it. Come back when you're ready." Then, more quietly, "I'm not really sure what I'm going to do."

Morgan stepped out of Claudette's embrace and put a hand on Felicity's shoulder. Now he felt this war was over, and the healing time really would begin.

Other Stark and O'Brien
Adventures from Austin S. Camacho

The Payback Assignment

Morgan Stark, is stranded in the Central American nation of Belize after a raid goes wrong. Felicity O'Brien is stranded in the jungle south of Mexico after doing a job for an American client.

When these two meet, they learn they've been double-crossed by the same man: Adrian Seagrave, a ruthless businessman maintaining his respectability by having others do his dirty work.

Morgan and Felicity become friends and partners while following their common enemy's trail. They become even closer when they find they share a peculiar psychic link, allowing them to sense danger approaching themselves, or each other.

But their extrasensory abilities and fighting skills are tested to their limits against Seagrave's soldiers-for-hire and Monk, his giant simian bodyguard. A series of battles from California to New York lead to a final confrontation with Seagrave's army of hired killers in a skyscraper engulfed by flames.

The Orion Assignment

Felicity O'Brien travels to her native Ireland to defend her uncle's Catholic parish. The job looks easy until they meet Ian O'Ryan, an IRA terrorist who believes he is the reincarnation of Orion the ancient hunter. He is determined to keep the violence alive in Ireland and to spread it throughout the island. Morgan and Felicity use their psychic link to alert them to danger. But against O'Ryan they face danger from an entire army of enemies.

Trying to separate patriotic mercenaries from heartless terrorists leads them to a sniper mission on the rocky Irish coast, a deadly high speed motorcycle race in Belgium, and a final confrontation on an island off the coast of France where Morgan could die by slow torture if Felicity doesn't find him in time.